THE CONFESSIONAL

THE CONFESSIONAL

J. L. Powers

Alfred A. Knopf

New York

THIS IS A BORZOI BOOK PUBLISHED BY ALFRED A. KNOPF

Published in the United States by Alfred A. Knopf, an imprint of Random House Children's Books, a division of Random House, Inc., New York.

KNOPF, BORZOI BOOKS, and the colophon are registered trademarks of Random House, Inc.

www.randomhouse.com/teens

Educators and librarians, for a variety of teaching tools, visit us at
www.randomhouse.com/teachers

Library of Congress Cataloging-in-Publication Data
Powers, J. L. (Jessica Lynn).
The confessional / J. L. Powers. — 1st ed.
p. cm.
SUMMARY: The murder of a student at an all-boys Catholic school in the border city of El Paso, Texas, throws the lives of a diverse group of friends into chaos.
ISBN 978-0-375-83872-9 (trade) — ISBN 978-0-375-93872-6 (lib. bdg.)
[1. Murder—Fiction.   2. Race relations—Fiction.   3. Catholic schools—Fiction.
4. High schools—Fiction.   5. Schools—Fiction.   6. Mexican-American Border Region—
Fiction.   7. El Paso (Tex.)—Fiction.]   I. Title.
PZ7.P883443Co 2007
[Fic]—dc22
2006024253

Printed in the United States of America

July 2007

10 9 8 7 6 5 4 3 2 1

First Edition

This book is for
Robbie,
Mikey,
Chris O.,
Marcos,
and Andrew,
with thanks.

MAY 5, 20—
JUÁREZ, MEXICO

To the President and People of the United States:

Let me tell you how it is.

First, I am a Mexican, not a terrorist. Yet when I am caught crossing the river to go to work, your Border Patrol makes me bend over, looking for explosives up my butt. They used to look for drugs. Now it's all about Al-Qaeda.

Has there ever been a Mexican terrorist? Never! So why did you put the Immigration and Naturalization Service under the Department of Homeland Security? Does "Mexican" equal "terrorist" because of what some Arabs did?

Second, I am not made of stone. You can't make me work all day in the hot sun picking chiles, then refuse to pay me and accuse me of being a terrorist because of some laws that don't make sense to anyone. I work in the U.S. illegally, but I am *working.*

Third, our women who work in the U.S. factories on the Mexican side of the border are dying. Our families are hungry, so these women work in the *maquiladoras* because they have no choice. Almost four hundred bodies have been found in the desert outside of Juárez. All *maquila* workers! When will you take responsibility for this slaughter?

My wife, Juanita, she was a *maquila* worker in Juárez. Two months ago they found her body. Facedown in the sand. She wasn't wearing clothes, nothing but her shoes. Ay, *Dios,* I can barely write this. She was pregnant with our first child. Just another wetback baby to you.

I wrote letter after letter. I called all your government offices. I lost two whole days' pay to wait in a lobby, and I never saw anybody! The only time someone spoke to me was to ask me if I'd cleaned the restrooms on the third floor. Whose ass do I have to look up to find some answers? Can anyone tell me that? How will your rich, fat country pay me for what I have suffered? With more abuse?

9-11 and Cinco de Mayo are now connected. One was the United States' day of reckoning. One was Mexico's liberation day. But today, the 5th of May, it will become your second day of reckoning.

So listen up and listen good to the sound of one proud Mexican making a stand! *¡Ya basta!*

¡Viva México!

Sincerely,
Jesús José Macías
Citizen of Mexico

ASSOCIATED PRESS
MAY 6, 20—
EL PASO, TEXAS

Yesterday, at 7:30 in the morning, Mexican national Jesús José Macías blew himself up while crossing the Santa Fe Street Bridge, an international bridge linking Mexico to the United States in El Paso, Texas. The explosion killed 32 Americans, including 3 Border Patrol agents, as well as 16 Mexicans, and wounded up to 100 people.

"We have found evidence that Macías walked across the bridge at 4 a.m. and, after being denied entrance to the United States by the Border Patrol, returned a few hours later with his bomb," said Border Patrol spokesman Manuel García.

According to García, the source of the explosive material is not yet known, but officials believe Macías was working alone. Damage sustained to the international bridge and inspection station is estimated to be several million dollars. The bridge will be closed until repairs can be made, which may take up to a year.

Border Patrol officials believe the Santa Fe Street Bridge was targeted because, like other international bridges that link Mexico to the United States, it is a conduit for trade and legitimate immigration between the two countries.

In response to the bombing, local residents have agitated for a 12-foot-high wall to be constructed along the El Paso section of the border.

Mexicans celebrate their defeat of the French army in 1862 each 5th of May. Cinco de Mayo is not Mexico's Independence Day, even though Macías called it "Mexico's liberation day" in the letter he left explaining his reasons for the suicide bombing.

APRIL 26, 20—
EL PASO TIMES

To the Editor:

Next week marks the first anniversary of the Cinco de Mayo suicide bombing. Much like September 11th, we will forever be reminded of this tragedy and the 32 Americans who died at the hands of a vicious terrorist.

We all know that the date happens to be a major Mexican holiday—no coincidence, since the bomber was Mexican and chose Cinco de Mayo on purpose so that every time Mexico celebrates its victory, the United States will be reminded of our loss, of our "day of reckoning." But what exactly is he blaming us for? What do we have to apologize for? To apologize would be like saying Jesús José Macías was justified in what he did!

Incredibly, the city of El Paso is going forward as it always has. There are the traditional plans for a Cinco de Mayo parade along Montana Street, and most of the area restaurants and bars are planning major celebrations. To me, it is the height of disrespect to go on, business as usual, only one year after the bombing. I am aware that the city plans a moment of silence and remembrance for the victims of the bombing before the parade starts, and I realize that several churches in the area are planning prayer vigils. But how does *one moment of silence* compensate for the loss of 32 lives? How can we have all these *parties* when our people died at the hands of a terrorist on this day? Don't you think the families of those victims have suffered enough? It seems to me as if we are celebrating terrorism rather than condemning it.

I propose that El Paso abstain from celebrating Cinco de Mayo this year. Perhaps next year we can party-party-party. But this year, there should be some suitable mourning and remembrance. It seems like the least we can do, out of respect for the memories of those who died.

Sincerely yours,
MacKenzie Malone
Junior, Jesuit High School

The Crime

MacKenzie Malone
Beating Up Bernie

As usual, Bernie Martínez greets me with some shit.

"Hey, Mac, heard your mom sucked Principal Rodarte's dick last night," he says, keeping his voice low so Mr. La Salle, first period, can't hear.

"Yo, Bernie, quit wasting oxygen," I say, slinking into my seat. "Slink" is the operative word. At Jesuit High, you never swagger anywhere, not unless you're one of those guys who's always running your mouth off. Which is Bernie, one hundred percent. I'm not really a violent person, but I could cheerfully cut off his air supply.

Bernie makes a sucking sound with his mouth. "It takes a whole lot of oxygen to suck a guy's—"

"You would know, Dirty Bernie," I interrupt. "I'm surprised you haven't drowned from all you've choked down."

I'm wired as soon as the words come out of my mouth. Bernie's got nerve, messing with my mom. Moms are, like, sacred, you know?

All right, then.

"One of these days, I'm gonna kick your *puto* ass," Bernie whispers. But this won't be the end of our little pissing match. He just called me a fag.

"At least *I'm* nobody's bitch," I say, opening my textbook to hide my face in a bunch of numbers.

Bastard's turning purple. I pretend to be reeeeally interested in the algebra problem Mr. La Salle writes up on the board.

Bernie's especially venomous this week because of that letter I wrote to the *El Paso Times*. Like a lot of the guys here, he lives on the other side of the border, in Juárez, and crosses the international bridge from Mexico to the U.S. every day to come to Jesuit. Cinco de Mayo is a *huge*-ass party for Mexicans. But this is America. I'm not trying to stop *their* celebration. They can celebrate *across the river* all they want.

Bernie finally shuts up and we both start paying attention to La Salle, who actually manages to teach algebra so it makes sense at 8:30 in the morning.

La Salle begins handing back our tests. I've always been one of the smart ones, like Chris "Carbon Copy" Cruz and Josh Alvarado. We kicked ass on the SATs last month. So I always open my tests with a flourish, as if to say, "I don't care if you see it because whatever it is, it's gonna be good." But today, while Bernie looks over my shoulder as I open it up, he starts *laughing.*

A 66%? How'd that happen?

Asshole. To be *so* continued.

♣ ♣ ♣

I step out of first period, on my way to second, and Sergio Camarena shoves a little Mexican flag halfway up my left nostril.

"We've got a special Cinco de Mayo celebration next Tuesday just for you, *amigo,*" Sergio says, making explosion sounds.

Is this jerk mimicking the bomber?

"You threatening me, Sergio?" I ask. Are they planning to mess me up?

"Oooooh, is Fa-ther Mac-key scared of a little Mexican holiday?" Manuel Hernández asks.

I *hate* that nickname. "Shut up." I try to move along but he chases after me in the hallway, waving his little flag and yelling, *"¡Viva México!"*

This whole week it's been impossible for me to avoid getting accosted while walking through the hallways between periods. I know it's just dumb stuff, but I can only take so much.

Yes, I'm aware that I pissed a lot of these guys off, but I'm *not* against all Mexicans or their holiday. They should *know* that. Some of these guys were my friends, until I wrote that letter.

Besides, a *lot* of Jesuit students—Mexican Americans, not just white students—are thinking about having a sit-down protest if the administration forces us to have a celebration. So far, the faculty has gone forward as planned. Bunch of PC pussies. If September 11th was a major Islamic holiday, would we celebrate *that*, too?

✦ ✦ ✦

Gregory González is my best friend. We live next door to each other in Kern Place. Yeah, sometimes I feel kind of self-conscious about that, like when Jesuit's only *cholo*, Rafael "Rafa" Najera, tells me to shut up—what could I know about real life when I live in a mansion? It's not a *mansion*, but Kern Place is one of the richer neighborhoods in El Paso. Anyway, Greg and I have known each other since we were little kids, cruising through Madeleine Park on our Big Wheels. We played soccer on the same team (go, Thunderbirds!) and our moms were in the El Paso Junior League together. I know his family like it's my own.

"¿*Cómo 'stás,* homes?" he greets me.

"*Como* crappo," I say.

"*Como* yo mama," he says.

"Leave my mama outta this."

We jostle each other in our seats until Mrs. Mendoza, our religion teacher, comes in. Mrs. Mendoza always looks like she's pinching her nose together 'cuz of our bad guy-smell.

I have this suspicion I'm Mrs. Mendoza's favorite. Now, there are some teachers I wouldn't mind if I were their favorite—Ms. Meadows, for example. Ms. Meadows, our economics teacher, is young and pretty and she walks up and down the aisles wearing these short skirts. Everybody's paying attention in *that* class.

The reason I think I'm Mrs. Mendoza's favorite is 'cuz she always has me hand out the homework. And I always get an A in class participation. Maybe she just has a thing for good-looking dudes—ha! The thing is, she knows I know my stuff. Being a priest, actually having to do that for a living, every day—there's no way. My father would kill me. But some of the theology shit really makes sense to me. Sometimes I think I'd like to go into philosophy or something. That would be cool.

So I'm handing out the homework when Rafa snickers. "The homo's handing out the work. Homowork. Get it?"

Rafa is *always* telling dumb jokes, then saying, "Get it?"

"Now, boys, this is religion class," says Mrs. Mendoza. "You're supposed to behave like the good, pious young men God meant you to be."

Today we're talking about whether the Iraq war is a just war or not. A lot of El Paso troops went over, so it's been a big issue here. We've been talking about that and how the U.S. has responded to having a terrorist from right across the border—yeah, that freak who blew himself up lived in Juárez and used to pick chiles just outside Las Cruces.

Mom says she gets nervous every time we drive past the chile fields now. I don't. But if we need Mexicans to pick chiles, shouldn't we figure out a way to make their labor legal? Otherwise, it's not really fair and we're just asking for trouble.

My dad's one of those businessmen who hires a lot of cheap Mexican labor. His exploitation will pay for my college, so my whole future will be built on a morally iffy foundation. Should I feel bad about that? Or do something about it? Like what?

"Um, miss, what exactly does the war have to do with religion?" asks Jim Hill. Jim's an okay guy, just a little strange sometimes.

"The concept of a morally just war has a long and serious tradition in Catholicism," Mrs. Mendoza says.

"Well, I don't think we should even be there," says Isaiah Contreras. "It's not a just war if we can't prove there was an imminent danger aimed at us."

The guys get off on talking about war way more than talking about sin and the usual stuff, but don't they realize, in just two years, we have to *register*? What if there's a draft? That scares the *shit* out of me.

"Who asked you, Ish?" Omar Chavarria asks. Omar's dad is totally military.

"It's a class discussion, Omar," Chris says. "He doesn't have to be *asked*."

"There are other options besides war," Mrs. Mendoza interrupts. "Pacifism is also a strong tradition in Catholic theology."

"What's that?" Greg asks.

"It's applying nonviolent resistance," says Chris. "Refusing to use guns or other kinds of physical force."

"But how do you do that if they're provoking you or attacking you?" Greg persists.

"Yeah, how, Carbon Copy?" Omar asks.

Chris rolls his eyes at them. "Look, man, I'm just trying to give an explanation, not defend it." We call Chris "Carbon Copy" Cruz 'cuz he has an older brother, a senior, who looks just like him. The other brother's name is Steve.

"So, if you're against war, if you're a pacifist, does that mean you can't defend yourself?" Isaiah asks. He's always making things personal.

"If you don't defend yourself, then you deserve to get beaten up," Omar says. "A country has to protect itself."

"Why do we have to have countries at all?" Isaiah asks.

"You have to have countries," Omar says, staring him down. "You can't not have countries."

"Says who?" says Isaiah. "We act like we've always had countries, but there was a time when there was no such thing and people survived."

"*Lo-co.*" Omar uses his index finger to make circles in the air near his ear.

Mrs. Mendoza jumps in with "Pacifism may not be a rational solution, but that doesn't mean it can't be effective. It was effective for Gandhi."

"Yeah, but Gandhi was dealing with rational people," I chime in. "Eventually, the British realized the truth of what

Gandhi was saying. If we'd tried to deal with Hitler that way, the Nazis would have taken over the whole world."

"Yeah, and terrorists are hardly rational," Chris adds. "If we don't do something to stop them, they'll just keep harming innocent citizens."

"I say, just nuke 'em," says Omar. "That'll stop terrorism."

A lot of cheers, but I notice they're not from Isaiah, who slides down in his seat.

I cheer, too, but I know it just has to be more complicated than bombing everybody to death till the Americans are the only ones left, which is what our foreign policy would be if it was run by people like Omar.

I'd kind of like to see pacifism in action sometime, to see if it works. Would pacifism have worked against Saddam Hussein? In Bosnia? Or Rwanda? Peaceful resistance . . . what a concept.

♦ ♦ ♦

The beaners are waiting for me outside second period, only this time they have a gigantic Mexican flag. It takes three guys to hold it upright! I can't believe the administration is letting them carry this monster. They're bound to whack somebody with it as they sweep through the hallways.

"What'd you do, steal the flag over by the free bridge?" I ask.

A few years back, the Mexicans hoisted an enormous Mexican flag over by the free international bridge. You can see it everywhere in El Paso, except for the west side—the Franklin Mountains hide it. Anyway, a lot of El Pasoans were upset.

They thought it was a deliberate in-your-face gesture. Nothing ever came of it, but people were talking about hoisting an even more enormous American flag on the American side. *Up yours, Mexico,* right? *Nyah, nyah, we're bigger than you are. . . .*

Sergio looks like he's about to reply, so I say, *"¡Hasta luego!"* and take off before they drop it on my head. Deliberately.

♦ ♦ ♦

I usually fall asleep in third period, no joke. The teacher's really old and forgets stuff a lot. Like, last year, she forgot to fail Greg. She just sits up there at her desk and talks, doesn't even get up and look around. No clue. Somebody told me I snored real loud once and she said something like "What's that?" then got real quiet and embarrassed because she thought maybe it was a fart and she'd just pointed it out.

I sling my backpack onto Dirty Bernie's desk like I'm going to leave it sitting in front of him. Then I sit down at my desk.

"Yo, *puto,*" he greets me. "You just *put-o* your books on my desk."

Hardy-har-har.

"Hey, Bern," I say, sniffing loudly. "Did you crawl through the sewage tunnels to get here this morning?"

It takes him a second. Then: "You smell like shit 'cuz you're a sack of shit," he hisses back.

"Aw, Bern, can't you come up with something . . . less pathetic?" I ask. "Something smarter?"

"You think all us Mexicans are stupid, don't you?"

I'm so sick of guys like Bernie playing that damn race card. "Yeah, that's what I think," I say, my voice *dripping* with sarcasm.

"That's *exactly* what I think." Then, really low: "Hey, Bernie, why don't you stay where you belong? Huh? Get yourself a nice *Me-hi-cano* education."

Trust Bernie not to figure out that I'm using an obviously stupid cliché just to stir him up. "I wouldn't live in the U.S. if you fucking paid me," he spits back. " 'Cuz of people like *you,* who don't want *my kind* here."

Dude's right about that. A lot of people *don't* want Mexicans on this side of the border.

Even before the bomber, I don't know how anybody slipped through the extensive web of security wrapped around this town. It's just like that freak said—we do kinda act like every Mexican's a terrorist.

After the suicide bombing, they shut the border completely. That lasted about five days. Then people like my parents started complaining about how they missed their maids and cheap child care. For businessmen like my dad, it stopped a lot of lucrative NAFTA trade traffic. So the president hired an additional two hundred Border Patrol agents before they opened it back up. Plus, they started plans to build a wall along the Rio Grande! A wall, can you believe it? My dad says it's gonna be an eyesore.

These days, there are so many cops, Border Patrol agents, and DEA agents, not to mention military, it's hard not to feel paranoid.

"You know what, Bernie?" I whisper. "I don't want *your kind* anywhere."

Look, I'm not talking about Mexicans, I'm talking about people who smear their shit in my face. This is a free country and I have the right to live in a shit-free environment, right?

"Or maybe I'm just not the *right kind* of Mexican," he says suddenly. "I mean, I'm not carrying any *la coca* in my backpack to sell to stupid *güero* users."

How the fuck's he know about that? Before I know it, I've jumped chairs and tackled him. I've got the upper hand but he socks me in the eye just as I hear Rafa whispering, "Yo, homes, Ms. Smith's here."

Bernie jumps back like I bit him.

It takes me a minute to get up off the floor and sit in my chair. Metallic blood taste in my mouth. Must've bit my tongue.

Ms. Smith doesn't even notice. She just suggests in her old-lady voice that all of us "work silently in our notebooks."

Bernie's sitting at his desk, hands all folded on the top, a little prick angel. How did he find out about the coke? And how dare he mention it in front of everybody? Yeah, he's gonna get his.

It's on.

◆ ◆ ◆

Even before third period is up, I'm aware that news of a Fight with a capital F has spread via cell phone text messages. Random guys are telling me I should beat the shit out of Bernie. Now that the word is out, I'm going to go for it. There's no other choice.

See, I used to get into fights a lot. Once I bit this kid's ear so hard, my parents had to pay for his plastic surgery. After that, they decided no more public school for me.

Whenever they want to rag on me, they always bring up the fact that they had so much trouble getting St. Pius to accept me, they had to agree to drug me with hefty doses of Ritalin and "donate" hefty sums of money to the school's building fund.

As a side note, Ritalin and cocaine—they don't feel all that different. Same thing, different packaging. In fact, they're so much the same, I stopped taking my meds a couple weeks ago, traded them in for some coke—it's reduced my debt to Josh by, like, a third.

I guess I might be . . . half a freak? A semiviolent kid who likes Mass?

When they bong the little gong, wave the incense, and sing that "amen, amen, amen," I feel like there's something bigger than myself in the world, something that can help me. I don't know if it's God exactly. Maybe it's just the Church, the institution. There's something comforting about the fact that the Church has been around for 2,000 years and is going to stay around, come what may. I'm glad to know there's something steady in this world, something that's not going to crumble in two seconds.

✦ ✦ ✦

Lunch period. I've got 30 minutes to not chicken out. Shit.

So, of course, I do it: put on the whole gangsta attitude, swagger over to Bernie. He starts to rise—guess he thinks I'm going to start things right here—but I just say, out of the corner of my mouth, "I'm gonna let you finish that nice little sandwich, Bernie, and that's the last thing I'm gonna *let* you do." It just pops out of my mouth, like in a bad movie.

Outside to the basketball courts. Wait until he comes out.

There's a crowd already. Greg takes a seat by Josh, who's

talking to Rafa. Jim Hill sneers at me, then gives me a thumbs-up sign—such an odd boy. Somebody laughs, somebody jeers. Everybody's watching out of the corners of their eyes. I'm surprised nobody's selling popcorn and those giant foam fingers.

What am I supposed to do while I wait? Meditate? Rouse the crowd to a fevered pitch of coliseum-gladiator-style excitement? Pray?

"No fighting dirty, *pinche*," Bernie calls from the doorway.

Like I'd go near his filthy balls.

I think for a second about how there are rules for regular fights and rules for bigger fights, like war. Isn't that weird? No matter how many people you kill, as long as you don't mistreat your prisoners of war or target civilians, you can't be tried for war crimes. You're considered an honorable killer. It's not a sin or anything.

"Get out here, you bitch," I yell.

"I mean it," he repeats. "No fighting dirty, you fuckin' fag."

He's *always* calling me a fag. "You're just jealous 'cuz I'm so pretty," I tell him. "I'd rather be a fuckin' fag than a fuckin' Fronchi," I add before turning to the crowd and yelling, "Yo, what's worse, a wetback or a homo?"

"*¡Oye! ¡Bolillo!*" Rafa calls back. "Why you gotta drag us into this? Eh, *ése*? We just wanna see the fight!"

Did he just call me *"bolillo,"* white-bread?

Just as I turn my head back toward Bernie, he spits a full-frontal loogie. It drips down my nose and onto my lip. Can't help gagging.

Crack! I throw the first punch, right across the jaw. His head whips around, I hit him so hard. *Better not break the fucker's neck.*

He comes back with a weak punch and then brings his knee up to my nuts.

Unbelievable.

I block it. "Thought we weren't fighting dirty, Bernie." Grabbing him around his waist, I throw him down and his head clonks against the pavement. *Dude! Isn't he going to protect himself? Cool it, Mac. Pace yourself.*

From his position on the ground, he starts kicking me right in the balls. Asshole!

That's when something breaks in me and suddenly I start kicking back and I don't give a fuck anymore and he's yelling something but I'm, I'm just kicking—*crack—thump—krrrk*. I can't even see him anymore, I don't hear the crowd, I'm just aware of the rhythm beating inside my chest. Crack. *Thump.* Krrrk. Crack. *Thump.* Krrrk. Crack. *Thump.* Krrrk. *Get him, Mac. Get him, Mac. Get him where it hurts.*

Father Raymond is screaming like a wildebeest in my ear, shoving us apart. "MacKenzie Malone," he yells, his index finger pressing on my windpipe until I feel like I'm going to puke. "Are you trying to send this boy to the hospital? Bernardo! Bernardo! Are you all right? Speak to me! Child, are you all right?"

Bernie's crouched in a corner against the wall. I must've kicked him all the way across the court to the wall. Nobody's saying a word, they're just staring at me. I've been kicking and kicking, just kicking him over and over, and now he's lying there, not saying anything, but I think he's still breathing. Thank God.

MacKenzie Malone
The Seven Deadly Sins

At a Catholic high school, the point of waiting in the principal's office until your mother shows up is to give you a chance to reflect on your sins.

Where *is* she? The school is five minutes from our house.

The secretary is chewing gum in synch with her typing. She stands up and goes over to a file cabinet in the corner. She's wearing pantyhose and a short skirt, and you can see where her thighs part just below the skirt.

Chubby chicks aren't really my thing, but she's still cute. If she leaned forward, I'd see up her skirt. *Come on, darlin', lean forward, lean forward. Just a little bit. Just a little—oh, yeah. Oh, yeah! Oh—ah, damn it.* She's coming back to her desk.

I wonder if she has her own fantasies about any of us guys here at the school?

When she sits back down, I lean forward in my seat and say, "Bet you think I'm a real bad kid, don't you?" I wait until she looks my way. Then I wink at her.

She opens her big, red-lipsticked lips, rolls her gum around, and sort of spits, *"Tsk tsk."* I thought that kind of thing just happened in books.

"That's probably what my mother will say," I try again.

"But I thought a pretty young lady like you would have a soft spot for young boys who were just trying to defend themselves."

She shakes her head, then says, "I need to get this done before your mother gets here."

Sourpuss.

So, what should I repent? I know have a loooong-ass list of sins to contemplate. But what I'm mostly thinking about is this: where did I go when I beat Bernie into a bloody, pulpy mess? No easy answer for that. Guess I should start making a list of my sins instead.

"Sin" is a word whose sound masks its true meaning. The word is actually pretty, sort of musical. I'm not kidding. It's fun to say it: sin. Sin-sin-sin. See how fun it is to press the tongue up against the top of the mouth to make that *s* sound? So actually, the word sounds just like it should. Sin, after all, is pleasurable. Why else would we sin so often? Why do I?

My Checklist of Sins:

ANGER. Beating up Bernie, probably harder than I had to.

LUST. Maybe it's 'cuz I'm still, well, ahem, a virgin. It's probably kinky to think about having sex with the married secretary at an all-boys Catholic school. But there are frankly not that many attractive females on the premises. Did you ever think about how the word "lust" oozes out of your mouth? It's almost like there's a direct correlation between the sound of the word and the actual meaning. Lust is an oozy, gunky, sweaty, oily feeling.

PRIDE. Hey, I know I'm a good-looking guy. And girls like cockiness, right? Except this damn secretary.

SLOTH. Daydreaming or fantasizing instead of studying. Why should I, when, after all, I can usually make A's without trying?

ENVY. Wishing Ms. Meadows would look at me the way she looks at Josh, lucky dog. So I guess that's also "coveting."

CURSING. Saying dirty words all the time. I don't think that's a major sin or anything, but I doubt it's winning me any points with the Big Guy.

DISRESPECTING MY FATHER. Dissing my dad every day, especially when he tells me to start living in the "real world." I don't know if that's a deadly sin or not, but it's against the Ten Commandments.

DISRESPECTING MY MOTHER. I know I should take my meds 'cuz Mom believes in them so much. I feel like a real jerk selling them to Josh when she's paying for them and assumes I'm taking them religiously. Oh, well. What she doesn't know won't hurt her, right? Or . . . is it possible I lost it with Bernie because I stopped taking Ritalin a couple weeks ago? Oh, God. I have to stop thinking about this right now.

The only deadly sin not on my list is GREED. But why should I be greedy when I can have anything I want, when I want it?

If I was Catholic, I could confess my sins to a priest, be absolved, and then just live my life. You'd think with a last name like Malone we'd be Catholic, but my father's line came from a dissident Protestant faction. That makes us outsiders here in El Paso, where practically everyone is Catholic.

When Mom finally walks in the door, I notice her skirt is a little too high and needs to be tugged down and her blouse is a little askew. Where's she been?

"MacKenzie," she says right away, "your father will be furious."

"Maybe if he believed in God, this wouldn't have happened," I say, just to be weird.

"Quit being a jerk, MacKenzie," she responds.

Now she's smoothing her hair, probably wondering what our principal, Brother Rodarte "El Fartay," will think of her if she looks like she was just getting it on with some hot dude. *Damn it.* Where do these ideas come from? But seriously, what do I know about my parents' sex life? I know they're practically never together and when they are, they fight a lot. So maybe she's . . . lonely?

Mom smiles at the secretary and says, "I'm ready whenever the principal is."

The secretary gets up with her nice round ass, opens the doorway to his office, and leans in just a little, enough so I can see a bit more of her legs underneath her skirt. She says, "Brother Rodarte, Mrs. Malone is here now." Then she waves us in.

What am I going to say if Brother Rodarte asks me why I did it?

Rodarte gestures for us to take a seat and starts right in. "Mrs. Malone, MacKenzie is an exemplary student in many ways, which is why this incident concerns us so gravely." He goes on, but the only phrase that stands out is this: "three-week suspension." *Fucking A.* That means cleaning out the urinals for three weeks and getting zeros in all my homework, tests, and everything. And this is junior year, when my grades really count for college.

"Well, I think we should consider that school is almost over for the year," Mom says. "If MacKenzie is suspended for three weeks, he will miss some of his final exams. Doesn't that seem a little excessive—sir?" Ha! I love the way she tacks on that "sir." Guess I can learn a few things from good ol' Mom.

"I'm afraid not," Brother Rodarte says. "After all, we had to send the other student to the hospital with a broken arm. It seems extreme measures are in order, Mrs. Malone. MacKenzie is generally a good student, but we won't risk a repetition of this behavior."

"His father and I can absolutely guarantee this will never happen again." Mom glares at me.

"I'm sure you will do your best, but it's important that our students know that this action received an appropriate punishment. Here at Jesuit, safety and respect for others is our first concern."

Sports are first priority here. If I was a basketball star, I'd get a "strong warning."

El Fartay stands and announces, "Also, we've arranged for the school counselor to meet with MacKenzie every day at 3 p.m. for the next three weeks. If you would prefer to hire a private psychologist—"

"No, thank you," Mom says, glaring at me again. "I'm sure between the school counselor, his father, and me, MacKenzie will learn what's what."

Mom stands up and tugs at me to stand as well. The two of them shake hands and Mom hustles me out of the room.

As soon as we get to the parking lot, she grabs my ear and starts pulling me toward the car.

"Ow, Mom. Ow!" She's pinching my ear with her sharp fingernails.

"Wait until your father gets home, young man," she says, like some stereotype.

"Let me go, Mom," I say.

Isaiah, Omar, Josh, and Rafa are standing around near Rafa's lowrider. Ish gives me a halfhearted wave before Mom shoves me into our car.

"You didn't even listen to my side of the story," I complain, trying to look pathetic. Hoping she'll see that I'm hurt, too.

"Oh, you have a *side* to this little story?" she says. "There's some terrific *excuse* for what you did? Some kind of reasonable *explanation* for beating someone until they end up in the hospital?"

"Mom, I just, I didn't mean to do it!" I grab her arm, trying to get her to look at me. But she shrugs me off. Damn it. I hate it when she won't look at me. Like I'm that *unbearable*.

But then she says, "This is just like all those other times."

"I haven't gotten in trouble since forever!" I protest. "You know that!"

"Remember that time you beat that kid up while his face was against the fence?" she continues, inexorably.

"Mom, please," I say.

"That boy, he had lacerations all over his face," she says. "I bet he has scars to this day. And then there was little Johnny Bradford."

I can't think about Johnny Bradford right now. The ear dude. "Mom. Please." I think I'm going to be sick.

"Maybe we should have named you Mike Tyson Malone," she says in her bitchiest tone.

I've heard that one too many times. I slump down in my seat.

"I'm so ashamed," she spits out. "Your father will be so ashamed."

"What's he going to do, give me a spanking?" I ask.

"MacKenzie Meredith Malone." Her voice has become all hoarse and whispery, different.

We're passing Madeleine Park. As a kid, I used to play there all the time. Greg and I still hang out there until two or three in the morning some Saturday nights with a few of the neighborhood girls. Veronica especially. Well, she's been busy lately.

"Look at me, young man."

I keep staring out the window.

She slaps my knee. "MacKenzie!"

I. Am. Not. Going. To. Give. Her. *Any*. Satisfaction. "Isn't that such a pretty park?" I ask. "One of the nicest parks in El Paso. So green. So peaceful."

Mom pulls in to the driveway, turns off the ignition, and leans back in the driver's seat. We sit like that, motionless, for an eternity. I can't read her silence.

"Well, time for my daily dose of penance," I say as I start to open the door, but she stops me.

"Mac." She reaches out her arm and holds me back. "Can I sit here for a second with my son? Please?"

I sit back with a *whomp*.

She turns sideways then and cuddles up against the seat like we're two corny teenagers sitting in the car gabbing. Her anger has dissipated. She just looks, well . . . fuck, she looks *sad*.

God, I don't know if I can have this conversation. She's gonna make me cry, I can tell just by looking at her face.

"Mac, do you remember when you were little, we'd drive all the way to Colorado to see Grampy?"

I nod.

"It was only a ten-hour trip, but it took us two days to do it. Do you remember why?"

"Not really. I just remember it seemed like it took forever."

"That's because it did. We had to stop every *hour* to let you burn off your excess energy. I remember stopping at McDonald's in Albuquerque once. You were, I don't know, four, maybe five years old. You kept banging your head against the wall, over and over and over again. I kept trying to stop you, thinking you were going to hurt yourself, but you wouldn't. You even said, 'It feels good, Mommy!' Mac, you bruised your own head so badly, people could see the lumps. They thought I was abusing you! Whenever we stopped at a parking lot, you ran in circle after circle after circle on the pavement, trying to make yourself dizzy. I would think to myself, 'Who is this child and why is he like this? Did he really come from *my* body?' This was *after* we had already stopped in Elephant Butte and gone swimming for two hours, *after* our stop to climb the mountain in Socorro. I sat down on the sidewalk to watch you and it was half an hour before you even *paused*. I remember thinking, 'When will this little boy *ever* run down?' "

I open my mouth to speak, but she holds up her hand.

"Just listen, honey."

I scrunch farther down in my seat. I'm not gonna look at her.

We both watch her hands, which she holds perfectly still in her lap, palms up. I remember the touch of those hands when I was little, how she'd wipe smudges of dirt off my cheeks with her spit and thumb, how she'd wipe away the hair from my eyes with her fingers. Her hands have always been soft and pretty, with long, polished nails. Looking at them now, I can see that they're getting wrinkled. Yeah, she's getting on up there in age. This thought pulls me toward her. I feel—

"MacKenzie," she says, "maybe you're mad at us for putting you on medication and sending you to Catholic schools. But I ask you, what else could we do?" Our eyes finally meet.

"You could have tried to understand me a little more," I say, and I swear I'm not whining, I'm really not. Just telling the truth.

She's crying now, tears dripping down her nose and quivering on her chin. "Understand *what*?" she asks. "Understand that if we let you keep going the way you were going, there were going to be even more emergency hospital bills? Understand that some parent somewhere someday is going to sue us? What is it that we should understand? That you want to destroy yourself? That you can't help yourself—or control what you do?"

"Maybe if I felt you were on my side," I say. "Maybe if you explained things to me and trusted me a little. I could, I don't know, control myself! And I have! Haven't I been better over the past few years? Don't you trust me at all?"

She shakes her head, and the tears quivering on her chin patter off onto her blouse. Can't tell if that head shake is her answer.

"I don't know what to do with you, Mac. I just don't know *what* to do with you. I don't know *what*."

And the thing is, I don't either. I feel like I've suddenly lost my home, like it was a temporary shelter, like it's been washed away in some gigantic tsunami. It's just gone, and I don't know if I'll ever get it back.

✦ ✦ ✦

Greg comes over around five. He looks weird, a little tousled, like he's been sleeping. "Hey, homo, *¿cómo estás?*" he says.

I'm hungry. "*Como* burrito."

"*¿Cómo, cómo, cómo?*"

"*Como* shitola."

"Ah, *grass-i-ass para la explanación.*" Then he jostles me. "Didja know some of the guys went to see the Fronchi?"

"Fronchi" is what we call Mexicans from Juárez. It's because they're from Frontera Chihuahua, the state in Mexico where Juárez is located. Fronchies come over and go to Jesuit or UTEP for school. At Christmas, Cielo Vista Mall is so full of Fronchies, you can hardly get from store to store.

"No, I didn't know." I don't want to ask, but maybe Greg will figure out I want to know anyway.

"Bernie's okay," he says. Good ol' Greg. "Ish says a broken arm, a concussion, that's it."

"Cool." I don't want to let on how relieved I really am.

Greg hits me on the arm. "You scared me today, man. What happened?"

"Dunno."

"I thought maybe there was some epistemological explanation," he says. Ha! He didn't even know the meaning of that word until last week, when *I* used it.

"Yeah," I say. "There is: it was an out-of-body experience."

"Serious?"

"Yeah. I was contemplating the mysteries of the third heaven."

"What's the third heaven?"

Masturbation, I almost say, but instead, "St. Paul. Second Corinthians 12:2–3. 'I was caught up into the third heaven fourteen years ago. Whether my body was there or just my spirit, I don't know; only God knows.' "

"How the hell do you remember these things?" Greg asks. "And besides, that doesn't tell me exactly what the third heaven *is.*"

"According to Dante, paradise was made up of nine levels," I say. "Hey, don't you learn *anything* in your confirmation classes?"

"Sit, stand, kneel, cross ourselves, blah blah blah," Greg says. He hates being Catholic. "So why are there nine levels? Is each level for different levels of goodness?"

"Sort of. I think it's for different *kinds* of goodness. Like level one, the moon, is for people who had faith but weren't constant with it, people who broke their vows. The fifth sphere is Mars—those who fought for Christianity. So I guess that level of paradise would be, like, for the martyrs in the Crusades."

"So, which of the heavens would you want to go to?"

"Wherever Vero is!" I say. "And that's *got* to be the third heaven—Venus!"

"Yeah, baby!" Greg's got a thing for Veronica, too. Once last year, we were hanging out at the park. It was late, and after we drank half a bottle of whiskey Greg swiped from his parents' liquor cabinet, she showed us her tits. But now she's got a boyfriend over at El Paso High, some hotshot lowrider, a *cholo,* José Cuervo or something like that, and we haven't seen her tits since. They were nice, though, full and round and cream-colored. "But isn't that an Islamic idea?"

"You mean that if you die during jihad, heaven's full of chicks dying to screw you? Yeah."

"If it is, man, make me a Muslim." He grins. "At least,

as long as I can get it up. Can you imagine how frustrating heaven would be if you were impotent? Kinda defeat the purpose, huh?"

"They probably have rooms stocked full of Viagra and Mexicans out on the sidewalk trying to hawk it to every guy who walks past, just like in J-Town."

Greg hits me on the shoulder and laughs. "Damn." Then he says, like he's morbid and obsessing about it, "Well, I'm glad nobody made it to heaven today, you or Bernie."

"What? Did Bernie really look that bad?"

"No, it was you, man. You looked like you were going to kill him."

"You think?" *Please don't say yes, Greg.* Scares me enough knowing I went somewhere in my head so far away, I didn't even know what I was doing.

"Yeah," Greg says. "He barely touched you and you looked like you were going to obliterate him."

Wish I knew what to say to that. It's weird to think about how other people see you when you can't see yourself. Greg acts like I looked, I don't know, demonic or demented or something. Maybe I should look at myself in the mirror more carefully. But what if I can't handle what I see looking back?

MacKenzie Malone

A Fag Moment and Hasta la Bye-bye

It's almost 9 p.m. and my dad still isn't home by the time my buddy Dan from school stops by to see if I want to go see his band play.

I leave Dan tapping his toes on the porch while I tell Mom I'm going out.

"Your father doesn't even know what you did yet," she says. "Until he and I discuss it, you can't go."

"Well, why don't you call him at work, then?" I ask, but I already know Mom never calls him at work. He doesn't like to be disturbed unless it's an emergency, the Big Important Man.

She shakes her head.

"Then *I'll* call him," I say, picking up the phone in the front hallway and starting to dial.

"No!" she says, grabbing the receiver from me and banging it back down on the phone. "You know that he's busy!"

"Oh, come on, Mom, he's got a million minions to be busy for him. He'd just rather be there than here," I say. Instantly, I feel shitty, protective, and mean all at the same time. "Wait, I'm sorry, Mom, I didn't mean it."

"Well, you're grounded, young man," Mom responds, a bit hysterically, her voice strained and cracked.

I put my arm around her like we're best buds, we're just joking around. I'm six-foot-three, got those typical white-boy basketball genes. She's so little, a feeling of wanting to protect her surges inside of me.

"Mom, you know the grounding can start tomorrow," I wheedle. "I need to get away for a while. I won't be late or anything."

"You can't go out after you just sent some kid to the hospital," she says, her voice quivering with tears. "We can't reward you for that kind of behavior."

Echoes of something . . . where have I heard that before? Wait! Didn't I say something like that in my letter to the *El Paso Times*?

"Mom," I say. My arm's still around her, and I lean down to kiss her. "I know I'm going to be grounded. You're not rewarding me. But how can you even start punishment before you talk to Dad?" Before she can respond, I open the front door and add, "We'll talk about it tomorrow. I promise."

"This'll go poorly for you when your father comes home!" she threatens.

"Later!"

Dan's waiting out on the porch. I heave the door shut and lean against it, panting like I've just narrowly escaped a war zone. "I know the 'rents love me," I tell him, "but I don't think they love *me,* you know what I mean?" My voice cracks.

"Yeah, guess so," he says, jangling his keys. He seems nervous. 'Cuz of me?

"So, I've never heard your band play," I say as we head to his car.

"We have a CD out," he says. "I'll put it in on the way over."

Dan and I are in choir together. He has a great voice and you can tell he loves any kind of singing. As soon as he puts the CD in—"Whoa," I say. "Does Mr. Torres know you sing like that?" Mr. Torres is our choir director.

"Nope." Dan turns onto Mesa Street. "But he might come tonight. If he does, he'll find out."

It will be so weird to see our teacher in a bar. The only bars I've been in are in Juárez, and that's another country, and a whole other scene. Anyway, Mr. Torres is one of the "cool" teachers. He's kind of fat, but he's young, in his thirties, and he really loves what he does.

"Does he know you're suspended?" Dan asks.

"Not that I know of," I say. "Hey, don't mention it to him either." Choir practice is at 7:30 in the morning. "Maybe I can sneak into choir before I have to go clean toilets."

I've never been in downtown El Paso after dark except during the holidays to see the Christmas tree in San Jacinto Plaza. I thought it would be crawling with hookers, Mexican transvestites, and junkies. But it seems really normal, except for one girl who's wearing thigh-high boots with a skirt that barely covers her ass. She gives us the eye as we walk inside.

"Maaaan," I whistle to Dan as we pass through the door. "Think I'm in loooove."

Dan jerks his chin at the girl like he knows her. "There's lots more T-and-A inside," Dan tells me. "If that's your thing."

He greets the bartender, then heads up to the stage. I don't know anyone here. Wish I had a beer, something to hold in my hands. There's an empty chair at the bar so I sit down and order a Coke.

Dan and his band are getting set up. He looks out at the

crowd every few minutes, but it's like he's seeing something none of us can see, a curtain pulled back that allows him to glimpse the beyond. Or maybe more like he's seeing nothing at all; he's so much into his zone. I can relate. Sometimes when I'm losing it, my medicinal substitute gives me that same kind of focus.

Some hot chick sits down at the bar next to me. I nod at her, she smiles, and that makes me feel brave. "So, are you *into* growling?" I ask, tilting my head toward the stage, where Dan's testing the mike.

She giggles. "Why? You want me to sit on your lap and growl at you?"

Hell, yeah! "Well, what are you doing sitting all the way over there?" I ask. "So very far away?" I pat my lap, hoping she'll leap onto it.

Just then, Big Boyfriend sits down next to her, slinging his arm around her shoulders. "What up?" he says, lifting his chin at me.

"Nada," I say. *Shit.*

Mr. Torres wanders in, wide-eyed and alone. I stand up to motion him over. He grins, waves at me, and jogs over. "MacKenzie!" he says. "So, together we shall find out what there is to know about Dan and his band." He slings his arm around me in a side hug for just a second, his way of saying, *I know what happened and I'm sorry.* It makes me feel better, for just a second.

But now it's just awkward to be standing here in a bar with a teacher. *Hurry up, Dan,* I beg.

As soon as the bar DJ says, "Let's give it up for Voz!!!!" Dan crashes onstage, shrieks into the mike, his leg and guitar contorting upward. He's a raging maniac! He runs, jumps into the air, his hair flying every which way. At one point, he even throws his guitar on the floor like he's having a temper tantrum. Who knew? Their music is loud and hard-hitting, of the "I'm gonna puncture your eardrums" variety. Dan lets his voice crack on high notes, then drops to a low growl. Quite sexy.

I can't understand everything, but it sounds like he's singing, *"I walk by your 7-11 heaven. So drunk, you don't even know who I am. What made you forget? Not the booze, not the crystal meth. This song's my gun. Gonna blow your ass to kingdom come."*

Mr. Torres and I look at each other and smile. He shouts, "Not exactly his choir-boy image, is it?"

"Nope!" I shout back.

And we both laugh.

At school, Dan's really quiet and well-mannered, always respectful to the teachers. Doesn't cuss much. Moves slowly, like he's considering whether each movement will waste energy. He seems almost shy, except it's more like he just isn't going to talk unless he feels like it.

The band is up there for an hour and a half and the crowd is really into them. Three or four girls get up and start dancing in front of the stage. They coax Dan to step off and then, when he's surrounded, they paw him while he sings until he breaks free and jumps back on the stage. Jeez. Wish *I* was in a band. I mean, those girls are hot! I don't play an instrument, but I can sing, sort of—so, why not?

When the show's over, I see Dan take a few minutes up on stage to calm down. Then he pushes his way through the crowd toward us.

"Hey, Mr. Torres," he says.

I note that Mr. Torres punches him on the arm. No quick side hug for Dan. You would think *I* would be the leper after today.

Some light goes out of Dan's eyes, but he recovers quickly and asks, "What'd you think?"

Mr. Torres lifts both his arms in a "how can I put this" gesture. "You know . . ." He trails off.

But Dan is grinning at him and that light's back on. "It's okay, Mr. Torres, you don't have to like it," he says. Where does that shine come from? It's got to be partly from being high off the show and the fact that it went so well. But it feels more like the light is coming from *this conversation.* "Thanks for coming anyway."

"Well, I have to get a move on," Mr. Torres says. "Thanks for inviting me."

"Sure thing," Dan says.

Mr. Torres practically sprints out the door and Dan's light is snuffed out once again. "Want a beer?" he asks.

"Sounds good."

Dan goes over to one of his bandmates, whispers something in his ear. A couple of minutes later, they set a nice frosty Heineken in front of me. Cool.

"The band always gets free beer," says Dan.

"Do you all get smashed afterwards, then?"

"They do." He nods at the guitarist, bassist, and drummer, who are roaming the room, brews in hand, chicks by their sides. It's such a cliché—but a good one.

"You don't drink?"

"My dad's a drunk," he says. "So, I'm careful." He's drinking a Coke.

I down my beer. Dan raises his eyebrows at the drummer and my empty glass is removed and replaced with another, full to the brim, just a light layer of foam across the top. Nice.

"I'm in deep shit," I tell Dan.

"It'll all be good," he says. "These things work themselves out."

"Look, I don't want a cheerleader, Dan." I find I'm staring at another empty glass already.

He grins. "Okay, but why'd you beat Bernie up like that?"

"It was like—like I wasn't there," I tell him as somebody sets another brew down in front of me. "I don't even know where I went. I don't actually remember anything until it was all over and stupid Bernie was lying on the ground."

"You were scary," he says. "A wild man, swinging around, punching Bernie over and over, and then you were just stomping his head and arm with your boots. A couple of guys nearby got blood on their shirts. You're lucky he wasn't hurt worse."

I try again to explain. I need someone to know, to understand. "Well, I was tired, tired of him shitting on me every fucking day," I say. "Why should he be allowed to shit on me? Am I just supposed to suck it up, day after day after day?" I can hear the girly whine in my voice and I hate myself for it.

"This happen to you a lot?" Dan asks.

"Yeah, maybe." I try to keep it in, stuff it down. I do. "I think I'm ready to go home," I say. I'm on the verge. No, I'm drunk.

Dan doesn't stand up, though, just says, "I'm sorry, man. I'm sorry you feel like you've been shit on a lot."

"Let's go, man. I gotta get out of here." *I will not fucking cry.*

Dan reaches out toward me with his hand and I see

something, way back, in his eyes. That light. That same light I saw around Mr. Torres. And I suddenly realize that his hand is on my knee. And that light, that shine, is in his eyes. *Fucking A. Dan is gay. Fucking fucking fucking A. He is fucking gay.* He can't help that hand. It crept onto my leg of its own accord.

And now he's leaning forward and fuck-he's-going-to-kiss-me! I turn my head at the last second and his lips land on my ear. *Rock. My. World.* First time I've been kissed on the ear and it's by a dude.

As soon as his lips hit my ear, he jumps back. I look at him. His light is snuffed out again. *Poof.* His eyes become black and cold, not even a wisp of smoke to suggest there was a fire there two seconds ago.

"Don't start bawling," he says as we stand up to go. "Somebody will think you're a pussy."

♦ ♦ ♦

On the way home, I try to be light, cool, nnoooothhhing happened. But, man, first thing I'm doing when I get home is calling Greg. *Yo, homes!* I'll say, *Dan the Man is a fucking fag!*

I won't tell *every*body. I don't want Dan to get *killed.* Most of the guys, if they know that about you, it won't matter how much they liked you before. Dan'll be dog meat for sure.

"I'll be there Monday," I say as I get out of the car. "But I might not see you. I'm a-gonna be making those porcelain beauties shine."

"Have fun with that." He's flat now. The fizzle is all gone. And we'll never talk about it 'cuz that'd make it real.

"Later," I say. "*Hasta la* bye-bye."

"See ya," he replies.

I step out of the car and Dan drives away. Three guys come out from behind a tree. One of them is Rafa, one of them is—

"Hey, dude, what's—" I start to say, and then I feel a sharp pain and something bubbling up into my throat.

Isaiah Contreras
Ganging Up on the Pacifist

I've never seen nobody lose it like Mac did except my dad—but Mac, I mean, he was savage in a really *calm* sort of way.

See, in my family, it works like this: Dad gets a little violent with Mom and we try to pretend like it was nothing—but it's not nothing. So then it's this thing hovering over us for days until one of them does something nice, like maybe they take us to the movies or we go get ice cream, and then we all pretend everything's okay again. And it is, for a little while, until the next time.

How will Mac act on Monday? Is he gonna pretend nothing happened? Will I feel a little weird being around him? The way he was, it made me think we don't really know each other, not like I thought we did.

Mac being suspended—this sort of *discipline* is why my parents sent me to Jesuit. It's one of my dad's favorite dinner table topics. "Schools today have no *discipline*," he'll say, pounding his steak knife on the table and making the milk in our glasses jump. "Kids bring guns or knives or anything else they want to school. Then something like Columbine happens." Except he says all this in Spanish.

He aims his steak knife at me and makes quick little jabbing motions into the air. *"Mijo,"* he says, "if you ever do anything at that school to make your old man ashamed, I will knock you from here to Chihuahua City. I'll hit you so hard, it'll make a man out of you, but quick. *¿Entiendes?"*

When he finally wraps up, it's always the same old same old. He thinks he's doing me a big fat favor.

Sure, Dad. You've made sure I'm so scared of you, the guys at school think I'm a total wuss. And I never do nothing bad.

He has no clue what I've learned at that place neither. Like, my freshman year, first week of class, I learned a entire list of dirty jokes, starting with the letter A and ending with Z. I learned how to say "fuck" out loud but under my breath so the priests don't hear and I don't have to confess it before taking Communion. And, yeah, we've *all* learned "it's a jungle out there," like our English teacher, Mr. Propp, always says. Each of us got to fight for ourselves. So fuck it if a whiner like Bernie gets hurt, right? Maybe Mac was thinking something like that?

After school, we all hang out in the parking lot until we see Mac drive off with his mom, then we pile into Rafa's car— Omar Chavarria, Josh Alvarado, Jim Hill, and me.

"I gotta call my mom and tell her where I'm going," Josh says, taking out his cell phone.

"Mama's boy," Jim snickers.

"Tu madre," Josh responds.

We all listen in as Josh tells his mother he's going to the hospital to see Bernie. Except he don't mention Bernie got hurt because of a fight. None of us will mention it to our parents, neither.

In the end, we all call our moms as we drive toward Thomason. We hear Jim's mom swearing at him for calling her at work. Then Rafa proves he's not so tough after all, no matter how cool he is in his smooth little lowrider. *"Mami,"* he says. *"Pues, yo voy al hospital.* Thomason. *Porque mi amigo Bernie está enfermo. Sí. No sé. Llamaré.* Okay, *Mami."*

My mom's not home.

"Man, I could really use some Chico's," says Josh when we pass Chico's Tacos on Alameda, right before the hospital.

"You eat that shit?" asks Jim.

Rafa turns around in the seat. "Are you saying our food is *shit?"*

"No, man, I'm just talking about Chico's Tacos, that's all." Jim backs off.

"I think the man has spoken," says Rafa. "I think it's time we stuffed him full of *la comida real,* the real stuff."

He pulls in to Chico's parking lot and we all pile out. I'm not really into this detour. Me, I don't like Chico's much neither. It's just greasy tacos in a little paper bowl, soaked in tomato juice. Kinda like tomato-taco soup. But you can't live in El Paso and not eat there. It would be like—well, like going to Chicago and not eating that thick pizza.

"Órale, pues, we're gonna get you three orders of tacos," Rafa says to Jim.

"Anybody got money?" Omar asks. Omar's dad is military. He never has money.

"Let's let Jim pay for it, man," says Rafa. *"El chingado* makes fun of our culture, let him pay."

"Why do you always assume I'm making fun of your culture?" Jim asks.

"Why do you always make fun of our culture?" Rafa responds.

"Ah, leave him alone," I finally say. "We had one fight already today. *¿Necesitamos otros?"*

"Hey, Ish, we're just teasing," says Josh.

Finally, we're sitting around eating tacos and that's when we start talking about The Fight.

"So, you see Mac's face?" Josh asks.

"Yeah. Did you see Bernie crumple? He's such a pussy," says Jim.

"Hey, guys, let's not talk about it," says Omar. Damn. That, coming from the military kid who loves his tanks and airplanes, bombs and bullets?

"What, are you a pussy, too?" Jim asks Omar.

"Shut up," says Omar. "You know I shoot guns on the weekends. But I saw Mac's face and it was, I don't know, really creepy."

I'm with Omar, just want to get this hospital visit over with, go home, watch some TV.

"Heard Mac's getting a three-week suspension," says Josh.

"¡Chingao!" Rafa swears.

"One of the teachers told me," Josh says, real cool-like, as if we don't all know about him and his "special relationship" with Ms. Meadows.

"How bad was Bernie hurt, anyway?" I ask.

"Bad enough to go to the hospital," Omar says.

"Yeah, but what does that mean? A broken arm? A coma?"

"Guess we'll find out."

I'm just pushing tacos around in tomato sauce. When I was really little and upset about something—maybe my soccer team lost or Dad had hit one of us or yelled about something stupid—Mom would take me to McDonald's. She still does that. McDonald's is "feel better" food for my family. Even when I'm not hungry, I can always eat McDonald's. These tacos—they just ain't cutting it.

* * *

"Yo, *vato*," Rafa greets Bernie as we all crowd into his hospital room.

"You look fuuuucked up," says Jim cheerfully.

Turns out, Bernie's not so bad, just a busted arm and a concussion, plus a lot of bruises all over his face. He's getting out tonight. But he's super pissed. So are his mom and dad.

"They're gonna make sure the racist motha gets kicked out," Bernie says, whispering. "Permanently."

Bernie's parents are talking in the corner. They look like your typical Mexican parents. The mother is short, plump, and dark, while his father is tall and looks more European than Indian. They're definitely upper-class Mexican. They have to be to send Bernie to school in the U.S.

"Look, man," Josh says reasonably, "I'm not saying what he did is right, but you *did* provoke him."

"Whatevers," Bernie says. He can *never* get the hang of that phrase. The other one that bugs me is "for reals." I'm not that great at grammar myself, but *dude*.

"It's *'whatever,'* Bernie," I hear myself say.

Everybody glances at me for a moment, surprised.

"Besides," I go on, "Mac's no racist."

"What about the whole Cinco de Mayo thing?" Bernie asks. "And then in math this morning, he told me he don't want *my kind* here. *Entonces,* the *pinche* white boy beats me up."

But, I mean, Gregory González is Mac's best friend. So why would he say that?

"Well," says Omar, in his best "patriotic American, my father is in the military" voice, "we probably *shouldn't* celebrate Cinco de Mayo this year—"

"Oh, get a life," Josh interrupts. "That's not the *point*. You know that's not the *point*. I don't think that's why Mac beat Bernie up."

"What *is* the point?" Jim asks. He fakes a punch at Josh.

"*¿Y qué?*" Bernie asks. "*¿Y qué?* Lemme tell you what the point is. Americans hate *Mexicanos,* that's what the point is."

"Dude, that is so wrong," Josh says. "I'm American, I don't hate you."

"How long you gonna be in that sling?" I ask, changing the subject.

"Doc says eight weeks," Bernie says. "But six months before I can use it like normal."

Josh whistles. "Guess that means you're out as goalie for the soccer team this fall."

"Yeah, but the doctor says I can play next spring." Bernie winces as he moves his arm around. He says to his mom, *"Mamá, ¿puedo jugar fútbol ésta primavera, sí?"* His mom nods, and he says, "Yeah, this spring. Hey, did you see the homo go after me? I thought he didn't know how to fight, man, and then he just—it was like he wanted to kill me or something."

Bernie's in a sling, there's a bandage on his forehead—blood is even seeping through, creating this deep purplish stain—and I'm ticked off at *him,* not Mac. "Shut up, man," I say. "Just quit calling him a fag all the time. Don't you *ever* get it?"

Bernie don't get it, though. "Hey, I call everyone 'homo,' " he explains. "You guys know that. Father Macaroon just can't handle it. Probably 'cuz it's true." He snorts.

Sometimes when we were kids, Mac was so serious, and so good, we'd call him "Father Macaroon" or "Father Mackey." They're just old nicknames 'cuz he's a thinker. I remember riding around with him and Greg on our bikes, Mac talking about what it would have been like if our parents had married other people and half of us was in one person's body and half of us was in another person's body and would we know it, would the essential Mac know that he was ripped in two? I mean, what kind of sixth grader talks about stuff like that?

Bernie's mom comes over and tells us we better go now, they have to finish some tests so they can go back to Juárez before it gets too late. We all yell, "*Hasta luego,* Bernie," and "*Ciao,*" and Jim throws him a quick "*Hasta* you basta."

"*Nos vemos,*" he says, waving with his good arm, and we all leave the hospital room together.

Jim whistles. "His forehead was messssssed up."

"Hey," Rafa says. "You really think Mac did this because he don't like Mexicans?"

"No way," I say. "Gregory González is his best friend."

"Greg's Mexican *American,*" Omar says. "There's a difference."

"How so?" I ask. It's not that I'm stupid, but I never quite get this. I mean, I'm American because I was born here but both my parents were born in Mexico. So am I Mexican *and* American or Mexican American?

"It's an identity thing," Omar says. "Are you loyal to the homeland, the United States—or the motherland, Mexico?"

"Somebody should talk to Mac," Josh says. "Find out what really happened."

Jim claps me on the back like we're all buddy-buddy. "Josh, you're right. And Ish is just the man for the job."

"Me?" I ask. "Why me?"

" 'Cuz you the peacemaker," he says. Just like that.

I am? I mean, at home, for sure. I'm always Mr. Peace-maker. Like Mom and Dad would never shut up if I never asked them to. But I didn't think that spilled over into school.

"Does that make him one of those pacifists?" Omar asks. "I'm gonna have to beat him up if he's a pacifist. Defend my dad's honor and shit like that."

"I ain't no pacifist," I say.

"Ish is like one of those old freak hippies, his brain fried on LSD. All he wants is to grow pot and commune with the earth in Taos," Jim says. He closes his eyes, presses his thumb and index finger together in a circle like he's meditating, and hums, "Ohhhhmmmmm."

"Look, I just don't think violence solves everything," I interrupt.

"No?" Jim giggles, a creepy baby's giggle. "I tell you what, Ish. I'll fight you. Right here. Right now. You win, you're not a pacifist. You lose, you're whatever I say. How about it? You want to fight? Come on, paci-pussy."

He starts jabbing at me with his fists. One of them hits me right in the ribs.

"Fuck, Jim, that hurts! Cut it out!" I'm, like, moving away from him, but it's not like these hospital corridors are very wide. What'll I do if he throws a real punch? I've had to defend myself before. From my dad, when he gets mean. If he's drunk enough, it don't take much to make him fall down. Now that I'm older. But I never do that unless he forces me.

"Chickenshit," he says, sneering.

"Scaredy-cat," crows Omar.

"Shut the fuck up, all you *vatos*," Rafa interrupts. "Josh has a good idea. *Pues, ándale,* Isaiah. You should be the one to talk to Mac, *ése*. And it takes *cojones* to talk to somebody who can fight like that, so shut up with the pacifist chicken bullshit, eh? *¡Ya basta!*"

It's decided that I'll go to Mac's house. Tonight. I'll ask him if he really told Bernie that he don't like Mexicans and I'll try to find out why he lost it like that. Then I'll report back to the guys whatever I learn. *¿Por qué? No sé.* For why, I don't know. But it's on.

Isaiah Contreras
Mr. Predictable?

Every time I think about talking to Mac, my stomach hurts. Maybe Chico's didn't go down right? Mom makes enchiladas for dinner, my favorite, and I only eat two. "*¿Mijo?* What's wrong?" Mom asks. "Are you feeling okay? *Pues,* let me get the thermometer and take your temperature."

Dad tells her to leave me alone. "You want something to feel bad about?" he asks me. "I'll give you something to feel bad about."

I swear I'm gonna pick up the phone and call Mac. But I can't talk to him as long as Dad's sitting around drinking beer and eyeballing me.

So I play video games instead.

The phone glares at me. But shit. Dad's practically passed out on the couch. What'll happen if I call Mac and Dad gets pissed 'cuz I wake him up?

So I play video games in my bedroom. Then I fall asleep in my clothes. Another Friday night.

My weekends are . . . I guess I'm a predictable kind of guy. I'm gonna be one of those Mexican dads who has sixteen kids 'cuz I'm always around. The guys never call me to hang out on Friday nights or nothing. If they go clubbing in Juárez, we all know this chubby baby face'll never make it past the bouncers. I'd just ruin the guys' action.

Someday I'll find a nice, quiet girl who don't like to party so much, the kind that'll go for my kind.

My mom likes to spend Saturday afternoon with my *tías* over in Juárez, eat posole, go to Mass. She takes my little sisters and sometimes she drags me along. Dad almost always stays home. Sometimes my *tíos* come over here and they all drink beer and watch sports in the living room. If I'm around, Tío Gordo, Uncle Fatty, who's my skinniest uncle, will take me outside to smoke with him. When Dad gets mad, Tío Gordo says, "Ah, leave *El Pobrecito* alone, Moreno. You taught me to smoke when I was thirteen." *El Pobrecito* is my nickname. Poor Little Guy. I hate it. Sometimes to escape them I go play basketball with my brother. He lives in an apartment near UTEP. He calls it "JUTEP," making fun of my parents' accent.

This Saturday morning, Mom rouses me out of bed at 7:30 and tells me two cops are downstairs. "Wha—?"

"They wanna talk to you, *mijo*." She has all these little wrinkles in her forehead. "*Pues,* you need to get up and go downstairs right away."

I roll out of bed, put on some jeans, and stumble downstairs. *Whoa!*

I like cops. I do. They keep the peace. But these guys are standing there with their big old guns, arms folded across their chests. They have the hugest arm muscles I've ever seen.

Why are they here? Did I do something?

My stomach gurgles and grinds, flip-flops around. They're staring at me. What if I accidentally fart in front of them?

"Isaiah Contreras?" the younger cop asks. They're both

Mexican American. Tight crew cuts. Just the hint of a mustache on the younger guy. Wish I could grow one of those.

"Yes, sir," I say. What would happen if I started freaking out and confessing all my sins?

They indicate that I can sit down, so I do. One of them takes out a notepad and the other a tape recorder.

"Am I in trouble, sir?" I ask. "I got a parking ticket last month, but I gave Mom money for it and she paid it. Didn't you, Mom?"

"You're not in trouble, son," says the older, bigger cop. "We understand there was a fight at Jesuit High School yesterday."

"Yes, sir." Guess Bernie's parents are pressing charges.

"Can you describe what happened?"

"Yes, sir. Bernardo Martínez, he's the one got beat up, is always insulting MacKenzie Malone. I guess Mac got sick of it, so he beat Bernie up. At least, that's what I think happened. Some kids think it was a race thing, that Mac don't like Mexicans, but I don't think so."

"Did Bernardo Martínez make any threats to MacKenzie Malone after the fight?"

"No, sir."

"Are there other people that you know of who might have a grievance against MacKenzie Malone? No other enemies that you know of?"

"No, sir. Mac's all right. Everybody likes him all right. I don't even know why Bernie's insulting him all the time. Mac has a temper. He'll hold it in, hold it in, and then let it out all at once, just like yesterday."

"What about Alexander Gold? Does he get along with Mac?"

"Who?"

"Alexander Gold."

"I don't know who that is, sir," I say.

"Okay. Well, what do you know about Bernardo Martínez? What sort of guy is he?"

I don't want to be a snitch. "Bernie's like most of the guys, sir."

"What does that mean?"

Mom's standing in the doorway, my little sis right behind her. I really wish they'd go away. But she says, "Tell them, *mijo.*"

"Uh, locker room jokes all the time," I say. "Foul language. He makes some racist comments sometimes about white boys—*gringos, güeros,* you know. He likes to pick on people, and Mac Malone is his favorite target. Mac's better-looking, richer, smarter."

"Has Mac ever done anything like this before?"

"Maybe once." I'm thinking about the time Greg came to school with a black eye. He wouldn't talk about it, just said he teased Mac too much. But there were lots of times at school when Mac just exploded. There wasn't a fight or nothing, just lots of yelling. Bernie loved to see Mac get all red-faced and blustery and indignant. Mac could be, what you call it, "self-righteous."

"Who did he get into the fight with the other time?"

"His best friend, Gregory González." I wish I hadn't said nothing. Why are they taking so many notes? "But man, that happens sometimes, you know?" I add. "Best friends fight sometimes. It's no big deal. It's just normal guy stuff."

Dad's like that with his *compadres.* At home, too, except he don't usually hit me 'cuz I don't talk back like Mom. Maybe I *am* a pacifist, like Omar says. Or just a pussy-chicken? Still, if Dad went after Leti or Angie, he better watch out. My sisters, they're the big exception.

"And what about your teachers, son? Do they ever do anything to stop it, this escalating teasing?"

What would they do if I started calling them "Dad" the way they call me "son"?

"The teachers pretty much ignore it," I explain. "Some will punish you, but most of them don't do nothing."

The cop holding the notebook looks like my Tío Gordo, who spends a lot of time in bars, even though he's married and has a little baby at home. "One last question," he says. "Where were you last night?"

"Here, studying, sir. All night."

Mom speaks up from the doorway. "*Es* true, Officer. I was here with him."

The cop holding the notebook closes it and the other cop turns the tape recorder off. "Thanks," says the tape-recorder cop. "That'll just about do it."

"Can I ask a question?" I ask. "I mean, am I allowed?"

"Sure, son." The cop with the notebook folds his arms over his chest.

"Why are you investigating a stupid high school fight?"

The older cop sighs and says, "I'm sorry to be the one to tell you this, son, but your buddy Mac Malone was stabbed to death in front of his house last night."

"What? No fucking way!"

"Yes, son. I'm afraid so."

Mom draws in a deep breath and says, *"Dios mío."* She's

already by my side, her arm around me, murmuring, *"Mijo, mijo,"* and I just want to shove her off.

"Leave me alone, Mami." I look at the floor. This is just not possible. I mean, *dead?*

Mom walks the officers to the door. I'm stuck to the couch. I want to leave, but I can't move. Bernie's in the hospital, Mac's dead. *Dead.* What the fuck is going on?

"Bueno pues." Mom comes back to the living room and stands in the doorway. "I better go give Mrs. Malone a call. *Mijo,* you going over there?"

"Should I? I mean, will they want to see me?"

"You should go, honey. He was your friend."

Just like that. *Was* my friend.

✦ ✦ ✦

About half an hour later, the phone rings. It's Chris Cruz.

"Hey, Ish. *¿Cómo 'stás?*"

"Carbon Copy, you heard?"

"Yeah, man."

"Shit, huh?" So then I add, "Somebody's got to call Greg," hoping he'll offer.

He's quiet. No offer.

I push the guilt up a notch. Peaceful resister or manipulator— or are they the same thing? "He must be hurting bad. Mac was his best friend."

"You call him," Chris says. "It's your idea."

I make sure Mom's not in hearing distance this time. "Fuck." Such a nice, all-purpose word.

"You can say that again."

In the end, we decide to meet at a coffee shop, El Paso Loco, then go to Greg's together.

"Don't chicken out," I tell him before hanging up.

All I want to do is crawl back into bed and sleep like there won't be no tomorrow.

Isaiah Contreras
Reincarnation Shit

Dad wakes up, Mom tells him about the cops, and he immediately starts hassling me. "What did you do, *mijo?*" he asks again and again, and no matter how many times I protest that I didn't do nothing, he don't believe me. If I stick around, he's just gonna get madder, so I tell him about how Chris and I are gonna go see Greg.

He takes a swipe at the back of my head as I bolt out the door.

There's some band playing at El Paso Loco so Chris and I hang around for a while pretending to listen.

"Hope he's not home," Chris says finally.

"I'm not gonna mention Mac," I say. I feel like I'm about to call some girl I'm crushing on. *Jeez. It's just Greg. Get a grip.*

"You can't do that," Chris says. "That's like, I don't know, ignoring the nude woman standing in your living room. You have to say *something.*"

I never had no best friend the way Greg and Mac were best friends. When we were kids, I used to hang out with Jim Hill some until the day his mother gave him a BB gun and me and him, we went into the desert, Arroyo Park, and shot at jackrabbits. Well, Jim shot at rabbits. It was sick, seeing those rabbits hopping all over the place, trying to get away with their injured legs and bleeding butts. I didn't even try to hit nothing. It was kind of a relief when he went to juvie a few weeks later. It provided a natural end to our friendship. When he got out, we still hung out a bit, but not like before.

"*Ándale. Vámonos,*" I say.

We get in Chris's car and head up the road. It's too short a trip. Greg's house is right next to Mac's house. We just sit there. For fifteen minutes.

"Fuck."

"Yeah," Chris agrees. He never swears, so I have to swear for him.

I'm trying to breathe. My little sister has asthma and sometimes she has trouble breathing. I'm wheezing just like she does.

"You gonna die?" Chris asks. "If you're gonna die, get out. I don't want you to die in my car."

"I'm nervous," I say, inhaling slowly, exhaling, before I get out of the car.

We walk up the pathway to the porch. The curtain's moving. They know we're here.

Greg's mother opens the door. "Hi, boys," she says in a weird, cheery voice, like her son's best friend didn't get stabbed to death in this supposedly "safe" hood. A few blocks south, where I live, it's way rougher, a lot more drugs, a few *cholos,* gangs.

"Hi, Mrs. González," we both say.

"You're here to see Greg?" she asks. She don't invite us in, but Greg shows up and she disappears back inside.

He's wearing the same clothes he was wearing yesterday. His eyes are bloodshot, his hair greasy and sticking straight up.

"You need a shower, man," I tell him.

"Dude," he says, "first thing you do when you see me is insult me?"

"Just an observation," I say.

He grins and shoves me a little.

Then Chris brings it out in the open. "I'm sorry, man."

You can actually see something sag inside of Greg.

All of a sudden, I want to scream at Greg because he'll always be a reminder of this from now on. But all I say is, "Yeah, me too."

Greg seems to find the porch floor really interesting. He says, "We were at the hospital until five a.m. this morning, just waiting and waiting out in the hall with all these nurses and doctors running in and out and Mac's mother crying and trying to get into the room. A security guard was keeping her out. They finally came out and told us, you know, he'd died and all." Greg looks at us for the first time since he came outside. "We all went into the hospital room and Mac was lying there, all waxy and white and shit. Have you ever seen anyone dead before?" He doesn't wait for an answer. "Me neither. Mac didn't look like himself at all. He was just lying there."

Jesus, Greg looks like he's going to start to cry. *Quick, think of something, Ish, think of something so he won't cry.*

I'm stuck. Then, just before Greg starts blubbering, Chris says, "Hey, I bet Father Macaroon is up there talking theology with God right now, you think?"

That makes Greg grin so we're safe for at least another second or two.

"Last night at the hospital," he says, looking around to make sure nobody's listening, "my mom shoves me over to Mac's mom and says, 'He'll be your son now.' "

We all laugh at that one. Anglo moms are the worst, 'cuz

they're all hysterical and uptight like they have some sharp stick up their asses. The only thing worse than an Anglo mom is a Mexican dad, 'cuz they swagger around and try to pull shit on you all the time. What you want is a Mexican mom and an Anglo dad. Then you can pretty much do whatever you want. Both my parents are Mexican. Chris's mom is a *güera,* but he's not offended. He knows the deal.

We scuff our toes on the porch floor until I hear myself say, "Well, guess we better go." I almost say, "Have a nice day." *Dumb.*

Greg says, "Right," and then we shuffle down the sidewalk, get in the car, and drive away.

"Whew," Chris says as soon as we've driven away from the house. "I mean, is it gonna be awkward the rest of our lives? Will we ever know what to say?"

"Don't know."

"Do we have to go to the funeral?"

"My mom's gonna make me go." Truth is, I want to go. It's not that I like funerals, I hate them; they remind me of my *abuelita* who died three years ago. But this is Mac. I've known him most my life. So I can sit, stand, kneel, say amen at all the right times. For him. Mac could be a good friend. Once he caught me cheating—really caught me, like, red-handed—and never told no one. He just said, "Yo, *amigo,* don't do it again if you don't want to go to hell." After that, my grades fell from B's to C's 'cuz I stopped cheating. I sort of appreciated that he called me on it without ratting me out.

"Do you think Mac's in heaven?" I ask.

"There is no such place," Chris says. "It's illogical."

"You think Mac just don't . . . exist anymore? He's just snuffed out?"

"Yeah, I do. You?"

"I don't know about heaven, but I think Mac's still out there somewhere. Who knows, maybe by, like, reincarnation? Somebody dies and their soul enters a new body? So maybe Mac's already having his ass wiped by somebody on a diaper table somewhere."

Chris laughs. "He'd like that."

"Maybe you have to enter the body of a baby born near where you die, so maybe Mac's a Mexican now," I say. "Bernie'd *love* that."

"If Mac returned as a Mexican," Chris says, "it'd definitely give him something to shit his diaper about."

I contemplate this for a sec. "It's totally possible, 'cuz souls don't know boundaries, *ey*? Unless they have borders in the afterlife," I say.

"What's the last thing you'd do if you knew you were going to die today?" Chris asks.

"Go hug my mom, my sisters," I say. "Probably pray, go to confession. You?"

"I'd read a really good book," he says.

"What book?"

"The dictionary," he says. "Seriously." No wonder he does so well on exams.

What would I *really* do if I knew I was gonna die today? Sure, I'd hug my family. But I guess I'd also let my dad have it. I'd unleash—a little payback for all these years of just sitting back and taking it, for every time he hurt my mom. *Then* I'd go to confession. But only after he begged me to stop. Yeah. That's what I'd do—in my dreams. Just dreams.

Isaiah Contreras

Mexican Moms Feeding Their Kids

Chris drops me off. Mom's in the kitchen cooking. She greets me with a kiss. *"Mijo,"* she says, *"¿cómo va?"*

"Fine," I say. I don't usually answer Mom in Spanish. I mean, we're in America, right? She gives me another kiss.

"I made burritos," she says.

She makes the tortillas from scratch. I follow her into the kitchen and sit at the table while she piles a mound of burritos on a plate and sits it in front of me. This is what Mexican mamas do best—feed their kids. Food is the answer to everything. Guess that's why so many of us are pudgy. Okay, yeah, I could lose some weight. But jeez, who really cares? I'm a guy.

She sits beside me at the table and watches while I eat. "So how was it, *mijo*? How was Gregory?"

"Fine," I say again.

"Oh, Isaiah," she sighs. "He was not *fine. ¿Cómo lo* dijo*?"* How can you *say* that?

"Maybe 'cuz I *want* him to be fine," I admit. "And I know he isn't." I've stopped digging in to Mom's burritos. It's hard to eat and have a heart-to-heart at the same time. *"Ey, Mami,"* I say, "you don't think Dad would go that far, do you? You know, like, to stab one of us? When he's mad?"

"Ay, *mijo,* honey, no," she says. "Your father loves you."

"I'm not worried about *me,* Mom."

"You think Mac's dad did this?" she asks me, in Spanish.

I shake my head. "But this wouldn't have happened if he hadn't done nothing. I think Mac's demons caught up with him."

She don't know what to say about that, so she tells me, *"Voy a orar por su alma."* I'll pray for his soul. Then: "Eat," she urges me. *"Es importante para comer."*

"They're having a rosary for Mac tonight," I tell her.

"Pero, mijo, los Malones no son Católicos, ¿sí? Why are they having a rosary?"

"I think Greg's mom arranged it."

"Vamos a ir," she says. And before I can say anything, she adds, *"No comiences conmigo.* We're going. He was your *friend."*

But here's the thing: was Mac really friends with anybody but Greg? I mean, we all got along, except for him and Bernie. But when somebody gets murdered, they start to feel like a stranger. Maybe he was the victim of random violence? But who would go around stabbing random kids like that? What would be the point? I think he must've done *some*thing.

"I'm gonna go call Mrs. González," Mom says. "I'm gonna find out about the rosary. *Mijo,* put your dishes in the dishwasher when you're done."

I hate it that my mom always calls the other mothers "Mrs. This" or "Mrs. That," like maybe she isn't good enough to call them by their first names. My friends all call her "Mom." Sometimes they call her "Mrs. Ish." She likes that. Loves being "Mom" to all the guys.

My little sister Leti comes in and sits down beside me.

"You got a dead friend. *Mami* told me," she says. "What's it feel like?"

Leti is why I want lotsa kids. I'd like a little girl just like her, or Angie, my other little sister.

"Let me think a minute," I say. So far, I guess it's kind of like watching a movie. It don't seem real. But that don't really describe it. "You know how it is when there's something you really, really want? And you're looking forward to it for weeks? I mean, something *important*."

She nods her head. So cute, with her little dark curls and black eyes.

"You're just waiting and waiting. You don't want nothing else, just this. It's the only thing you can think about."

She nods again. She's tracking with me.

"So then, pretend, it don't happen. It don't happen at all. Whatever you wanted. And you have this sick, lonely, lost, homesick kind of feeling at the pit of your stomach."

"Oooooh," she says.

"That's what it's like."

"Really?" she says.

"Yeah."

"I'm sorry." She scoots her chair really close to mine and leans in to rest her head on my shoulder. She pats my face with her little hand.

Suddenly I'm crying into my damn burrito. Buckets. Damn little kid.

Isaiah Contreras
Mijo, Behave Now or Pay Later

I jack off just before we leave for the rosary. I feel kinda guilty about it but I need to relieve some of this pressure.

When I walk into the cathedral, the first thing I see is Chris, standing in the corner with a long face. I start fake laughing at him, but then I get all serious when I dip my fingers in the holy water and make the sign of the cross. It's one thing making fun of Chris, another of religion. Besides, Mom's digging her elbow into my side, hissing, "*Mijo,* behave now or pay later."

Man, there must be forty guys from school here. I wonder if we all have the same sick feeling in our stomachs. It's like how I felt years ago when Jim got arrested. For days I was all lost and lonely just thinking of him locked away, wondering what he told his mom the first time he saw her after being picked up.

I notice the cops at every single freaking doorway. One of the cops who came to my house is staked out at the front, near the altar.

There's plenty of empty seats and everything, but Mom has to head right to the front of the church, dragging us behind her. I know the drill—kneel, make the sign of the cross, follow my little sisters into the pew.

In the front pew, Mac's mom is sitting beside Greg's mom and a man who must be Mac's dad. She's crying, he's not, but he has his arm around her. There's a cop right next to them. I scan the whole church, but I don't see Greg nowhere.

The priest stands up at the altar and we begin. I mumble with the rest of them. *"Hail Mary, full of grace, the Lord is with thee. Blessed art thou amongst women and blessed is the fruit of thy womb, Jesus. . . ."*

I glance up in the middle and realize that Chris Cruz is looking back and making a goofy face at me, and all I can think is, *Please, dear God, don't let Mac's parents look up just now and see that and think he's making fun of Mac, 'cuz I'm pretty sure he isn't.*

And now my mom is nudging me and I realize that I've fallen off the Hail Mary's so I start up again. . . . *"Holy Mary, Mother of God, pray for us sinners now and at the hour of our death. Hail Mary, full of grace. . . ."* And where is Mac's best friend at "the hour of our death," anyway? Even Jim Hill's here, way in the back. He came alone. What's he doing here? Weird.

We start praying in Spanish. *Dios te salve, María, llena eras de gracia, el Señor es contigo. . . .*

God, these pews are hard. Why can't Catholics create more comfortable seats?

Am I going crazy? I better get serious and spiritual, pronto. *God, Carbon Copy, will you quit grimacing at me?* What is he getting at? Wish I knew.

I find out later, after the service. "Can you believe Bernie came?" he says as soon as we meet in the foyer.

"What?"

"Yeah. Some balls."

"Did he stay for the whole service?" I ask.

"Not only that, he even went up and kissed Mac's mother, you know, at the end, when everybody goes up to do that."

"He's lucky he didn't start another fight right in the middle of the rosary." Shit. I can't believe he came. I mean, *crap*. I'm still in church. I can't believe I just thought the word "shit." I mean, *"crap."* I just thought that word again. *Fuck* this. This is *exactly* why I hate church. Having to be careful all the time about what you think or say or how you act.

"I wonder if Mac's parents know who he is," I say.

"His mother just kissed him like he was another Jesuit boy," says Chris.

Jim walks over with Omar Chavarria in tow. "Hey, Ish, Carbon Copy. Can't believe Bernie showed his face around here. Like he wasn't just threatening to take Mac on yesterday. I'm gonna go beat that fucker up."

"Don't say that in church," I say quickly.

"Why not?" he asks. "Anyway, God doesn't care."

"Yeah, he does," I say. Jim and Omar both give me this weird look.

"And you know that how?" Jim asks.

Then Omar adds, "I never knew you were so religious, dude."

"I'm not," I protest. But you have to stand up for some things, right? "Shi-iiit," I say, finally, just to get them off my back. "Let's get out of here."

I can make a confession about swearing in church later. That's the beauty of confession: no matter what you do, you can be absolved. It took me a long-ass time to figure that out but now I'm virtually guilt free. Ha-ha. If only.

"So, dude, you all down with taking him on?" Jim asks.

"No way, man," I say. Chris shakes his head, too.

"Look," says Jim. "The bastard can't think he can just come here, to this place, and it's okay. The Fronchi probably had Macaroon killed."

"Aw, man, we just had a *rosary,*" I say. "What about all the cops, anyway?"

"We'll be careful, man," says Omar. The two of them head out the front door.

I think I'm gonna puke any second now. Fuck, here it comes. Where's the damn bathroom?

What do they think they're doing? Do they *want* to start a war with the Fronchies?

Alexander Gold

Member of the Mermaid Garden

The days go on and on . . . they don't end. . . . All my life needed was a sense of direction, a sense of some-place to go. I do not believe one should devote his life to morbid self-attention, but should become a person like other people.

—Travis Bickle, *Taxi Driver*

I'm sick of the way all the teachers look at us guys like we have some sort of disease. And having to goddamn pray before every class. Most of us just sort of mumble, make the sign of the cross, and glare if someone seems too happy about it like that sicko Mac, who's gonna make a perfect priest someday.

Sometimes at school, it's all so depressing, I think about killing myself—but there's too much going on at home. I don't know what Mom'd do if I was gone, with Dad being the way he is. How can people change so much in one year?

I thought about this while watching Mac slam Bernie's head into the cement. I wasn't cheering either one of them on, just watching.

The thing is, I don't know which one I hate more. Mac's al-ways had a thing for Vero, this girl I like. A few months ago, he talked some shit about her, that she showed him her tits or something. And Bernie's just Bernie. An asshole. The only thing he ever said to me, ever, and we've been going to the same school for three years, was "You think you're better than us *Mexicanos,* don't you?"

The whole school's on edge these days. Nah, it's not the Cinco de Mayo thing. That just highlights it.

And in the midst of it all, I am invisible, the Invisible Man of Jesuit. I'll see one of the guys at the mall and they just walk on by. The teachers never call on me. I was on the wrestling team last year. Not only did the coach never let me compete, sometimes he'd forget to call on me in practice.

I'm a little bit like Travis Bickle in *Taxi Driver,* a movie I used to watch constantly with my dad: *"Loneliness has followed me my whole life,"* says Travis, *"everywhere. In bars, in cars, sidewalks, stores, everywhere. There's no escape. I'm God's lonely man."*

Not that I'm altogether like Bickle. Nah, just in some ways—like I'm alone all the time. And I want to do something big that will prove my importance. I want other people to know I'm here, that I matter.

But of course, there is an upside to being invisible: I see *a lot.*

Like Dan Tucker doesn't know I know he's gay and in love with MacKenzie Malone in the worst way. And with that choir teacher, Mr. Torres, who's also a total flamer.

I know Rafa's in some El Paso gang called Los Chucos. I don't know if it's a real serious gang or not—a *Blood In, Blood Out* kind of thing—but it *is* a gang. Still, one likeable thing about Rafa—he keeps telling dumb joke after dumb joke, and even though nobody laughs, he keeps telling 'em. I heard him in the hall the other day telling some kid, "You know you're a Mexican if you use your lips to point something out!" Then he laughs and says, "Get it?" Nothing gets the guy's spirits down.

Then there's Jim Hill, who, when he thinks nobody's watching, fucks with people in bad ways. I saw him burn a hole in Greg González's T-shirt once with a match. Greg thought he was getting bit by some fly until he discovered the hole.

And everybody thinks Isaiah Contreras is such a saint, but he cheats on tests *all the time,* usually from Chris Cruz or Josh Alvarado 'cuz they're the ones sitting just up from him. He's been cheating off those two guys for years, since eighth grade. I know 'cuz I've been watching. Good ol' Father Mackey caught him once and confronted him about it.

At least Isaiah's sober—Mac sure as hell isn't. I caught him snorting something once in the restroom. Gets his shit through Josh. Josh, who pretends to be Mr. Goody-Goody Drug Dealer—claims to sell a little harmless hash, cannabis, and nothing else, but I know for a fact that he'll hook you up to any dope you want.

And that's Today's Report from Jesuit's Invisible Man.

◆ ◆ ◆

When I get home from school, I can tell Mom's crying. She stops and quickly says, "Hey, Alex," and gets up to look in the refrigerator. She swipes her eyes and I pretend not to notice. "After-school snack?" she says, turning around and giving me this bright kind of look.

This is our routine.

"Yuperoo," I say. She just needs to do something for

somebody. "Going to the computer room," I add, and I go make myself comfortable while Mom putters around the kitchen.

One time, Mom accused me of spending all my time cruising porn on the Web. Sure, I've done my share of dicking around online, okay? But mostly I'm in chat rooms for video games or I'm looking for Web sites that experiment with weird digital technologies.

Dad comes home around seven. I grew up with a "normal" dad. He used to yell at the umpires during my baseball games. Went to all my karate matches. Last month, when I earned my black belt, he just stayed in bed. He spends most days sitting in some coffee shop, reading the newspaper.

You know that Disney movie *The Little Mermaid*? There's this scene where Ursula the Sea Witch shows Ariel her mermaid garden. There's this close-up shot of all of these once-beautiful mermaids who have shriveled and dried up like mushrooms. They're missing teeth and their eyes are huge in their tiny, wrinkled heads. You hardly have to look at their eyes to know their fear, to taste it, the same kind of fear I used to feel as a kid when I knew a kidnapper was creeping down the hallway to get me. My dad looks just like that, one of the living dead, a member of the mermaid garden.

"Hey, Dad," I say, but he passes by, wordless. A few seconds later, the mattress creaks as he slumps onto the bed.

Mom wanders by a few minutes later and smiles at me, distracted, but pretending she's not worried. "Doing your homework, Alex?"

"Of course, Mom."

Why does she think I do homework in here? She's seen my

grades; didn't even ground me when my report card came last week. Wasn't even mad.

I decide to call Veronica. I've known her since elementary school, but she just sort of popped open last year. I don't think she knows what to make of my phone calls.

"Hey, Vero," I say as soon as she picks up.

"Who's this?" she says. I picture her on the other end of the phone, her long, hooked nose that she hates, her dark *café con leche* skin that she hates, her dark almost-black eyes that she hates. *I'd* hate it if she had white skin, blue eyes, a tiny nose. She's perfect just the way she is.

Maybe she's curling up on her bed with the phone and looking at the ceiling, where she has pictures of her favorite band, The Fatal, local boys who've made it big. One of the guys in the band, Angel, used to go to Jesuit and lived in my neighborhood. I used to see them taking basketball breaks between band practice, before they went on the road.

"It's Alex," I say. "Alex Gold. What're you doing?"

"Homework."

Vero's an El Paso High girl. I didn't think she *had* homework. "Yeah, like what?"

"Spanish verbs."

There's this long silence. *What should I say?* Girls in public school, they have a freedom and looseness. We try to be all cool and dirty-mouthed at Jesuit, don't get me wrong, but it's in an uptight way, like we're all playing against some stereotypes that we can't get beyond, because they're true.

"So, what're you doing?" I say. *Shit.* I'll always be Milhouse, trying to talk to Lisa Simpson.

"Told you."

"That was thirty seconds ago," I say. "You might be doing something different right now, like picking your nose."

Why the hell did I say that?

"Do you think I have a big nose?" she asks right away.

"God, Vero, no, I *love* your nose," I say immediately.

"I'm going to get a nose job," she says, "when I turn seventeen. Mom says I can."

"Don't," I say.

"Why not?" she asks. "You want me to stay ugly?"

"God, no," I say, horrified to my toenails, but then I realize she just tricked me into saying she's ugly!

"You think I'm ugly?" she asks in a tough-girl voice.

"No! No! *No!*" I say.

"My boyfriend, José, thinks I'd look better with a smaller nose," she says. "I asked Mac Malone what *he* thought and *he* said, 'Don't change a thing.' Why can't you be like him, Alex? Why don't you like me the way I really am? Huh?"

Jesus. I don't even get the benefits of having a girlfriend but I have to sit and suffer through conversations like this one. Just for the *hope* of getting a girlfriend.

But I . . . I like this girl, that's all. I type her name on the computer screen. *Vero, Vero, Vero. Veronica, Veronica, Veronica.*

"Mac Malone got into a huge fight at school today," I say at last, to change the subject. "He sent this kid Bernie to the hospital."

"I don't know why you guys call him Father Macaroon," she says. "This is just more evidence that he's no priest. I showed him my boobs once and he, like, totally ejaculated. In his pants." She squeals as she giggles.

"God, Vero. Do I need to know that?"

"My boyfriend didn't want to hear it either. I was telling him and Rafa all about it and he was like, 'Bitch, shut up,' and I was all, 'Who you calling bitch?' What kind of boyfriend calls their girlfriend a bitch?"

"Probably all men think that about their woman at some point."

"*Their* woman?" she asks. "Like she's a possession? Like a dog? What are you, some kind of macho pig? You know, women's lib happened before your mother was even born."

"Vero?" I say. "I gotta go. My mom needs to use the phone."

"Okay. Later."

And we hang up. I sit back with a long *oomph.* She's so quick, I never respond fast enough. If I could do that, I'd write a book about it and make millions selling it to Catholic prep school guys who have no clue. Like me.

Mom comes down the hallway and smiles at me. "You haven't touched your milk and cookies," she says, and looks like it's going to make her cry. *Oh, Mom, do you really want me to be six again? Because even if I wanted to, I really can't do that.*

"I like the milk warm," I lie.

"Who were you talking to?" she asks.

"Just a friend." Mom'd probably be thrilled if she knew I was in love with some girl, but then she'd get all anxious and start thinking I would knock her up. I wish.

"I'm going to go get a movie," Mom says. "Want to come help me pick it out?"

Damn. I'm going to be stuck watching this thing with her. "Sure," I say. "What's Dad doing?"

"Sleeping. He's worn out. It's hard, looking for jobs all day."

Is she really trying to protect me from the truth? I wish I had a sibling. Then it wouldn't all be on me.

◆ ◆ ◆

Mom really likes classic films, classic romances especially. If I ever take a class on the history of American film, I'll definitely ace it. I've seen them all: *Battleship Potemkin, Singin' in the Rain, Midnight Cowboy, Rambo.* Between Mom's obsession with the classics and Dad's obsession with manly flicks from the '70s and '80s, you name it, I've watched it.

Tonight it's *Breakfast at Tiffany's.* Seen it.

It's one of those films where everything falls apart for the woman but at the same time there's a comfortable sense that everything will be all right in the end. This girl, she has all these men who love her and want to protect her, even though she gets into trouble and everything. It would be so much easier if life were like one of these movies. But Mom's no Audrey Hepburn. She's stuck with a depressed husband who couldn't protect her if he wanted to. Sometimes I want to say, "It's over, Mom. Why don't you just leave him?" But then she'd cry and I'd feel like a jerk.

Mom and I watch movies every Friday night. Even if I could go to J-Town and party, who would I go with?

◆ ◆ ◆

Dad's passed out on the couch when we get back. I poke him in the foot a little and Mom whispers, "Leave him alone, honey. We'll watch the movie in the bedroom."

I'm sticking the DVD in the player when I hear the first sniffle. Oh God, the movie hasn't even started.

I sit stiffly against the bed throughout the film, pretending I don't notice the tears. When it finally wraps up, she says, "You want to take it back tonight, Alex?"

My own mother, asking me to break the law! Curfew's at 11 for all seventeen-year-olds. "Sure," I say, all suave. I'm reckless, a daredevil.

Just before I reach the video store, I see Rafa and his hoods drive by. I'd know his car anywhere. Lowrider cars are always distinct. Rafa's is an old '78 Chevy Impala with a motor so loud you can hear it five miles away. It makes everything in the vicinity shake and rattle. He's painted the body a bright yellow, with red flames licking up the sides. Rafa's from Segundo Barrio, one of our poorest neighborhoods, but I swear there's got to be ten thousand bucks in that car. Guess there's more money floating around the barrio than in these classy neighborhoods sometimes. Drugs. Illegals. Smuggling shit and people. I've heard they just tuck the money away in things like old cars so nobody ever suspects. Spending that kind of dough, though, you'd think he'd find a way to make it stealth, smooth, quiet. I would. But I don't think that's considered cool in his lowrider world.

Wonder what they're doing around here? They don't generally venture onto this side of town. They're not cruising, though. As they peel past me, I catch a blurry glimpse of the back of two other guys' heads. The whole thing looks like trouble.

♦ ♦ ♦

I drive up Baltimore Street, thinking, *Maybe I'll see if the light's still on in Vero's room.* I cruise past slowly. Her bedroom's on the second floor, around the side.

Just as I reach her house, I see this guy get up from the grass a couple houses ahead and kind of stumble forward and drop into the street, almost right in front of my car.

It's Mac! Mac Malone! Oh God. Oh God. Oh God. Oh God.

I get out of the car as fast as I can, but he doesn't get up again, just leans against me when I kneel down. He's bleeding everywhere, all over the street, all over my shirt, just bleeding like a . . . I don't know, what do they say, a stuck pig?

"God, what happened?"

"Are you talking to me?" he mumbles. "Please, go get my mom," he begs, starting to cry. "Please go get my mom. I need my mom." He's crying and bloody and I don't even know which house is his. I stand up to go but he grabs my T-shirt and says, "Don't leave me! Don't leave me here!"

He's still gripping my T-shirt.

"I don't understand, do you? Why would that *ass*hole—?" He spits up a bunch of blood on my shirt and closes his eyes.

Ohfuckohfuckohfuckohfuck.

He's let go of my shirt and that is so fucking not a good thing.

I run up to the nearest door and start pounding on it and I guess it must be Mac's mother who answers and she sees all the blood on my shirt and she just screams, "Who are you???" and then she looks beyond me at Mac, who's lying in the middle of the street. She runs screaming back into the house and starts yelling into the phone.

She's left the door open and I am just standing there but I don't think I should go in. Should I?

I walk back to the curb and sit down, staring at Mac. I can tell he's stopped breathing.

I would hate to say he's dead but I think . . . he is.

Fuck.

This. Is. Not. Real.

The police arrive in about two seconds.

"Dear God!" the first cop says as he gets out of the car. Mac's mother is screaming in the background. Mac's father is now crouched down by Mac's body, Mac's head in his lap. He's crying, these great, gulping, wailing sobs. I've never heard a man cry like that before.

The fire truck comes next in a light-blinding, siren-wailing arrival, followed by an ambulance. Two paramedics jump out and run toward Mac and his dad. Gently, one of them steers Mac's dad away while the other turns Mac over and grabs for his wrist to check his pulse. They start pumping Mac's chest and breathing into his mouth. Then they move him into the ambulance and whirl away in a noisy blur.

I sit on the curb. Neighbors start to come out onto their front porches to watch. "I want to go home," I say to nobody in particular.

"I'm sorry, son, you can't go home yet," some cop standing nearby says.

"Why not?"

"You're a witness."

"But I just—I just found him like this, what you're seeing now," I protest.

"We still need a statement," he says. "Just sit tight."

Soon there's a whole group of cops standing next to me. One of them has the yellow police tape; he blocks off the crime scene.

Then one says, in this tough-guy dickhead police voice, "You'll have to come down to the station to file a report."

I'm like, "What? Can't you just take my statement here and let me go?"

But no. "You're breaking curfew," Dickhead Cop says. "We have to charge you."

What the fuck? So what that I'm breaking curfew? They've got a murdered kid on their hands.

They let me call my mom from the police station. She says, "I'll be right down, honey." She comes to the station in her bathrobe and everything, which should be embarrassing but I couldn't care less. I give her a strong hug.

"What's going on?" she demands. "Are you charging my son with something? We want a lawyer."

"No, ma'am," the officer explains, "we just need his statement and his clothes, which will be entered as evidence."

"Why do you need my clothes?" I ask.

"He won't make a statement without a lawyer," Mom says.

She's making me sound all guilty! *Thanks, Mom.*

"Mom, it's okay," I say. "Let's just make a statement and get out of here."

"Be *care*ful," she insists. "Don't let them trick you." And she eyes the police officer with enormous distrust staring out of her baby blue eyes. I feel almost . . . flattered?

I head into a room with two cops, Dickhead from earlier and an older-looking cop. I write my statement. "I, Alexander Gold, saw MacKenzie Malone stumble into the street next to his house. He was all bloody. I got out of my car, helped him to the lawn, where he uttered two phrases: 'Please go get my mom' and then 'I don't understand why that asshole—.' Then I rang the doorbell to get his mother. This was at approximately 12:15 a.m."

Even while I'm writing this, I'm wondering whether he said "*that* asshole" or "*those* assholes." That would make a big difference, wouldn't it? Our whole justice system is so dependent on people remembering little things like this. For a second, I think about withholding that information. I don't want to seem wishy-washy. Besides, I know I'm a suspect. But then I think about Mac. No matter what, he doesn't deserve this. So I should just be honest, stick my foot out, let them know the truth.

"You know," I say, "I don't remember whether he said 'that asshole' or 'those assholes.' "

"You don't remember?" Dickhead Cop says, then repeats, "You don't remember?" He leans back in his chair and stares at me like I'm some kind of punk. "A detail like that—it could make or break a case."

"Well, I'm sorry, but I was a little distracted." I did not ask for this.

"Hey, hey, it's okay," the other cop says. "Ease up, will ya?" he says to Dickhead.

"You guys don't need to play Good Cop, Bad Cop," I say. "I really don't have anything else to tell you."

It takes them so long to process this simple paragraph that I'm at the station until 4:30 in the morning. I'm like, "Aren't I breaking curfew?" at one point to Dickhead. Then I say, weakly, "Ha-ha," and he says, "Ha-ha back at you." *Dickhead.*

Around 4, some guy comes in and says, "I'm sorry to be the one to tell you this, but your buddy died about half an hour ago."

I knew it. When Mac spit all that blood all over my T-shirt, I knew I was seeing Death.

I wish I could feel sorry. But there was his thing about Vero. And he was this weird mixture of religion and phoniness. So I just sort of say, "Thanks," to the policeman, and "Can we go home now?" to my mom, who puts her arm around me like it's the saddest moment. I guess it is. *But I didn't even like him,* I want to scream.

♦ ♦ ♦

Finally at home. In my room.

Who can I call about this?

I wait until 7:30. Then I call Vero. She's totally sleepy and annoyed.

"Alex," she says. "God, why're you calling so early? Jeez."

"MacKenzie Malone's dead," I blurt before she can say anything else.

"What?" she says.

"MacKenzie Malone—he's dead."

"You're full of shit."

See, this is the El Paso High coming out in her. Normally, she refrains from swearing, like she's all cultured.

"He was stabbed to death last night. Right in front of his house."

"What?" Now she starts getting hysterical and crying, right away; all it took was one little sentence and she's weeping and wailing on the other end. "Oh my God, right in my neighborhood! Do they know who did it? Did they catch the guy? Are they looking for somebody?"

"Vero? Vero? Vero?" I'm going on and on and she's not even paying attention. "Vero, please. I *need* you."

"What? Oh, God, I can't talk right now," she says, and hangs up.

Mom gets up at 8 and comes down. "Couldn't sleep?" she asks. She puts her hand out like she's going to smooth my hair and then she stops herself.

"No," I say. I'm sitting at the computer. I haven't even turned it on. I'm just staring at the blank screen. I'm wondering whether dead guys get hard-ons. I'm wondering if you can see the hard-on through their clothes if they have an open casket. I'm wondering if I'm a real sick fuck.

"Alex," my mom says, and stops. Then, again, "Alex?"

"What?"

"Um, do you think you need to talk to somebody about what you saw last night?"

Oh, Mom. God. "No."

"Are you sure?"

"Yes, Mom, I'm *sure.*"

"Because I'd feel better if we maybe called your dad's shrink and made an appointment."

"Oh, right, because she's really done wonders with Dad!"

Mom looks like I just kicked her. She wanders away without replying.

Suck. Do I have to go find her now, talk to her, tell her I didn't mean it?

I get up from the computer. She's sitting in the kitchen with her head buried in her arms. I don't really know what to do—I'm not good at this—so from the doorway, I just say, "Mom. I'm sorry."

She waves her hand at me to go away. So I do.

Alexander Gold

Clean Conscience

> **Personnel Officer: How's your driving record?**
> **Travis Bickle: Clean. Real clean. As clean as my conscience.**
>
> —*Taxi Driver*

Saturday afternoon someone knocks on the door. A cop. I should have left. Hopped out the window. Don't have anywhere to go, but should have left anyway.

Mom answers it and says, real cold, "May I help you?"

And the cop replies, in a smooth, warm voice, "I'm here to talk to your son, Mrs. Gold."

My little mom actually seems to swell until she fills the doorway, like she's the keeper of the gate. "He's already given a statement."

"Well, ma'am, this is not about the fact that Alexander found the young man who was killed. We are stopping by the houses of a lot of Jesuit boys to ask some further questions. I'm sure you want to help find out who did this terrible thing."

Mom thaws one tiny little inch, lets him in.

I sit on the rocking chair in the living room while this cop sits on the couch opposite me. Mom stands in the doorway, her hand on her mouth. The cop is leaning forward, not relaxed at all, and I'm just rocking and rocking.

"Alex— Can I call you Alex?"

Ah, the Friendly Cop game. "Sure." I have an odd impulse to yell, *I've watched every single movie on the face of the planet that deals with cops, so I know ALL your games, buddy. EVERY SINGLE ONE.*

"Alex, do you know anything about Mac that would help us figure out what might have happened yesterday?"

How about the fact that Mac could be a bully? That he got into other fights the administration didn't know about?

"Nope," I say.

"Okay." He makes a mark on the notebook. "Nothing at all? Who he got along with, who he didn't get along with, was he involved in anything he shouldn't be?"

I could tell about the drugs, but that could get Josh into trouble. Josh isn't a bad guy, even if he is a dealer. He's, like, the one kid at Jesuit who occasionally says hi to me or "excuse me" when we bump into each other.

The cop gazes up at me, waiting for me to respond. I shrug. "Not really," I say.

"Some other guys have told us he didn't get along well with a kid named Bernie. Do you know anything about that?"

"Nope." *They were both assholes, asshole.*

"Do you know why Mac and Bernie didn't get along?"

"Uh-uh," I say.

"Do you even go to this school?" he asks. Annoyed. Good. I'm getting to him.

"Yep," I say.

"Oh, wow," he says. "You actually know how to say something other than 'no.' "

"Sarcasm won't get you what you want," I say.

"Fine," he says. "Note to self: doesn't like sarcasm. Okay. All right, Mr. Doesn't Like Sarcasm, do you know anything, anything at all that might help us find Mac Malone's killer?"

"Nobody talks to me at that school and I don't talk to them, so why would I know anything?"

He jumps right on that. "Do you resent that?"

Fuckeroo. "Uh, no. I resent *you.*"

He almost doesn't catch it, I say it so low. But then he stares at me for a looooong-ass minute.

At this point, he stops taking notes, picks his head up, watches my every move.

"Do you wish you had more friends at Jesuit?"

"Nope," I say.

"Why not?"

"Just don't, that's all."

"Do you have a problem getting along with people?"

"No."

"Then why don't you have any friends?"

"Because they're all assholes."

"Do you wish you had been friends with Mac?"

"Mac was a jerk."

"A jerk to you or a jerk to everybody?"

You want to know what kind of guy Mac was? He'd just go along, go along, taking it from whoever, and then he'd suddenly have enough, and he'd lash out at anybody who crossed his path. Like that time Bernie kept giving him digs about being a virgin, so finally, in the bathroom, Mac grabs me and tries to shove my head in the toilet. I gave him a front snap right in the stomach. Shithead got what he deserved.

"To everybody," I say.

Mom is sitting on the couch biting her nails. Is she following this?

"Why were you there last night, anyway?" He asks this one casually.

"Just happened to be there."

"How did you 'just happen' to be in that neighborhood at that time?" Ooooh, a stray hint of sarcasm in that "just happen."

Here I am, the one guy at school that nobody notices, and now everybody is going to notice me. I bet they're going around to all the guys and asking them, *What about this Alexander Gold? What do you know about him? Did he hate MacKenzie Malone?* And nobody will defend me because they don't know who I am.

"I was returning a movie," I say. Didn't I go over this last night? Maybe not. Don't remember anymore. Haven't had any sleep. "I went up Baltimore to pass by this house where this girl I like lives. That's all."

"Did you see anything else unusual around the area?" he asks.

"No."

"No? Weren't you driving slowly and looking carefully at this girl's house?"

"Yes, precisely," I say. "I was looking *at her house.*"

"Then how did you 'happen' to see Mac lying in the street?"

He's painting this picture of me inside his head: a loner psychopath, the alienated kid who suddenly goes berserk and kills his arch-nemesis.

Surprise—Mom answers for me. "What are you getting at, Officer . . . Officer—" She locates his name on his uniform. "Officer *Loopeze?*"

It's almost like she's saying, *Take that, bitch!* She totally knows his name is López.

"Are you suggesting my son had something to do with this unfortunate murder?" she continues. "Because I don't like what I'm hearing, and let me tell you something, Officer *Loopeze*. A person guilty of murder does not knock on the door of his victim's house to wake up his victim's mother to go get help for that victim. A guilty person does not stick around until the police show up. A guilty person does not go obediently down to the police station to give a statement. No, siree. Are you people idiots or what?"

Yuperoohoohoo! Go, Mom!

"If you people would learn how to use basic common sense in your investigations," she continues, "you would have figured this out already. I'm sorry to have to point this out to you. I think that will be quite enough of my son helping the likes of you." She's standing up and pointing toward the door. "Thank you very much for coming, Officer *Loopeze*."

She closes the door behind him, then glares at me. "This isn't something you should be snickering about, Alexander Gold." She disappears down the hallway.

I *did* feel like snickering for a moment.

But now I'm thinking, *Damn Mom for making me her mama's-boy movie date. Damn Vero for being so sexy. Damn Vero for living near Mac. Damn Mac for being the kind of asshole that gets killed.* Why does everything and nothing happen to me?

Sometimes I feel like I want to do something, you know? Do something bad, something that's not easy for me to do but maybe could be if I pushed myself hard enough. Like Travis Bickle.

You know, in that classic Martin Scorsese film. Bickle is

this dude who can't sleep, so he takes a night job as a taxi driver. He'll drive anybody anywhere, no matter if they're uptown or lowlifes. The more he drives, the crummier he feels about the city, the more he thinks it's full of people who should be just wiped out. He tries dating this woman, Betsy, but that doesn't work out because Travis really doesn't know how to behave like a normal person. He doesn't know the difference between taking Betsy to a regular movie or to porn and that's why Betsy, this blond ice-queen type, breaks up with him. The loss fills him with despair and he wants to do something, anything, something bad. He decides to assassinate the presidential candidate Betsy works for. But even in his badness, he still wants to save the world. And the person he ends up saving is this twelve-year-old prostitute, Lily, played by Jodie Foster. He saves her by pumping her pimp full of bullets.

Some people say it was this movie that made John Hinckley shoot Ronald Reagan, to impress Jodie Foster. So maybe movies make people do dumb, extreme things. *"Are you talking to me?"* That was the phrase Travis Bickle kept repeating to himself, looking in the mirror, right before he tries to be both the hero and a killer. And I don't believe it's a coincidence that that's what Mac said, too, just before he died: "Are you talking to me?" Jesus. I mean, shit, he *couldn't* have been quoting from the movie. I mean, it's not like I think it's a clue to the killer's identity or anything. But I felt like Mac was talking to *me,* telling *me* I had to do something, something only I could do for him. Maybe I'm closer to being Travis Bickle than I thought.

Daniel Tucker

Fag Moment Revisited

> This plane is definitely crashing. . . .
> And my heart has slowly dried up.
> —Modest Mouse, "Shit Luck"

It sounds totally gay to say it, but my favorite part of school is choir. Mr. Torres, the choir director, kicks ass. It's a completely different kind of singing than the kind I do for the band, but something about singing Handel's "Alleluia" every Christmas makes me feel clean and good, I don't know why. When I sing for the band, I just feel cool. Okay, sometimes I feel a little stupid, especially if people in the audience are just standing there talking. But I always put on a good show anyway. I jump in the air, do splits, throw my hair around—what little hair I have, that is, since we have to keep it short for Jesuit. During the summer, I'm growing it long. We'll have more gigs then anyway.

"Move with the rhythm, boys," Mr. Torres says, and most of us try to sway more while we sing. He cuts his eyes toward me, then back to the rest of the guys. Even when I step out for my solo, he keeps his eyes on everyone but me.

Everybody stares at Mr. Torres while we sing, like we're little angels, like we're not going to revert to our usual trash talk as soon as class is over.

Other than Mr. Torres, I don't give a rat's ass about school. And as for the guys? The only guy I like, hetero, is Josh Alvarado. He's been my buddy since first grade. Malone's cute and interesting but I mostly ignore everybody else. If I could quit and just play music, I would. Hang out with the band. Refuse to take showers for weeks. Just sing and play.

I wait around until everybody leaves, then I approach him. "Hey, Mr. Torres, I have a gig tonight at The Underground with my band. I was wondering if you'd like to come see me play."

"Um, sure, Dan," he says, looking a little nervous. Jeez, it's not like I'm asking him out or anything. "Where's The Underground?"

"Downtown El Paso," I say. "You know, right near San Jacinto Plaza, on Oregon Street. It's got that big yellow sign?"

"Oh, yes. Isn't that a bar?"

"Uh-huh," I say. But isn't it pretty much the same thing as if he was going to some student's basketball game or speech competition? "I mean, you don't have to come or anything," I add. "I was just asking. You know. If you don't want to, that's cool. I understand, it's last minute, you probably have plans. It's okay if you can't make it."

"No, no," he says. "I'll come, for a little while. What time?"

"Band sets up at nine. We'll start playing around ten."

"All right then." He smiles at me, all kindness. He's not really my type—at least, I don't think so. I've never even had a date. In El Paso, it's not easy finding gay teens who are out. Especially when you have to keep your identity a secret at school like I do. I'm always trying to figure out if any other students at Jesuit are gay. You'd think we'd find each other. You know, birds of a feather.

✦ ✦ ✦

Ma never comes hear the band play, but she'll take in some of my choir performances. She thinks we're all sweet and nice when we sing choir music. She worries, when I'm with the band, that I'm hanging out with all of these older guys in bars. "Don't be like your dad, Danny," she always tells me before I head out on Friday nights. I've *told* her I don't drink or do drugs. But she doesn't believe me. My pops lied to her all the time. Thanks, Pop.

I'm not friends with Mac Malone or anything, but I'm dropping by his house on my way to the gig to invite him along. I saw that fight. Thought he might prefer not to be alone tonight.

"Hey, man, you want to go hear my band play at The Underground?" I ask real fast as soon as he opens the door. I'm nervous around all the guys except Josh. Oh, yeah, and my band members. But they're like brothers to me.

"Why?" he asks.

"I don't know why," I say. "Just thought you might want to, that's all."

"I'm supposed to be grounded," he says.

"Well, say your buddy needs some support or something like that. Tell your mom I've been expecting you to go for weeks." *Jeez, man, don't make me beg.*

There's something about Mac—this sadness way back in his blue eyes. It makes him seem really sensitive, a total turn-on. Queers will dig that hangdog look, too, even though he's straight. I think.

"Just a sec," he says, then leaves me standing by the door.

Why am I even bothering? Guess I don't want Mac to feel like a pariah. Despite the fact that he beat Bernie to a bloody pulp. Or despite his little Cinco de Mayo letter last week. For God's sake, Mac, what'd you think would happen?

I wander to the edge of the porch and look out at Madeleine Park. Mac lives in a nice part of town and his house is really cool. I like this wide porch, with the ivy hanging over it. It makes the house seem kind of secluded and private. If I lived here, I'd get a hammock, some plants, probably do all my studying out here. Well, whatever studying I had to do. Did I mention how much I hate school?

Why is Mac taking so damn long? What if he thinks I just asked him on a date? Ah, shit. But I need him to say yes so that if Mr. Torres comes, he'll see that I didn't just ask a teacher because I don't have any normal friends. Josh has other plans tonight that involve dope and some chick.

I hear a little yelling inside.

Mac slams the door shut behind him and leans on it like he just escaped. "Yeah, it's cool."

"How long you suspended for, man?" We start heading toward my car, parked under the cottonwood tree in his front yard.

"Three weeks! But I'm gonna protest the decision. They're fucking with the rest of my life. If I miss three weeks of school right now, it'll look bad. College applications. All that shit."

I whistle. "So what're you going to do? A letter campaign?"

"Yeah, plus placards and posters and protests after school," he says. "Gonna make sure I'm real visible. Gonna make sure I'm a pain-in-the-ol'-Catholic-ass."

He seems real revved about this, so I let him rant on while I get in the car. Then: "I think Mr. Torres is coming," I babble. Mac's in choir with me.

Mac shifts in his seat a little, like he's uncomfortable. "Mr. Torres, huh? He's cool. Hey! Do you ever think about teachers having lives outside of school? I mean, besides the obvious fantasizing about Ms. Meadows."

"I ran into Brother Rodarte at Albertson's once," I say. "He and Sister Mary Marie, the nun at the cathedral—they were stocking up on beer and wine. They had an entire cart full of the stuff."

"No shit," Mac says. "One time my mom and I stood behind Mrs. Smith in the checkout line at Wal-Mart. I said hi but she didn't remember who I was. I snuck a peek in her cart. Guess what she was buying?" He doesn't wait for an answer. "She had eight cartons of cottage cheese! Oh, and some hair dye. For the next week, I wanted to ask her what she had brought to school for lunch, cottage cheese or cottage cheese."

"Did you?"

"No guts."

We're quiet for a long time, and just as I'm starting to get nervous again, he speaks. "I want to believe they're human, you know?" he says.

"Who, teachers?"

"Teachers. Moms and dads." He sighs. "It's like they never *listen* but they still make all the fucking decisions for us. It's kinda like this whole three-week suspension. Have they thought about the consequences for the *rest* of my life? No, they just act. Decide. Like little gods, lording it over our lives. Not 'cuz they're smarter, just 'cuz they're older."

"Sometimes I get the feeling I'm marching blindly toward something I don't want to be," I agree.

"You are," he says. "It's the inevitability of turning eighteen and becoming an adult." And then he adds, gloomily, "But we don't have a choice. In real life, nobody loves Peter Pan, the boy who never grows up."

♦ ♦ ♦

Mac sits at the bar drinking Coke while we set up. There's already a crowd of people laughing and drinking. Some of them keep heading to the bathrooms to snort or shoot. They always come back with their eyes all glassy. My pops used to look like that before Ma kicked him out. Then he went to jail. I've seen him once or twice since he got out, but it's embarrassing. He's not all there. He calls me "Danny Boy." Like I'm four years old. There's this Circle K near school where bums sit around drinking all day. I've seen him over there. He always hangs with losers.

Hey, there's Mr. Torres. Cool! He came! I should warn him. Wonder if he'll question my singing abilities after hearing me grunt and screech tonight?

He joins Mac and puts his arm around him for just a second, a quick second, then drops it. Most of the guy teachers do that. I guess they're afraid of getting sued if some student takes it the wrong way. It'd be nice, though, if one of them sometime just put their arm around us and left it there, in a normal way. I'd never think Mr. Torres was coming on to me just because he put his arm around me for a few seconds.

We warm up with some numbers we're not sure about yet

but that we've been working on for a couple of months. We're building an enthusiastic fan base in El Paso. So, maybe we have a chance to achieve our rock-star fantasies.

When we finally get going, I'm already down, into it. I look up once and realize Mr. Torres is watching some girl stick her hand on my ass. Fuck!

I whip around and jump up onstage, crashing to the floor in a semi-split, then jump back up into the air and end with a howl.

Afterward it takes me a couple minutes to cool down, and besides, the stage gets crowded in seconds with our groupies. I say hi to a couple girls but I'm eager to find out what Mac and Mr. Torres think. My two big crushes at school, both here. God. Makes me feel all giggly and nervous. I'm *such* a girl.

"Thanks for coming," I say when I reach them.

"All those chicks," Mac says. "Lucky dog. Think I need to learn to play guitar."

"Great job, Dan," Mr. Torres says. No arm around for me. I probably make him nervous 'cuz he's a fellow fag. Gaydar. "But I gotta go. Things to do, people to see." He smiles as he makes his way out of the bar.

"What'd you think?" I ask Mac.

"Fantastic, man. I can't believe you can still talk after all that screaming."

"Want a beer?" I ask. "I can get one of the guys to get it for us."

"Sure."

So we sit in a corner, watching the next band. They're really tight for the first three songs, then the guitar player loses it and starts going all over the place. The beer's starting to go to Mac's head. Instead of that deep sadness thing way back in his blue eyes, there's something else, a dazed what-the-fuck-have-I-done kind of look. I get him another two beers.

"Shit," he finally says. "I'm so fucked."

"I know." He looks really cute and available, a little lost dog. I really want to do something right now. Why am I thinking about this when he's trying to tell me his problems?

"My parents are so pissed, they're never going to trust me again."

"Your mother let you come out with me tonight."

"No, I came despite her."

"Or *to* spite her?" I ask.

"Both."

Am I really here with Mac? I should be siding with Bernie. He's actually all right. He's the only guy in the school who knows I'm gay and he's never said anything to anybody. Okay, he can be kind of an ass, like the rest of them, but overall he's a good guy. I guess you can be an ass and a good guy at the same time.

Mac taps the table twice with his fist, then holds the fist in the air for a second before he crushes it to his mouth. "My mother—she knows exactly how to mess with my head. She makes it sound like if I've been defective ever since I was born."

"Isn't that part of a mother's job description?" I feel like his priest all of a sudden.

"You know what she told me today?" he asks. " 'We wanted more kids,' she said. 'But you're all the children we could handle.' "

We talk a while longer. Mac's starting to look really drunk, and like he's about to cry.

"I don't really know what's wrong with me, you know," he says.

And I say, "Hey," soothingly, putting my hand on his knee, just to let him know it's okay. It's just an impulse. I don't know why I do it. Suddenly, without even thinking, I'm leaning toward him, my lips ready to kiss him. He jerks his head aside and my bottom lip brushes the soft bony flesh of his upper ear. His hair smells like strawberry. Weird. Maybe he uses his mother's shampoo?

His knee jerks and his head whips back around so he can look at me and I see all his pain deep down—and a realization. He's thinking, *Shit, Dan's coming on to me.*

I snatch my hand away quickly, like his knee is really hot. My God. Did I just make a pass at MacKenzie Malone? *Fucking, fucking stupid.* Rule #1: Never let anyone at Jesuit know you're gay. Rule #2: Never let anyone who knows someone at Jesuit know you're gay. Rule #3: Never let anyone who knows anyone who knows someone at Jesuit know you're gay. *Stupid, stupid, stupid.*

Mac is getting up, walking out to the car. He's not looking at me. I'm surprised he's even willing to get in my car.

I swagger out to the car after him. Have to act tough and unconcerned or something. Should I insult him so he doesn't think I'm a homo? Except I am. And now he knows it. And he's going to tell everyone. *Hasta la vista,* my life.

Daniel Tucker
Lights BUrn Like Scars

You better listen while you can
It's a very thin line between animal and man.
—Dead Prez, "Animal in Man"

My boy Josh comes over Saturday afternoon, stoned. The thing is, the guy is brilliant. He could go to Harvard Law School tomorrow and hold his own. But he'd rather deal, smoke, and screw chicks than do something worthwhile with his life.

I've told him, "Look, man, don't be a loser like my pops." Don't get me wrong, it's not like I'm into law and order or anything. But drugs can wreck everything. I've seen it. I know it. I do. Sometimes, though, I'm jealous of Josh's freedom.

As Josh sits in the corner, the band practices in my garage. There's four of us in Voz—me, the lead guitarist and singer; Matt, the other guitarist; Alfredo on bass; and Manny, the drummer. Josh is our groupie, but he's not always loyal. Take last night, for example.

"Hey, Josh, I've got a new song I'm working on; a cover, but we'll put our own spin on it," I say. "Tell me what you think." Sometimes he can have real insight when he's in that openness that apparently comes with weed.

Strumming a few chords on the guitar, I start to sing a wailing tune from Sparta:

Piece this together
And it's always a fight
This puzzle's intact
And you're always right
The sky could fall
The bliss of beginning replaced with an end
And the sky could fall
It's always it's always the same

And it ends
From a scream to a whisper
Can you free me from these words and let me forget?
And it ends
From a scream to a whisper
Can you free me from this world and help me forget?

I'm singing along and then I realize that Josh is—*crying?* Oh, God. What . . . ? I blurt into the mike, "Josh, man, what's up?"

He chokes, then: "It's Mac. Mac, he died last night."

"Mac Malone? I was just with him last night. Are you sure?"

"He got knifed like twenty-five times or something. Died early this morning at the hospital."

I should stay. But I have to leave. Now.

I rush out of the garage, leave the band and Josh without saying a word. Go inside to my room and lie facedown on the bed. When Josh follows me in, I say, "Go away," and he does.

But now I wish he was here. Last night, I tried to kiss Mac Malone. He didn't want that and I knew it, but I did what I did and now I can't change it. Ever. God, who did this to him? I need to talk to *somebody*. But who?

My mother comes to the door and says, "Hey, Danny, there are two cops downstairs. They want to talk to you. So tell me first. What'd you do?"

"*Thanks,* Ma," I say.

"I'm just asking," she says.

Why can't I just lie here in bed forever? Maybe listen to some Blonde Redhead or Modest Mouse. Jack off and then sleep for a thousand years.

"They're *waiting,*" Ma says, tapping her foot on the floor.

"Okay, okay, don't get your panties all in a wad," I say. I've always wanted to say that.

She swats my butt as I go out to the living room.

Officer Rodríguez and Officer López shake my hand. "Do you know why we're here, son?" Officer Rodríguez asks.

"I just found out about Mac. About twenty minutes ago."

"We understand you were with him last night? Before he died?"

"I was."

"What did you and Malone talk about? How did he seem to you? Was there anything you noticed that seemed odd?"

"Um, which question do you want me to answer?"

"All of them."

What should I tell them? "I, ah . . . He seemed bummed out about getting suspended from school."

"So you guys talked about that? Did he indicate he was worried about possible revenge from Bernardo Martínez?"

"Not really. He just said he didn't like getting shit on."

I answer the questions, they go away, Ma freaks out.

"Daniel," she's yelling, "were you involved in this horrible thing? Were you? Huh? Tell me!"

She starts to slap me and I put my hands up to protect myself. "No, Ma. I already told you."

"You're turning out just like your father—" she starts.

"You *know* I'm not like Pop at all," I interrupt. "And that's just the problem! That's *why* you don't get me! It does explain why you're so fond of Josh, though. He's *just* like Pop."

"What?" she screeches.

Oops. Time to shut up. "I'm going to bed," I say, and leave her fuming.

Now Josh is waking me up in the dark by shaking me, shaking me hard and whispering, "Hey, man, I need your help."

"Wha—? What're you doing here, Josh?" I poke around for the alarm clock and stare at it. It's 2:17 a.m.

"Greg's fucked up," Josh whispers. "He had a bad trip. He's pretty calm now but kind of a zombie. I don't think he can walk yet. I need to get him into his house, into his bed, without his folks waking up."

"Crap. How are we going to do that?"

"Bedroom window. Just need some extra muscle."

"Fuck, Josh. Why do you always get me into these things?"

He grins and hits me on the shoulder. " 'Cuz you my boy," he says. "You my main man. You my boyfriend." And he does this little wiggling of his hips, purses his lips like he's going to kiss me, and waggles his finger at me in a come-on gesture.

"Shut up, you faggot." I'm already up and putting jeans on. Josh is, like, the only guy who will ever see me in my underwear until I have a boyfriend. I can't risk getting a hard-on with anybody else. But Josh is kinda like a girl to me. There's no attraction. So weird. "I don't like it when you look at me that way. It makes me nervous."

He laughs. "Are you homophobic, Dan? Do faaaaaags scare you?"

God, Josh—what would you do if I told you?

"Yo' mama," I say before we open the door, sneak down the hallway, gently ease the back door open, and walk over to his Jeep.

* * *

Greg's half zonked, half weeping in the car. He doesn't even notice when I sit right next to him.

"So how'd this happen?" I ask.

"He freaked out just when he started to fry," Josh explains. "He thought I was the one who killed Mac."

"Shit. No way. What'd you do? What'd he do?" We speak quietly so as not to disturb the patient.

"Well, we were out in the desert, so he just takes off, starts running in circles, like he has all this excess energy to get rid of. And I just let him run. And he's yelling. Then he tried to choke me."

I glance at Josh's neck. "Are those his finger marks on your neck?"

"Nah, just hickeys," he replies. "Anyway, I just talked in a real calm, soothing voice to him until he removed his hands from my neck. Then he freaked out and started sobbing in this really high-pitched scream. I've never heard anything like it. He was just wailing and wailing, like some Jew at the Wailing Wall."

"What?" Josh is beyond me sometimes.

"You know, the wall in Jerusalem, the wall that's left of that temple?"

Whatever, Josh. He can be so random. "Do they actually wail there?" I ask.

"They pray there, man. It's the closest they come to the temple, their holy place."

"Okay, how long did he freak out like that?" I ask.

"Three hours, give or take. Since then, he's been crying and talking to himself. When he calmed down, I brought him here."

"What do you think he saw?" Damn—I regret the awed way I phrased that and the hushed voice I used. As if I think acid is a "religious" experience, a visionary thing.

"Himself," Josh says. "You always see your true self on acid. You just usually see more than you want to see. So it all seems distorted."

See what I mean? He's not your normal stoner. The guy should become a poet, a psychologist, a scientist.

We pull up near Greg's house and stare at it like it's a damn fortress.

"You don't think he needs to go to the hospital?" I ask.

"Nope," Josh says. "For a while, I thought maybe, yeah. But he's good now, he's off it, he's not hallucinating anymore."

"You're sure?"

"Yeah."

" 'Cuz you can *die* on LSD—"

"That's such anti-drug propaganda bullshit, Dan," Josh interrupts. "Nobody's ever died from an LSD overdose. *Ever.* As long as you keep people from doing stupid things while they're tripping, it's all good, man. Why do you think I babysat him?"

He reaches into the backseat and punches my shoulder. "LSD isn't your dad's smack. So stop worrying."

I scrunch down in the seat. How'd he know about that? "Right. What's the plan?"

"I'd ask him if there was a key hidden under a rock," Josh says, "but he's not gonna be much help. Watch." He pokes Greg in the leg, prods him on the shoulder, grabs his cheeks and smushes them together, the way parents do to a baby, and says, "Ootchi googi Greggy, did ums have a good trippy? Did ums find out itty-bitty singies about oos-self zat oos didn't likeums?"

Yeah, Greg's lost in his own world.

"Man, you shoulda known better than to give him acid after his best bud was murdered."

Josh pulls a remorseful face. "True." Then he grins, remorse gone just like that. "What a trip, huh?"

As Ma always says, "That Joshua, he's incorrigible." True that.

* * *

So we figure that since I'm sober, I should conduct reconnaissance. I creep out of the Jeep and head toward the side of the house, moving right in between Mac's and Greg's houses. Aren't the cops keeping an eagle eye on this street? Jeez, Mac died in this yard, right where I dropped him off. Someone must have cleaned off all the blood. Did Mac's mom have to do that? If you were just some stranger walking past, you'd never know. Mac's life—just washed away. By Monday, his locker'll be emptied, and next semester somebody else'll be using it. Maybe it'll be known as the Dead Guy's Locker, and everybody will make up ghost stories about it.

Are there really ghosts? Will Mac's ghost haunt this spot where he was killed? If there were such things as ghosts, I'd try to work up the guts to tell Mac I'm sorry. But if ghosts have power and he was mad about what I did, he might hurt me. Gay guys get bashed on a lot and I don't really want to be the gay guy with a ghost after him. Unless it's a hot gay ghost?

I poke around in the grass, trying to find a way to lift myself high enough so I can see inside the windows and figure out a good room to dump Greg in. Preferably his bedroom.

By placing my hands and feet on the side of Greg's house and the wall that separates his house from Mac's, I can scoot upward, sort of like a rock climber, to see into the window. That's when I notice that there is an identical window on Mac's house. I look inside Greg's window and bingo! It's his room. And bingo for the second time! The window lifts. Yippee-ai-ay. I didn't know what we were going to do if that didn't happen. Leave Greg on the porch and ring the doorbell? Nah. We couldn't do that to his parents, not on the night after . . . I don't know how we'll shove Greg in there but we'll manage. We're strong, tall, strapping young men in our primes.

I drop down in the grass and start to head back to Josh's Jeep when I glance over at Mac's house. I crouch inside the bushes to be sure nobody sees me. Just as my back starts to itch from all the little bush spines sticking into me, I realize I can see right into what is obviously Mac's bedroom. Mac's mother is sitting on his bed, just sitting there. She's not crying, as far as I can tell, not covering her face. She's just sitting in the dark, in her dead son's room, just—sitting. All alone in the dark.

I want to jump inside that room, throw myself at her feet,

confess, express all my frustration and sorrow and how I *wish to God* I had done anything else. Anything but try to kiss her son.

But first, I have to shove this lardass through his tiny little window.

* * *

Next day, Sunday. I can't stop thinking about Mac's mother. I wonder if she knows what an asshole her son could be. Or how great he was. Do any of us realize the million stupid truths about the people we love? I hope she never finds out how some people think he was a card-carrying member of the Aryan Nation, just because of that newspaper letter.

Four-thirty in the afternoon. Can't sleep, can't play the guitar, told the band to go home 'cuz I can't sing worth shit today. Need to stop thinking. Gotta do something, anything.

"Why don't you eat something?" Ma asks. "You seem jittery."

"Not hungry."

Mac's mother, in the window, sitting on Mac's bed. Mac getting out of my car. Me driving away. What if I'd stopped, turned around, gone back?

Does Mrs. Malone need to talk to somebody? Do I need to talk to her?

"I'm gonna take the car, Ma," I say, positioning myself over the keys so even if she says no, I can grab them and run.

"You got a hot date?" Ma asks.

Wonder what she'd do if I told her?

"NO!" I say, drumming my fingers against the countertop. I pick up the keys.

"But you're showing all the classic symptoms," she persists.

Go to hell, Ma.

"Okay, okay, go, go," she says.

The car won't start. The engine keeps trying to turn over. What am I doing wrong? I hardly ever drive.

Ma starts tapping on the living room window, gesturing for me to come back inside. The car chokes and starts so I take off.

Takes a mere two minutes to get to Kern Place from Sunset Heights. First time, I drive past the house slowly. Then I drive past again, ultra-slowly. I should stop, get out, knock on the door. I should I should I should. But I can't. I think I can I think I can I think I can I think I CAN'T. I am not some Little Engine That Could . . . or will.

Circling around the block again. That picture stuck in my head. What exactly was she thinking about, sitting there in the dark?

I circle the block a zillion times. Stop once. Twice. Head back home.

◆ ◆ ◆

Now it's 8 at night and the seconds are ticking by so slowly, I feel like I'm counting 'em. I wonder if this is why people start drinking? Why they can't stop?

"Ma, can I borrow the car again?"

She sighs. "Danny, remember your father. Always out and about, running around, looking to score or party."

"Aw, Ma, I just need to go somewhere, that's all."

"Okay. Fine. But be back in an hour."

Yes!

So now I'm right back where I started. Right outside the

Malones' house. Stuck. Why am I such a coward? What am I doing here? What do I think I can provide to Mac's ma?

Finally. Out of the car. Knock on the door. A very light knock.

Mrs. Malone whips open that door like she was waiting behind it. "Hi!" she says. "You must be one of Mac's friends from school!"

I nod, mute. *Why is she so . . . exuberant?*

She reaches out her hand and pulls me inside. "Come in."

I find myself sitting in an uncomfortable wooden rocking chair in the front living room. Mrs. Malone positions herself across from me to the left and Mr. Malone wanders in with a glass of, I'm guessing, whiskey in his right hand. He shakes my hand and sits across from me to the right. They both focus on me.

"I went out with Mac the night he died," I start.

Mrs. Malone's hand goes to her mouth. Mr. Malone takes a swig of his drink. He sits on the edge of the chair like some earnest guidance counselor, his knees spread apart, one hand on a knee, one hand holding the whiskey. He's tall with curly blond hair. Just like Mac.

"I just wanted to say I'm sorry about what happened," I tell them. "I've already talked to the police. I'm sure they'll find out who—"

"Was he upset?" Mrs. Malone interrupts. "That night? When you guys went out?"

I could lie. "Yes, ma'am," I admit. "I'm sorry."

She lets out a tiny little sound, a cry so quick and high, it's like a hiccup. Mr. Malone collapses back in his chair.

"It was a bad day," I say. "I—I wasn't on my best behavior

either. I'm kind of ashamed of that—" What am I saying? I can't tell Mr. and Mrs. Malone what I did to their son. This visit isn't about *me*. "Uh, I just feel bad," I continue lamely. "I don't have a dad so I—I know what it's like to, um, lose someone." God, I— "Hey," I say, finally. "I'm writing a song. For Mac. Because—well, because I'm going to miss him. I will. He was a good guy."

I look desperately from one adult to the other, Mac's parents, Mr. and Mrs. Malone. You never really think about other parents, about what goes on in their heads, until something like this happens. Isn't that what Mac said? How he wanted to think of adults as something more than just parents and professions? Right now, they look so incredibly frail and human, I'd do—whatever they asked me to do.

Mr. Malone clears his throat. "Thanks, son. That's—that's real nice."

Mrs. Malone is openly crying now. She pats the sofa beside her and says, "Honey, come over, please. Come here. I'm glad you came. Don't feel bad about yesterday. It wasn't my best day either. I wish—I wish I could tell him I love him one last time, that's all."

So I get up and go over to the couch and I sit there beside her. "Thank you," she says, putting her arms around me. "Thank you for coming." Her tears soak the shoulder of my T-shirt.

◆ ◆ ◆

At home again. When Ma's gone to bed, I sneak downstairs and open the photo albums. I don't know what I'm looking for. There's a few pictures of us all together when I'm, like, four

112

years old. Dad has a goofy look on his face when we're posing outside of Disneyland. There he is at my birthday party when I'm three, wearing a clown wig and outfit. The Christmas I'm six, the pictures don't lie: he's clearly bombed out of his head. By the next year, he's in jail, so it's just me and Ma in front of a much smaller Christmas tree. I was ten when I caught him coming out of an adult video store. I didn't even know he was out of jail. So when I saw him, I didn't know what to do. "Danny Boy!" he called, and came running over. He smelled like BO squared and his teeth were brown, like you could scrape layers of scum off of them.

We don't have any pictures of him when he looked like that.

I slap the photo album shut. What was I hoping to find? Insight? Shit, I don't know why I'm so worried about Mac's ma. I should be worried about me. It's been ten years since I lost my dad and I still haven't figured out how to deal with it.

Gregory González

Death Scene

I was gonna hang out with Mac after dinner but his mom tells me he's gone out with a friend. She says this from inside the door, her hands crossed over her chest, which Mac tells me is a "posture of defiance and anger." Where *does* he get this stuff?

"Greg," she asks, "do you think Mac is stressed about grades or something?"

You don't always know when you have to be a best friend. This is one of those times. "No more stressed than the rest of us! He's fine, Mrs. Malone."

But truth is, Mac has seemed different lately. Wired. On edge. But what she doesn't know won't hurt her, right?

"Thanks for trying to make me feel better, but I suspect it's much more than that, Gregory," she says. Her whole body sags as she closes the door.

My dad suggests we go see a movie. "We haven't done that in a while, Greggy," he says.

Garrgh. "Dad, I'm sixteen years old. I'm not little Greggy anymore."

"Sure thing, Greggy," he says, winking at me.

Double garrgh. "Dad!"

We go watch a movie called *Northern Lights,* which is

supposed to be a freaky new thriller about demon possession. I keep giggling throughout the movie. Fuck, the priests in the movie are *nothing* like the tons of priests I've known my whole life.

"Well, that was spectacularly dumb," Dad comments when the lights come on and the credits are rolling. "Best part about that movie was the popcorn and sour gummy bears."

"You always say that." It's true, he always says that.

"How about some suds and mud?" he asks. We go to Jaxon's for this. Dad likes their microbrewed beer and I like their Mud Pie. We never come here when Mom's with us. She doesn't care if Dad has a few beers, but she thinks I should drop a couple sizes. Dude, the last thing I need is my mom looking over my shoulder while I eat.

We sit at the bar and watch ESPN on the big-screen TV. After Dad's had one beer, he says, "So . . . I hear Mac got into a pretty big fight at school today."

"Can I order a second Mud Pie?" I ask.

"I don't see why not," he says.

"Is this like a bribe?" I ask. "Are you saying yes so that I'll talk to you about Mac?"

"Curses, you've seen right through my clever scheme." He waves at the bartender, Eric, who sets a beer in front of him. "Thanks."

During football season, the two of them are all buddy-buddy. Dad went to Texas A&M and Eric's from College Station, the town where the school is located. Dad's rooting for me to go there, too.

"So, about this fight," Dad says, all fake casual.

"Mac feels really bad about it."

"Does he? I understand he sent that other kid to the hospital. . . ."

"He didn't mean to. I mean, Bernie was insulting Mac's mom. Saying some bad stuff. Mac had to do *some*thing. He couldn't just take it."

"You don't have to solve these sorts of problems by fighting," Dad says.

"God, Dad." At this point, I'm picking at my Mud Pie, having totally lost my appetite. "This is as bad as you calling me 'Greggy.' "

"I'm your dad," he says, spreading his arms in a "what can I do" gesture. "I just have to make sure your moral compass is pointing in the right direction."

"Isn't that what those dumb catechism classes are for?" I grumble. "Besides, *I'm* not the one who got in a fight."

He sighs and pats me on the back. "Okay, son."

♣ ♣ ♣

Mac and I are building a huge fire underneath the tree house he used to have in his backyard. Mac has painted his body green and he's dancing around the bonfire in a bathing suit. I have this sense that there's a girl around somewhere but I can't see her. I hope she doesn't come back and think we're satanic, but I go along with Mac's plan. 'Cuz I always go along with his plan.

"Greg! Wake up!"

"Huh? Wha—?"

Dad's voice is low. "Mac's been hurt. Some kind of a stabbing incident. The ambulance is on the way to the hospital. Your mom and I are going there to be with the Malones. Do you want to come?"

I'm already out of bed, putting on my pants. "I'm coming!"

Mom's waiting for us in the car. As soon as I sit in the back-seat, she reaches around and rubs my knee with her hand.

Off we go. Nobody says a single word.

When we walk into the emergency room at Thomason Hospital, Mr. Malone is bellowing at the nurse in charge, "I have to be in there with my son, do you understand?" His face is all red.

In a firm but definite whisper, the nurse says, "That is not policy or procedure and we simply cannot allow it." She motions to a security guard, who bounds over and stands just behind her so Mr. Malone knows she means business.

Mrs. Malone sits in the plastic chair with a faraway look on her face. My mother sits next to her, holding her hand and stroking it.

We all just stare at the floor. My mother keeps stroking Mrs. Malone's hand. Somebody walks by and we look up to watch them pass.

Doctors and nurses rush in and out.

The other people in the waiting room look just like us.

"How long do you think we'll stay?" I whisper to Dad.

"Son, we won't leave until we know how your buddy is, don't worry," he replies.

Fucking A. What would Mac make of this? He'd probably start pondering the irrationality of hospitals keeping people from their loved ones just when they most need to be with them.

I go sit in a corner for some privacy and start dialing a couple people I know. Why am I so eager to spread this news? I call Jim's house but nobody answers. Neither does Josh. Third try.

"Yo, Raf."

He's grumpy. "Why'd you wake me up, hey, *Chuco*?"

"I'm at the hospital," I announce. "Mac got stabbed."

"Oh, yeah?" He seems wide-awake all of a sudden. "*¡Chingao! ¿Qué pasó?* Do they, like, know who did it or what?"

"I don't know, dude, but they're not sure he's gonna live."

"Shit. Call me in the morning if that *puto* don't make it, okay?"

I'm about to call somebody else but Dad comes over and says, "That's enough, Greg. Let it wait till morning."

I have to go back and sit beside Mr. and Mrs. Malone. Mr. Malone has stopped harassing the nurse. He's sitting back in his chair, glaring at the floor.

I hunch over in my seat. Whatever it is that Mr. Malone finds so interesting on the floor, I can't see it.

At ten minutes to three, the emergency room goes suddenly, deathly quiet. Not a nurse in sight. *What is going on?*

Mr. Malone gets up and goes to the double doors that lead to the area where they are working on Mac. The security guard silently steps in his way.

"I just want to see," Mr. Malone begs. "I just want to see. Please. That's my only child in there. My son. I just want to see. Look, everybody's gone." He gestures toward the empty waiting room. "Nobody will know if you break the rules. That's my boy. Something's happening to him. Please. Let me in."

"I'm sorry, sir."

The pleading sound in Mr. Malone's voice makes me feel sick. I can't look at anybody, can't look around the room. Does everybody else hear that sound in his voice?

Dad puts his arm around my shoulders. I'd like to lean against him but I stay in my hunched-over position. Frozen.

When the doctor who went in with Mac comes out of the

doors, his body sagging and defeated, I know what he's going to say. We all do.

"Everybody here is family, Dr. Mathias," Mr. Malone says.

But I'm not sure any of us really hears the doctor's words because Mrs. Malone starts screaming as soon as he opens his mouth. Mom moves over to her and hugs her, as if that will stifle the screams, and then she grabs me and I'm stuck in that double-mother-hug while the doctor repeats, "I'm truly sorry for your loss."

We silently follow the doctor to a hospital room. Mac's lying on this bed and he is totally, one hundred percent dead. But he still looks alive. Except he doesn't. He's all—white. God, of course he's white, he *is* white. His mouth is open. I can see his teeth, all the cavities in his lower molars.

My mother reaches over and closes his mouth.

That's when I run my fat self right out the room. I can't handle this, I really can't.

I sit down in the hallway until my dad comes over. He gets down on his haunches to talk to me face to face.

"Seeing Mac like that," he says, jerking his head back toward the open door, "is more than *I* can handle. A kid your age . . . you're not supposed to ever see something like this, son. I'm so sorry, Greg."

Let me breathe for a few minutes, okay, Dad?

"Do you want to talk about it?" he asks.

"I just— Look, I need some space."

The clock. It's one of those big electric ones with red numbers that tells the seconds. I keep looking at it to figure out how many minutes Mac's been dead. The doctor said he died at 3:34 a.m. and 6 seconds. Why are they so precise? What's the point?

Mac's been dead for less than half an hour and I'm just standing out here in the hallway, watching time continue to tock. Dad goes back into the hospital room. From my position in the hallway, I can see the four of them gathered around the foot of the bed, silent like they're in church. And I can see the foot of the bed. But I can't see Mac lying on it. Dead.

Here they come. They step outside the room and Mom grabs Mrs. Malone and they stand there, weeping in the hospital corridor, holding on to each other for forever, like they're not going to let go.

Suddenly Mom detaches and propels me toward Mrs. Malone, who is dabbing at her eyes with a tissue that's been used so much, it's falling apart, leaving little bits of white tissue paper on her face. Mrs. Malone grabs on to me with this iron grip. She's clamped down so hard, my nose ends up right in the middle of her boobs.

I don't want to be thinking about Mac's mom's boobs. It's hard to breathe inside this hug. But I can't move because if I do, she'll be hurt, like I don't want her to hug me or something.

And then Mom goes, "Merle, Gregory will be your son, too, from now on."

And now Mrs. Malone weeps even harder. *Shi-iiit. Two moms, as if one isn't too much.* Awkward, I rub Mrs. Malone's back and try to catch my dad's eye. But he's just looking at the floor, and Mr. Malone is tracing circles on the tiles with his toe.

I can still see that damn clock. Mac died thirty-five minutes and thirty-six seconds ago.

Gregory González

Mac in Heaven

Isaiah Contreras and Chris Cruz are walking up the driveway to my house. *They weren't Mac's friends, not really. What are they doing here?*

I walk out on the porch and we just stand there, looking at the park where Mac and I used to ride our tricycles when we were kids. *Jesus, this hurts.*

"Hey, man," Ish says. *"¿Qué haces?"*

"Nada," I say. "Just hanging around. What are you guys up to today?"

"Same old same old," says Chris.

"My mom's gonna make me go to the Mass," Ish volunteers.

"Me too," I say.

Except for school, I haven't been to Mass in three years. But I want to go today. Mass at least is larger than me, grand and impersonal somehow. I'll be invisible and nobody needs to know what happened to me.

"Someone's arranging a rosary for Mac at the cathedral tonight," I add. A rosary is, like, specific—everybody will be there for the same purpose so everybody will know what you're thinking, what you're feeling. It's gonna be so awful. On the other hand, Mac deserves a rosary, he really does.

So finally, "I'm really sorry, man," Chris says.

"Me too," Ish offers.

"Not your fault." Dumb thing to say. But somebody *is* at fault, somebody *did* this to him.

Was there something we could have done to prevent this? Maybe if Mac hadn't fought Bernie? Or if he hadn't gone out last night? Or was it just his time to die? I hate this thought. Mac and I used to talk like that. Could you prevent your death or change your fate? Was everything foreordained? Mac should have been a priest with the way he liked to talk about this stuff, but he liked girls way too much.

"When did you find out?" Ish asks.

"I was at the hospital last night," I say.

"Rough," Chris says.

"Really was." After we came home last night, Dad grabbed me in another bear hug. His body shook. I mean, he was *crying,* just like Mr. Malone cried at the hospital before we found out Mac was dead. Then he shoved me away, said, "You know I love you, son," but before I could bolt, he grabbed me again, said, "I love you, Greggy. My son." Then he shoved me away again. "Go to bed. Get some sleep. We'll talk tomorrow."

No sleep for me. Kept looking out my window at Mac's room, just across from mine. All these years, living so close, we passed messages back and forth, used flashlights and Morse code. When we got older, we'd text message on our cell phones. That is *never going to happen again.*

I would have gone out with him last night, but he was supposed to be grounded. If I'd been there with him, would I be dead, too?

Chris and Isaiah have said everything they know to say. The three of us are all talked out.

"Well," I look back at the house, "I think I better go inside. My mom's been crying all morning."

After they leave, I tell Mom I'm going for a walk and head over to Jim Hill's apartment. We aren't the best of buds, but sometimes he'd hang out with us, me and Mac and him and Ish. He's kind of the closest thing to a Mac type of friend I have right now—a little bit crazy, likes to hear himself talk. You know.

Jim lives in these tiny apartments near Cincinnati Street with his mom and little sister, who just started high school this year. His mom is this frazzled white woman who's smoked too much, so she has that wrinkled, washed-out look, and a drawstring-bag mouth. She has a sexy voice, though. Too bad it doesn't go with the rest of her.

We used to tease Jim and call him Jim *Hell* but unfortunately, it's not much of a joke. Once, when we were little kids, I caught Jim frying ants with a magnifying glass. He kept the sun's beam on them until the little bodies burst in this explosion of steam. I even saw one ant burst into flames. That's just one of the reasons I don't hang out with him much. He set fire to his mom's car once, too, I remember, and then he got arrested for setting fire to his neighbor's garage. That was back in seventh grade. I think he was already doing drugs when we were, like, twelve. He says he parties in J-Town at least once a week.

His little sister is even worse. It's not that she does sick, sadistic things like Jim, but she's already the town ho. She started wearing a dog collar last year, and these little black leather skirts. No underwear. I *saw* it. She's a pregnancy-and-abortion waiting to happen.

Jim's mom answers the door. "Oh, hi, Gregory," she says.

It's obvious she's read the story in the paper or heard it from somebody.

"Is Jim home?" I say quickly, even though she's not the type to cry.

"Yeah. Hey, Jim!" she yells down the hallway. "Get your ass out of bed. Gregory González is here."

Jeez. Kinda glad she's not *my* mom.

Jim looks like he's just tumbled out of bed after a hard night. He joins me outside and we sit on the curb. "Wha's up?" he says, blinking rapidly, as if he's not really in the real world yet.

"Just came over to say hi," I say, wondering if he knows. Picking up a few stones, I start tossing them into the street. Jim's street is full of all of these cracks. When I was little, I'd follow the cracks splitting off into dozens of different directions on my street. Used to pretend that if I couldn't cross the street by following one crack to another crack until I reached the other side, then I was stuck on one side of the street. It gave me this great feeling to solve the problem of being stuck by figuring out the maze.

"Rough fucking night," he says.

"Too true," I reply.

"Shit." His eloquence always amazes me. "Shit. I can't believe it."

"Yeah," I say. "I know."

"Shit makes me mad," he says. He picks up a large stone, aims it at a car across the street and throws it so it hits its target. It leaves a little dent and chips off some paint. I can see it from here. "I want to go beat somebody up. You want to come with?"

"Jim, that's probably what got Mac into this in the first place."

"You think Bernie did it?" he asks.

"How could he?" I say. "His arm is broken."

"But he knows all those beaner thugs. He probably had Mac killed. You know those rich J-Town kids. They're all loaded down with drug money. You should have heard him at the hospital yesterday, saying stuff like 'That motherfucker's gonna get it.'"

"Yeah, but that's just trash talk. We all do that," I say. "You can't just go around accusing somebody of murder without proof. If Bernie knows people and got those people to kill Mac, we'd better just keep our mouths shut or we'll be next."

"No, man," says Jim. "I say we find out."

He's such a maniac sometimes. "Leave it alone, Jim."

Jim throws another rock across the street at a different car. It leaves another dent.

Somebody drives by in a new Hummer. "Think your grocery shopping will break your little Lexus so you need a badass Hummer just to haul your load?" Jim yells after it. "I hate those fucking cars."

"How come?"

"'Cuz people who buy them think they're better than everybody else."

My dad's been thinking about buying a Hummer since they first came out. I don't think we're better than anyone else. We just have more money than some.

"Whatever," I say. "So, you coming to the rosary tonight?"

"Fuck that. No." Jim's eyes have the same wild look I've seen before. "What's the point? Mac's dead, finished, terminated, totally fucked up to the point of no return. How's a rosary going to change that?"

"A rosary's so his soul can go to heaven," I say, good Catholic boy that I am.

Jim snorts. "You don't think Father Mackey's an automatic shoo-in?"

"He just sent Bernie to the hospital. Yesterday," I say. Why am I arguing that Mac may not make it into heaven? Jim, he stirs me up, that's all. "And anyway, Mac wasn't Catholic. He never got baptized."

Jim waves his arm to dismiss that. "Doesn't matter. Mac was practically a priest. He fucking went around all the time talking about sin and shit like that. In fact, he was such a self-righteous little prick, I kinda hated hanging out with him."

I stare at him. Mac wasn't like that. I knew him way better than anyone. So he was into talking about philosophy and that kind of stuff. So what?

"Well, I have to go tonight," I say at last.

"Yeah, buncha old ladies praying and weeping. *Fuck that.*"

"You're not even Catholic, are you?" I ask.

"Nope. Only reason I'm there is 'cuz my parole officer asked the school to give me a fuckin' scholarship."

"So what do you do when we pray at school?"

"Wait till it's over. I made up my *own* words to the Hail Mary—want to hear 'em?"

"Not really." I can just imagine.

"No, listen. 'Hell, Mary, who went down on God. Blessed is your pussy above all hos'—' "

"Shut up," I interrupt him.

"What are you, a little Holy Roller, too?"

"Do you really say those words when we're all praying?"

"Fuck yeah."

"Nobody's ever caught you?"

"I just mumble 'em," he says. "They don't care. Just so long as you look like you're doing the right thing."

I stand up. "I gotta go. My mom'll get worried if I'm gone too long today."

"Mama's good little Catholic boy," Jim snickers. Then he gets a serious look on his face for just a split second and says, "Hey, man, I'm real fucking sorry, okay?"

I give him a friendly shove. Jim Hill's an idiot. A little bit creepy. But sometimes he's okay, you know?

Gregory González

A Little Trip to Nowhere

I'm walking back up to my house when this Jeep swings around in front of me and I see Josh Alvarado. Man, this neighborhood is crawling with Jesuit guys today. I haven't seen so many of them on the weekend since, well, never.

"Hey, man, want to go for a drive?" he says. "I got some bud to spare."

He's stoned, of course. Josh is always stoned. I don't know how he does so well in school. I study hard and I don't do half as well. "I could use some," I say.

So I hop into the Jeep and we start to drive. He's obviously driving just to get away, taking whatever road looks interesting. Eventually we end up on a dirt road in New Mexico, headed out toward the Potrillo Mountains. Mexico to the left, Texas behind us. I've been out here with my dad, hunting for rattlesnakes, just for fun. We haven't done that in a long time. I wish I could do that right now, just take a gun and go blow the heads off a bunch of snakes. If I knew who killed Mac—I could blow *his* head off.

"Do you know where Kilbourne Hole is?" Josh asks.

"Dad and I've camped at the edge of it a few times," I tell him. It's this gigantic hole in the middle of nowhere, created by a volcano that imploded instead of exploded. Mac explained that to me once. "It's to our right and up a bit. Why?"

"I'm thinking of pushing this Jeep over the edge," he says. "And just leaving it there."

"Sounds like fun. Except then we'd have to walk thirty miles to get out of here."

"Right," he says. "Bad idea." Then: "I have some LSD. Want to try it?"

"Sure."

He pulls over off the side of the road. "Okay, man, have at it. I'll babysit."

"Thanks." *Just give me some release. If it's stupid and I die, then let me die.* But still, I ask, "Am I going to be able to go to Mac's rosary later if I do this?"

"Sure, why not? It might even make it endurable."

He hands me this little stamplike thing with a picture of Bart Simpson on it. What *is* this?

"It's a blotter," he says. "Stick it on your tongue and let it dissolve."

I place it on the tip of my tongue.

Then he says, "Stop! Are you sure you want to do this, Greg?"

"Yeah," I say.

"Just so you're sure." He sits back, like he has all the time in the world.

It tastes funny, sort of sugary and mediciney at the same time. "What's supposed to happen?" I ask.

"Just wait," he says. "You'll see."

"What is this shit, anyway?" I ask.

"It's lysergic acid diethylamide," he says. "It's a synthetic chemical derived from ergot alkaloids, which comes from the ergot fungus, which grows on rye. So, if you want to justify it," he continues, "rye is a grain and grains form the base of the

FDA's Food Pyramid. You're just getting one of your daily nutritional needs."

"I've already taken it," I say. "You don't need to sell me."

"Hey, Greg, sit back and relax," he says. "You're supposed to enjoy this."

Suddenly I realize I'm sitting forward, tapping my fingers everywhere.

Wow. Every time I tap my finger on the dashboard, my finger makes a dent and light ripples outward from the dent in the plastic. Cool!

I wonder if LSD allows us to see what the afterlife is like? Wish I could ask Mac. By now, he'd know.

"Look at this!" I tell Josh, tapping on the dashboard. The light flashes over to his face, lighting it up like a big glowing bulb. Hahaha! "Ook-ah this." Something's holding on to my tongue and jiggling it so I can't say anything properly. I try to say it real slow. "Juoshhh, lew-ook-ah THIS." What's on my tongue anyway? Maybe the blotter made it all swollen. I look at the side-view mirror and stick my tongue out. OH MY GOD, it's like one of those freak shows! I saw this book once that showed pictures of a man whose balls were so big and heavy, they were like basketballs. Someone had to help him carry them up the stairs. That's exactly the way my tongue looks. "Juoshhh, lew-ook-ah mah ton-huh-huh—" I can't say "tongue." I try it several different ways. I would stick my tongue out and point at it but it's so huge, he can't miss it. It's spilling out onto the seat beside me. What if Josh were to grab my tongue and not let go? I mean, it's so swollen, he could do it easily. He could cut it off with a knife.

"Get away from me," I tell Josh. He's looming toward me, close and ugly, his hands reaching for my tongue. "Don't touch me!"

He's saying something but my head's underwater and I can't hear him. *Don't look at his head, Greg. Don't look at his head! Don't look! Greg,* don't look at his head! Oh, God. His head is split in two. He's been shot with a gun.

Oh my God. Did Josh just kill himself?

I don't fucking need this. What'll I do if he's dead? I just had one friend die and I don't even know who killed him. Maybe Josh killed him?

Who killed Mac? The wind takes my words and they come out sounding like *Whooooo killlled Maaaaaac?*

I ask the universe and God answers with a mighty *whoosh,* a wind of words ruffling my hair. I feel the Jeep shake at the sound of his voice. Can't understand a word he's saying. He's speaking in, like, Hebrew or something.

"God, don't you know English?"

"Yeah, I do, freak," Josh says.

"Josh, I wasn't talking to you. I'm talking to God. Didn't you kill yourself?"

This is said in a singsong voice. *Can't you hear him, man? Yo, God. Speak to me in English!* Whoa! What the hell is this? I KILLED MAC in big script across Josh's forehead.

So, you *did it. You've been lying all along, Josh. Great big fucking liar! You didn't kill yourself, you killed Mac! Hey, Josh, did you lie to God, too?*

Shit pops out of his mouth. Great big long strands of poop he thinks are words. *Pop. Pop. Pop.* But I won't listen to the words of the liar.

Mac!!! I hope you can hear me, man. Josh killed you and I'm gonna make sure the fucker pays.

Lalalalalalalalalalalalalalalalalalalalalalalalala! *I can't hear you! So if you want to say something to me, Josh, you'll have to write it. But I won't listen even then, because* you *are a killer!*

◆ ◆ ◆

I wake up in my own bed, early morning sun streaming through the window. I'm shivering, and what I remember most vividly is that Josh killed Mac. I can still see it, clearly written across his forehead in yellow ink; that is, when his forehead wasn't split by the gunshot wound. And I remember him confessing it, only his words, "I'm the one who killed Mac," sounded really slow and loud, the way it does if you play a tape when the batteries are winding down. What should I do about it? Who should I tell? Should I go to the police?

"Hey, Mom," I croak and get out of bed, padding down the hallway to find her.

She's sitting at the kitchen table, drinking coffee. She looks normal, maybe a little pissed. "You missed church," she says. "How could you miss the rosary for your best friend?"

Mexican moms sure know how to play the guilt card. "I'm sorry," I say. I want to go sit in her lap, have her stroke my hair, but I just pour myself a mug of coffee. Suddenly I throw the mug right at the refrigerator and it smashes in a glorious explosion of hot liquid and ceramic.

"Gregory González!" Mom stands up. "You clean that up right now!"

"Yes, ma'am," I say. My outburst done, I feel better. I go to the pantry and find the broom and mop.

She's still really upset. She stands there, staring at me, then at the mess, and then she leaves the room. I hear her go into her bedroom and shut the door, which means I'm not welcome, when what I really want to do is go in there and kneel beside her bed and put my head near hers so that I know that everything will be okay, I'll get through this. Somehow.

Dad walks into the kitchen and stops when he sees the ceramic and coffee splattered all over the floor. "What happened here?" he asks.

"I needed to smash something," I mutter.

"Where's your mother?"

I nod toward the bedroom.

"You need some help cleaning this up?" He scratches his bald spot. I hope I don't go bald.

"Nope." *Just go away, Dad. Just go away.*

He finally gets the hint. He walks to the bedroom and tries to open the door. It's locked. "Lucía?" he calls. "Lucía? Why is the door locked?" After a minute, she unlocks the door and he steps inside.

* * *

I remember laughing hysterically every time Josh told me he'd killed Mac. Why did I think it was funny? In the light of the morning sun, it is hideously unfunny. Could Josh have done that? Why would he tell me?

Did I hallucinate all of it? After all, he doesn't actually have I KILLED MAC written across his forehead. So probably he didn't say it. But what if he did? Should I call him up and ask? Should I go to the police and say, *Last night I dropped acid and discovered who killed my best bud?* Suuuure.

It is the day after the day after. It is 10:14. Mac is thirty and a half hours dead. Will I go on the rest of my life thinking things like *5 thousand, 4 hundred and 36 hours since Mac bit the big one?*

After I sweep up the kitchen, I give Josh a call on his cell. "What happened, man?"

"You don't remember?" he says.

"Not much."

"You freaked out. I thought I'd have to take you to the hospital."

"Why'd I freak out?"

"I don't know. Some people do. I'm sorry, man."

He's so casual. I hate him.

I hang up.

Taking that LSD has changed everything for me. Before this, I thought Mac's death was just some fucking freak accident that nobody could have predicted or prevented. But now I know: the guy who murdered Mac might be anyone, including someone I know.

Last night, I had this feeling I was in a long hallway and there were thousands of doors. I just kept walking and looking at all the doors. At the end of this hallway, there was an enormous door with a big M emblazoned across it in neon pink. I just knew if I made it to that door, Mac would be inside, but no matter how long I walked, I never got any closer. I remember telling Josh about the door and he said, "Maybe the M stands for 'murderer.' Maybe the guy who killed Mac is in there." *What do you know, Joshua?*

Bending down to pick up the broken pieces of ceramic, I get a distinct feeling of déjà vu. Like I'm still in that hallway, still walking along the corridor. Like I'm never going to get to the end of it.

The Kidnapping

Jim Hill

Machete and the Infiltrator Go Down

Things are not looking good. Sunday afternoon, I get a call from Gregory González, informing me that Josh Alvarado had confessed to the murder of MacKenzie Malone. He claimed that in a drug-induced state of otherworldly realms, God had appeared to him and told him that Alvarado was guilty; and furthermore, he claimed that in a moment of boasting weakness, Alvarado had in fact confessed.

Alvarado is an acquaintance of mine, and we had spent part of Friday night together. True, there had been a space of about half an hour during which we had been separated for reasons neither of us wished to discuss. Nevertheless, I decided I wouldn't dismiss the confession outright. Everybody's guilty of something, right?

I decided to go deep into this thing.

I have *always* been able to do this, become something or somebody else, for better or for worse.

I start my mission Sunday afternoon, less than thirty-six hours after Malone's murder. The night before, a colleague and I had attempted to coerce a statement from one of the prime suspects, Bernie Martínez. The Fronchi refused to crack. He claimed he knew nothing, had seen nothing, had done nothing.

So far, there was nothing I could pin on him. So I turned to my next target. Luckily, I appreciate a challenge.

Today, the first item of business is to contact Alvarado and establish if I am, in fact, his alibi.

I also need to determine exactly what potential motives for murder we can attribute to all suspect parties. And, while I'm at it, who exactly was with Malone during his final hours?

I call Alvarado. "Alvarado, I have a few questions for you."

"Jim? You sound funny. What's wrong? Why're you calling me 'Alvarado'?"

"Nothing." I clear my throat. "Can you tell me where you were between the hours of eleven p.m. and one a.m. on Friday night?"

"With you, dumbass."

"Can you verify that?"

"You were *there*. Did you get so stoned, you forgot?"

I clear my throat again. "I've decided to look into Malone's murder."

"Ha-ha," he says.

"Look, numbfuck," I say, "I'm trying to establish your guilt or innocence. You really should help me out."

"You know I didn't do it," he says. "Now leave me alone." And he hangs up!

Placing the receiver down gently, I reflect on how I need a sidekick, a Dr. Watson to my Sherlock. I call Alvarado back.

"Alvarado."

"Yeah?"

"How 'bout you help me out? Be my violent sidekick?"

"Sure," he says. "But only if you stop calling me 'Alvarado.' "

"Okay, how about calling you 'Machete'?"

"Machete?"

"Well, it's better than 'Scarface,' isn't it? Everybody does Scarface, it's so cliché."

"I don't have any scars on my face, Jim. Or anywhere else!"

"That's why Machete is better."

"Can't you just call me fucking 'Josh'?"

Hmm. Should I? "Fucking Josh" as a nickname has possibilities. "No. Josh is a name for refucktards."

"This isn't a *game*, Jim."

"I know that. You think I don't know that?"

"No, I really don't think you know that, Jim, and I don't want to be your sidekick. Go find somebody else."

"You're no fucking fun."

"Ah, but you know that I am." And he hangs up again.

I immediately call him back. "Fine. Fine. It's Josh. Now, will you *pleez* be my sidekick?"

"Grrrr."

I switch focus. "Hey, Josh, wasn't your buddy Daniel Tucker with Malone during the last few hours of his life?"

"Yeah." Now Machete sounds wary.

"Find out what Tucker knows. Find out if Tucker's guilty of anything."

By calling guys by their last names, I'm hoping Josh will catch on and start doing it, too.

"Dan is not guilty, Jim," he says.

"How do you know? Were you there?"

"No, I wasn't there, but Dan's a fucking girl. He's incapable of violence."

"Just find out. We'll reconnoiter later."

He snickers. "Yeah. We'll—'reconnoiter'—later. You *bet*."

His reaction is highly inappropriate. "Josh, have you forgotten so soon that our buddy has been slain on the battle-field of Kern Place? Is your sarcasm at the expense of his sacred memory?"

"Jim Hill, you are *weird.*"

It was time to move on anyway.

* * *

Through my extensive network of contacts, I learn that a Jesuit kid had, suspiciously, "found" Mac's body and been taken to the police station for questioning. I had never heard of Alexander Gold. None of my contacts had either.

"It's sooooo freaky," said one anonymous source. "We could have been going to school all these years with a psycho murderer."

"Who is this kid?" said somebody else. "Why did *he* find Mac?"

I had to know that, too. Further, I had to know precisely when he had arrived, why he had been there, and what he had seen before he found Malone. My best course of action was to follow up on this lead. But before interrogating Gold, I needed to talk to Dirty Bernie again.

However, in order to continue the investigation, I had to have a little conversation with my boss first.

"Hey, Mom, can I borrow the car this afternoon?"

"No, Jimmy. Last time you borrowed it, you wrecked it."

I hate it when she calls me "Jimmy." "Mom! That was a month ago."

"And you're still grounded."

"Aw, Mom."

" 'Aw, Mom' nothing. Now go away, you little waste case."

My boss is sometimes loving and kind and understanding. Sometimes she's a stone-cold bitch. This is one of those times. So I am dependent on Machete. I call him up. "We need to go interrogate a suspect, Josh."

"Is that a euphemism?" he asks. "Okay. I'll bring the 'suspect' and we'll 'interrogate' the hell out of him. I'm on my way."

Machete is disappointed to learn my true intention.

"Let's just smoke and forget about it," he says. "I don't know what you're gonna discover that the cops won't find out twice as easily."

"Cops are idiots," I tell him. "Cops would not be able to find anything, even if it was stuck up their ass."

"You'd have to be really flexible to do that."

"Exactly."

♦ ♦ ♦

The first order of the day is J-Town: Dirty Bernie and his crew. We can't take Machete's car, though. No way will it pass through Border Patrol smelling the way it does. If he's ever pulled over for speeding, he'll be so fucked.

"Maybe he'll meet us in downtown Juárez," Machete says. "We can walk across the bridge."

"You call him," I say. It's not that I don't *want* to call, but given our encounter at the church last night, Bernie might not be down with my presence. "Don't tell him you're with me."

"*Am* I with you?" Machete asks.

Hurrgh. I swallow my exasperation. I need him to cooperate.

Dirty Bernie agrees to meet Josh by the downtown bridge, but only after Josh guarantees nobody's coming to beat him up.

"You're not planning to beat him up, are you, Jimbly Wimbly?" Josh asks.

"Ne-ver call me that," I snap. "Cross my heart, dope to die, I won't beat him up, Joshy-Woshy."

After parking Josh's Jeep in a Park and Pay lot right next to the international bridge, we pay our twenty-five cents to the lady at the bridge and start walking across. Takes about two minutes and *voilà, buenos días,* downtown Juárez.

I've always liked crossing the bridge. It's like entering a different world. We usually cross at night, Thursdays or Fridays, on our way to one of the clubs on the strip. The clubs have specials on Friday nights called "Drink'n'Drown." Ten smackeroos lets you in the door and buys you all the liquor you can drink until the bar shuts down at quarter to two. Yeah, baby. Cheap way to get smashed.

Last time I crossed the bridge during the day, my mother and I were going to see one of her boyfriends, some dude who lived in J-Town but made his living ripping off convenience stores in the U.S. He'd cross the bridge, rob some store, then casually walk back across to Mexico.

But this is not about my loser mother.

Downtown Juárez is a hive of activity at all times of the night and day. Right now, street vendors peddle ice cream or fruit. Pharmacy owners stand outside their stores hawking Viagra. Taxi drivers offer to drive tourists to the market for souvenirs. Indian women in red-and-green skirts sit in doorways, babies on their laps, holding out little cups to passersby. It's all so colorful, I could kick a cat.

We spot a couple of crosses painted on random signposts. Each cross is a symbol of the murdered women of Juárez, the ones who work in the American factories, the *maquilas*. In the last ten years, they've found like three hundred bodies, and supposedly there's like another five hundred women missing.

"Who do you think is killing all those Mexican women?" I ask. "Do you think it's a serial killer?"

"How could one guy kill that many women?" Machete asks. "It'd be a full-time job. Besides, they arrested that dude, the Egyptian. But he's still in jail and they keep finding bodies. New bodies."

"Yeah, but they say he's directing the murders from prison," I say.

"Maybe." Machete won't commit himself to any kind of speculation.

How could you kill that many women in the same city and leave no clues? It's sort of impressive. *That's* true talent, total control.

We walk down the Strip. A Mexican man stands in front of one of our favorite clubs, handing out a small slip of paper, an advertisement, to each person who passes. I take one of the flyers and glance through it. Cool. Next Thursday, they're having one-dollar-margarita night. Maybe I'll come.

"The Cinco de Mayo Bomber said that Americans were killing the women," I point out. "I mean, are Americans crossing the border and killing Mexican women or what?"

"I doubt he meant that Americans are literally killing those women," Machete answers. "I think he meant that Mexicans aren't allowed to make a legitimate living. They can't cross legally, so they're forced to work in these American factories on the

Mexican side and they aren't paid enough to live on, so it creates the kind of resentment and crowded conditions and frustration that produces violence. The factories probably create some kind of violent culture without even intending it. And those women pay the price."

"You think it's just lots of different men killing their own women?" I ask.

"It's not what *I* think. But that's what I think the Bomber meant. You know what Mexicans say, right? 'So far from God, so close to the United States.' They feel like they have no help from God, but they can see all the riches and splendor and blessings of the U.S."

"Ha. That's funny."

Dirty Bernie's waiting for us outside Martino's, a restaurant on the Strip. "What's *he* doing here?" he asks Josh.

"*He's* the one that wanted to meet you," Machete says. "I just acted as the go-between."

Great echoes of the Mafia in Machete's choice of words. I can almost imagine an Italian accent. *He's da one wanted to meet choo. I just acted as da go-between, ya know?*

"Well, I don't have nothing to say to him," Bernie says.

I appraise my two companions before responding. Bernie has the dark skin of an Indian but he is dressed like an upper-class Fronchi: the ironed button-up shirt, the pressed Calvin Klein jeans, the dress shoes. Machete has the heavy-lidded look of the stoner. His skin is lighter, his T-shirt and jeans rumpled. He wears his clothes casually, but with confidence. And Machete *does* get laid.

"I'm sorry about last night," I say, deciding that concession is the key to gaining Dirty Bernie's trust. "You have to admit, it looked bad. Your fight, Mac's murder. But I thought about it and I realized that was just not the kind of thing a guy like you would do. I'm hoping you'll forgive me and help me prove your innocence."

People are passing us constantly, stopping to glance at us because we're standing on the street corner. Maybe we look suspicious?

"*Ándale, pues,*" Dirty Bernie says. "You hear anything about who did it?"

"Now that, my friend, is a mystery," I say. I have to be careful here. Dirty Bernie is not the smartest kid on the block. But even though Machete is a stoner, he's no fool. "But don't you think it's mighty suspicious that Mac got murdered the same night after he beat you up? Looks to me like someone is trying to pin the blame on Mexicans. Am I right or am I right? *¿Comprende?*"

I clap the fucktard on his back. Machete gives me an odd look so I clap him on the back, too, just to include him in the conversation.

"*Chingado,*" Dirty Bernie says. "What do you think I should do about it?"

"You could start by telling us what you know," I say. Finding out everything—that's my first goal. Seeing what the guys will do with what we dig up—that's my second.

"I don't know nothing about Mac's murder," he says. "But I know it wasn't no Mexican. That fucker is beneath us. We wouldn't bother."

"*Was,* Bernie, *was* beneath you. That may be, but I'm just telling you, word spreads fast, it gets around. People are already saying this is the work of the Fronchies."

"Who's talking?" he asks.

"Everybody, man," I say.

"Why would they say that?" Machete asks.

"Yeah," Bernie echoes. "Why?"

"Because they hate Mexicans," I say. "And you know what I tell them? 'Fuck you, racist pigs.' Who cares what they think, right?"

This is good. Bernie's getting all puffed up and red-faced. Kinda like Mac used to get.

"Just let anybody insult me or call my friends and family murderers," he says. "I'll fuck 'em up."

"Ah, you'll just make things worse," I say. "It's better to leave people alone." Reverse psychology. Always works.

"Jim," Machete says, in a "stop it" voice.

But Bernie's not fully cooked—yet.

"I'm outta here," Machete says, and turns around to head back to the international bridge.

"Be right with you, Josh," I call after him. Should I worry about his loyalty? I turn around and whisper to Bernie, "I wasn't sure I should tell you what everybody's saying, especially with Josh right here. But I thought you had the right to know." Then I go in for the double whammy. Why not, right? "Hey, man," I add. "I'm real sorry about beating you up last night."

"It's all right," he says. Then: "Thanks, man," and I'm already running after Machete.

Score one for the Infiltrator.

* * *

On the other side of the bridge, just before crossing into the United States, *La Migra* has the dogs out.

"Did you smoke today?" I whisper out of the side of my mouth.

"Shut the fuck up," Machete says softly, not looking at me.

A Border Patrol agent and his dog stop at my feet. A little sucker, a black lab with a squat body and brown, wistful eyes. I have an urge to smash it right between those cute little eyes.

I don't have anything on me, so I'm not worried. The pup stops for just a second, maybe gets a whiff of last night's weed, then moves to Josh. *That's* when she gets excited.

"Come with me," the Border Patrol agent says, and moves Josh to the corner.

I'm still in line. Should I join him or just split?

"You been smoking?" the agent asks.

"No, sir," Machete says. Voice of steel—but with a *lee-tle* crack in it somewhere.

"Are you sure? Because the dog smelled something on you. Do we need to search you?"

"Go ahead." His voice quivers, just slightly. "I haven't smoked and I don't have anything on me."

"Were you at a place where people were smoking, son?" he asks.

"I don't think so," Josh says.

The dog's finally lost interest. She's poking her head toward some other poor bastard waiting in line. Now the question is, how badly does Border Patrol want to harass Josh?

La Migra decides to let him go with a warning. "I have no jurisdiction over what you do in your own house, son, as long as you're free, American, and over eighteen," he says. "But sanitize yourself before you leave home. Take a shower, change clothes."

Did he really just say that? Fucking impossible.

"Did he really just say that?" Machete says, joining me. "Fucking impossible."

Scaaaaaary. Can Machete read my mind? If so, he'd know how pissed off I am at him because of last night. How I see it as a *betrayal*. How lucky he is I'm loyal to my friends.

"Citizenship?" the Border Patrol guy asks me in a bored voice.

"U.S.," I say, handing him my driver's license. He punches something into the system, probably my license number. That always makes me nervous. Sure, they have juvenile records expunged and all, but I still wonder what's going to pop up. But, like always, the guy nods at me and lets me know I can go through.

They question Machete longer, probably because they saw him get pulled aside for smelling like pot. "Purpose in Mexico?"

"Visiting a friend," he says.

"Really? What friend? What's his name?"

"Bernardo Martínez," Josh says.

"Where'd you meet him?"

"Downtown Juárez. Just across the bridge."

"Why were you meeting him?"

"Just wanted to hang out." Josh has been through all this before, I can tell. "We go to school together."

He's finally nodded through and we head back to the car.

"I don't know why they had to sweat you so bad," I say, but, Machete-like, he doesn't want to talk about it. *Okay, okay, I get the point.*

"Before we go anywhere else, we're getting stoned," he says. "I don't want to think anymore today."

♦ ♦ ♦

Damn it.

Dirty Bernie doesn't know shit. My sidekick is doped up. And other than Alex Gold, I have only one other lead, Daniel Tucker—and I have a feeling Machete will refuse to cooperate.

"Hey, Machete," I say, "did you talk to Tucker?" We're parked in an alley off of Montana Street. One of Josh's favorite places to smoke.

"Who?" he asks. "Oh. No. I came straight over and got you."

One good thing about the fact that he's doped up is it makes him receptive to his new name.

"Let's go see what old Tucker's up to," I say.

"Who?" he says again.

God, dope makes him dumb.

"I'll drive," I say.

"No," he says. "Marijuana does not impair your driving ability the way liquor does. I'm fucking driving my own Jeep. If you don't like it, walk." He starts the engine. "So, do you consider your little talk with our friend to be a success?"

I decide the proper response to his derision is to shame him. "Hey, at least *I'm* trying to do something for our buddy Mac," I say.

"We all have our own methods of dealing with it," he says. "But most of us don't get a crowbar up our ass about solving the crime and saving the world."

"A crowbar up my ass?" That makes me laugh. "That makes me laugh."

"Then why aren't you laughing?" he asks.

"I laugh internally. Privately. To myself. So nobody else can see."

"Where did you say we're going?" He practically runs a red light.

"Tucker's."

"Oh, right."

Yep, no impairment at all.

* * *

Daniel Tucker lives in Sunset Heights, an old El Paso neighborhood where the rich, poor, and bohemian commingle. Houses range from large renovated homes to crappy tenements where recent immigrants (legal and illegal) live. Tucker's house is in between these extremes, a small corner unit with a rock lawn and too many windows. I hate windows.

Machete marches around the back to a small garage separated from the house.

"He's not in the garage playing his guitar. If he's not doing that, then he's sleeping."

"Let's go find out if he's sleeping." The Infiltrator must be thorough.

Machete tramps right into the house. The man has balls. *That's* why he's my sidekick.

Tucker is not in bed. His mother, who is in the kitchen cooking chicken soup, says, "He borrowed the car twenty minutes ago and left. I don't know where he went or how long he'll be gone. He tells me nothing. He's a bad kid."

"He's not a bad kid," Machete says.

They have a stare-down.

"You're a bad kid," she says at last.

"True that," Machete says, waggling his fingers at her.

Then they both laugh and she gives Machete a hug. "Come back later," she says as we leave. "Come have a bowl of chicken soup."

"You're not so tough as you pretend to be," I say as we get in the Jeep. "Chicken soup? Hugging mothers?"

"I'm screwing her," Machete says.

"Yeah, right," I say with a laugh. He doesn't join in. Could it be true? Tucker's mother? I know there are rumors about Josh and our history teacher, Ms. Meadows, but fucking some bitch in her forties? That's sick, man. But kind of sexy, too. Shit, I'm jealous.

"What about Stacy?" I ask. Stacy's my sister. It's not like I'm real fond of her, but a brother has to be protective.

"What about her?" he says, as if he doesn't know what I mean.

Pisses me off, him acting all innocent. He could give my sister a fatal disease. He could, I don't know, hurt her feelings. Like, she's my *sister*. "I mean, if you're fucking all these other women, what about *her*?"

"Don't worry," he says. "She's my favorite ho."

I'll refrain from kicking him in the nuts. For now. I mean, I guess Stacy can do what she wants with whoever she wants, right? But I feel like at least she should ask me, if it's one of my friends. "I don't even know what you see in my little sister. She doesn't have much in the way of boobs."

Machete shrugs. "I don't want to talk about your sister's boobs, man."

"You were with her just last night," I point out.

"Jeez, Jim. She's your *sister*, not your girlfriend."

This stirs me up. Last night, it made me so mad, I had to

leave for a while. I took care of my feelings in my own way. But given what I'd done last night to cool off, I had to wonder what I might do if he ever makes me feel that way again. *We'll see.*

"You know she wasn't, ahem, a virgin before you," I say.

"Just shut the fuck up, Jim," he says.

I'm trying, I'm trying real hard to shut up. But it's been on my mind since yesterday.

"So, where to next, Detective?" he asks.

"We need to find out what this Gold's involvement is."

If I can find the most likely suspect, I can fan the flames. Imagine the whole school going up in smoke. That would be sweet.

"We could kidnap him," suggests Machete.

Now that's a plan. I look at his puny ass, then mine. For all we know, Alexander Gold might be some giant bruiser. "Yeah, but we'll need to get a few other guys involved." It takes me two split seconds to think things through. "Let's *do* this!"

Conspiracy

First order of the day: figure out which one of the guys will help us.

We try Rafael Najera. He doesn't answer his cell phone so we drive to his hood, Segundo Barrio, to see if we can find him.

Segundo Barrio is one of El Paso's oldest neighborhoods. If you don't speak Spanish, this is not your place. Situated right next to the Río Grande, just a stone's throw away from Juárez, it is a haven for immigrants who need to live in the United States but want to pretend they've never left Mexico.

As Machete and I drive through it, you can't blink without seeing Border Patrol. Uniforms everywhere, and I mean *everywhere.* Bikes, motorcycles, Jeeps. Watching everything and everybody. Creeee-py. It's become a full-on military zone since the bombing.

When I was just a little kid, my mother and her boyfriend would bring me and Stacy to the river near Segundo Barrio. This was long before 9-11 restrictions, so Mexicans still crossed on inner tubes to reach their day jobs in El Paso. We would all look through the fence and my mom's boyfriend would yell, *"¡La Migra! ¡La Migra!"* (That's the Spanish term for Border Patrol). It was hilarious to watch them scattering like cockroaches

do when you turn the light on. But that was a long time ago, before Operation Cinco de Mayo, the plan put into effect by the
president after the bombing. Now there's no way some stray
Mexican's gonna cross that river. Not and live to tell about it.

As we drive through the neighborhood, Machete seems real
nervous, but they don't care about us. He could pass for white,
if he wanted.

I was certain Rafa would be down with the mission—
I mean, he'd been on the scene last night, after he delivered that
ecstasy to Josh, and he'd been cool then—so I'm caught off
guard when we catch up to him and he says, "No way, I don't
want no involvement with that shit."

Rafa's a funny one—hard to tell how his mind works.
Sometimes he'll be as American as the rest of us, but when it
comes down to loyalties, Rafa's all into La Raza—solidarity
with other Mexicans. Last Fourth of July, we had a little party
at some guy's house, and I remember he took down the American flag and hoisted a Mexican flag in its place. Mac got all
mad and red-faced about that one, especially since it was so
soon after the Cinco de Mayo bombing. It was real funny. He
was totally flustered. "It's the *Fourth* of Ju*ly,*" he kept repeating.

Rafa was madder at Mac about the whole Cinco de Mayo
thing than most of the guys even realize. Last night, Rafa kept
saying, "It's fucking ignorant to go around behaving like all
Mexicans are terrorists, you know? Mexicans do everything for
Americans—we clean their toilets, sew their clothes, we even
wipe their butts—and this is how we're treated?"

Josh'd challenged him on that one. We're both Americans
and we don't treat him like he's a terrorist. (Actually, what Josh
said was "You don't wipe *my* butt," to which Rafa replied, "I
wouldn't go near *your* ass, *Chuco.*")

Rafa told us that ever since the Cinco de Mayo bombing, he gets pulled over by the Border Patrol at least once a week. One time, they even found some weed on him. They confiscated it but didn't arrest him. These days, it's all about bombs. "It makes delivering this X to you real interesting," he'd said.

So . . . Rafa isn't into kidnapping Gold. He stares at me for a long minute before we say goodbye and take off. Makes me a little nervous, but I'll deal with him later. If I have to. He knows what he has at stake.

We figure out our next best bets will be Omar Chavarria and Greg González. Chavarria's all about the military and patriotism and finding evildoers, and Malone was González's best friend. Greg is so messed up, we could have a loose cannon on our hands if something goes wrong. But he'll join us, of that I have no doubt.

"Cool," Omar says. "I have an awesome army knife we can use, if necessary. It cuts through diamonds."

"Whatever," Machete says.

"For reals," Omar insists. Wrong thing to do around Josh, the precision freak.

"The only thing that cuts through diamonds is diamonds, dumbass," Machete says. "Are you telling me your army knife is made out of diamonds? Because if it is, that is one expensive motherfucker."

Omar becomes real quiet after that comment. But I know his boasting will return. You can't keep a dumb prick down, right?

"Hey," he says as we drive over to pick Greg up, "I want a nickname. People always get nicknames for this kind of shit."

Now here is a man who understands the spirit of our venture. "We already got Machete here," I say, ignoring Machete's sour look. "So whaddya want to be called?"

"You could call me 'Mr. Bean,' " he says.

"Mr. Bean? Mr. Bean? What kind of name is Mr. Bean?"

"He's some British guy," Omar says. "He never talks."

"Hahahahahahahahahaha," says Machete. "But *you* never shut up."

"Will you two quit fighting?" I lean over and turn on the stereo, loud. "If we're gonna go kidnap Alex Gold, we have to maintain a united front."

When neither of them responds, I say, "Let's go recruit González. I'll come up with a nickname for you in a sec, Omar."

As we drive along, I consider the possibilities. Chavarria's a real fucktard. But Fucktard as a nickname is clearly out. What's the sort of name that would flatter him so that he'll do what I want?

I take stock of what I know about Omar. Appearance: dark curly hair, military-style crew cut, freshly shaved face; short, like Mexicans, but there's something unmistakably non-Mexican about him. Probably the fact that he already has to shave every day. Background: Lebanese mom, Mexican American/Lebanese dad. Family: military. Religion: Greek Orthodox. Go figure. That has *got* to be worse than being Catholic.

"Crazy Diamond," I say. "Omar, that's your nickname. You're going to be Crazy Diamond."

Omar lights up. Bull's-eye.

"From the Pink Floyd song?" Machete asks. "Aw, man, why couldn't you call *me* that?"

Only a stoner would think a Pink Floyd name is cooler than Machete. "No, dickwad," I tell him, hoping he'll shut up.

González lives in Kern Place, an area of town characterized by architectural class and professionals who have some money but not enough to display it in the ostentatious water-wasting style of the Country Club area. González's house is built of rock, with a winding staircase up to the second floor. Gazing around the side, you discover that his family has a sweeping panorama of downtown El Paso/Juárez from the backyard.

I don't know much about his family, but they are obviously doing okay.

All of my life, I have lived in the Kern Place area, but in crummy apartments next to Mesa Street. My mother works her ass off waitressing but she spends all her dough on shitty boyfriends and even shittier booze. I started cleaning up her morning-after vomit in kindergarten. What can I say? We got what we got.

González, standing inside his house with the front door barely cracked open, takes a little convincing before he decides to join us.

"Are you sure *you* didn't do it?" he asks Machete.

I observe him as surreptitiously as I can. His nickname in grade school? Lardass? Fatwad? Gregory González and Isaiah Contreras make a trio.

"If you want, I will swear on the Bible," Josh says. He holds out his hands to González, as if to say, *Look, no blood on them.* "Jim can verify my whereabouts on Friday night."

"Well," I start to say, "I don't know *exactly* where you went or what you did after you and Stacy went into her—"

"Enough," Josh interrupts. "Am I going to have to tie you up and gag you?"

But I am not done with this subject. Not yet. I still want to kick him in the dick. But that's not about sex or jealousy, it's just being protective.

González has issues with the plan. "Isn't kidnapping a felony?" he asks.

"Only if it's real kidnapping," Crazy Diamond says.

"What the hell is the difference between a real kidnapping and a fucking fake kidnapping?" Josh asks. "Huh, Omar?"

Wish Machete hadn't brought that up. Wish I were like Tyler Durden in *Fight Club. He* knew how to convince people to do what he wanted.

"Look," I say. "You three are involved now so it's already a conspiracy, which means this is a risky operation. But you guys can handle that, right? The thing is, we've got to keep this covert. Rafa knows but he'll keep his mouth shut. So, you in?"

"Yeah," they all reply, and Greg hops into the Jeep.

"So, Commando, what's the plan?" Josh asks as we drive toward Central El Paso, where Gold lives.

Damn it. "Machete, stop the car. We have to create a plan."

"Shouldn't we wait until it's dark?" Crazy Diamond asks.

Machete pulls in to Jesuit's parking lot. "Let's smoke a joint while we make plans and wait for it to get dark. That can be our first plan." He parks behind a wall, hidden from the main street. He opens his CD case on the floor. Inside, there are ten perfectly rolled joints.

"That's a lot of dope," González observes astutely.

Should have thought of this before. It's, like, perfect. Get 'em doped up, they won't think about what they're doing.

Josh lights the joint, takes a hit, tries to pass it to Crazy Diamond.

Omar refuses, says, "No thanks." We all stare at him until he explains, "My dad gives me random urine tests."

"Damn," Josh says. "Why?"

"It's a military thing. He caught me smoking a cigarette

once. Made me smoke the entire pack right in front of him. I got so sick, I puked all over his shoes. Then he made me clean his shoes. Told me if he ever caught me doing drugs, he'd ship me off to military school faster than I could say, 'oops.' "

"So you *never* smoked dope?" Josh asks.

Josh and I glance at each other. We've been smoking since we were like nine.

For a few minutes, we sit there, passing the joint around between the three of us. Crazy Diamond opens a window and practically hangs his entire body outside. How can someone named Crazy Diamond refuse to take a hit?

González breaks the silence. "Do you think penis size really matters?" he asks.

"Is this something you're worried about?" I ask.

"I'm just asking."

"It matters," Josh says.

Seeing as how Josh is probably the only one of us who has had any experience—I don't think my childhood thing with my sister counts—we all wait for him to explain. "Women like big dick," he says, finally.

"What's big?" Omar asks.

"Anything over six inches."

"What's yours, man?"

"I'm not telling." Machete takes a hit, blows smoke right at Omar. "You'd just get all jealous."

I haven't measured mine. Should I? What will a girl say when she sees it? "Is that six inches when you have a hard-on or when you're limp?" I ask.

"Limp," Josh says. "Oh, and did you know that women care about balls, too?"

"No way," Greg protests. "That's such a lie."

"I'm not fucking with you." Josh grins. "The bigger the balls, the better the sperm."

"That's absurd," I say. "Enough dick talk. Let's come up with our plan to get Gold."

"We should wait until he's asleep," Crazy Diamond suggests. "Then we'll crawl into his bedroom, someone'll hit him on the head, and we'll drag him out."

"No good." I nix that idea. "What if his mom *hovers*? Or his dad has a gun?"

"Okay," González says. "Somebody lures him out of the house, somebody else waits in the bushes and hits him when he comes out, then we drag him to the car."

"Yeah, but we have to knock him the fuck out," I say. "We don't want him screaming and alerting the entire neighborhood."

"That works for me," Machete says. "Omar? Greg?"

"Hey! *I'm* the one in charge of this operation," I say.

"How can we forget it? You remind us every two minutes."

"All right, all right," González intervenes. "Let's not forget the purpose here is to help find Mac's killer. So stop fighting, you guys."

"González is right." I want to assert myself more, but for the sake of tactics, I let it go. "Who's gonna lure, who's gonna hit, who's gonna drag him to the car?"

"I'll lure," González says. "Mac was my best friend."

"I'll hit," Crazy Diamond offers.

"With your knife that cuts diamonds?" Machete snickers in a peculiarly un-Machete-like way.

"Shut up." That Crazy Diamond, always so eloquent.

"I have a better plan," I say. "No offense, Crazy Diamond,

but how about I lure him and you and González both hit him? We need something heavy to hit him with. Then you'll drag him to the car."

"How come Omar and I are doing all the hard work?" Greg asks. "What's *Josh* doing?"

"Machete's the lookout."

"Does that mean if we're caught, he's more responsible?"

"We're not going to get caught." It wasn't totally dark yet but I was beginning to feel itchy. "Come on, men. It's time. Let's roll!"

Jim Hill
The Kidnapping of Alexander Gold

Turns out, Alexander Gold lives in Central El Paso, near El Paso High. His neighborhood is one of those classic lower-middle-class El Paso neighborhoods, where Hispanic families have lived in the same small pink and blue and purple adobes or red and yellow brick bungalows for generations. It's the sort of neighborhood where people would raise holy hell if the city ever decided to raze it for development. It's *too* charming, in an understated El Pisshole kind of way.

Gold's house is a bungalow, short and low, with a few scraggly bushes around it. I note the general air of neglect that permeates the house. Could mean a single-parent household, a loser father, lazy kids. Nobody's taking care of the lawn.

What sort of guy is Gold, to be at Jesuit for who knows how long, yet to be so invisible that nobody is friends with him or even knows who he is? What kind of anger would that create in someone? What angst troubles his young, tortured mind? Loners are always psychopaths. The cops gotta be thinking the same thing.

González and Crazy Diamond hide in the bushes just below the porch bungalow while Machete stays in the car. "I'm gonna smoke while I wait," he says.

Gold's mother opens the door. You can tell a lot about mothers at first glance. Take mine, for example. It's not just the booze and cigarettes. I mean, I know she loves us but we kind of ruined her life. Or my dad, who I don't even remember, did. Anyway, she always makes me feel responsible for that. The older I get, the worse I make it for her. She's a good enough mom, though. When I was in juvie, she visited me practically every day.

Gold's mother has a red and puffy face. She was probably pretty once, but now she's worn the fuck out. She looks like someone married to a schmuck. I'm guessing hers has not been a happy life. Does she think her kid killed somebody? Should I try to find out?

"What do *you* want?" she asks sullenly.

I don't know whether to call him "Alex" or "Alexander." "I'm a friend of your son's," I say.

Bitch actually perks up, her eyes brightening. "Oh, just a second," she says. "I'll go get him right away."

Sooooo, Gold doesn't have any friends. She's *too* happy to see me. *She* could be worked on. First, however, I have to work on this Alex.

Through the crack in the door, I see his tennis shoes approaching. Nike. Blue. New. Surprising, given the surroundings.

He opens the door suspiciously. Sandy hair, a bit too long, bangs in his eyes, freckles everywhere, from the tip of his nose to the collar of his T-shirt and probably beyond.

"What are you doing here, Jim Hill?" He knows me? He looks past my shoulder and says, "And what's Josh Alvarado doing in the car?" Then: "Smoking dope. Big surprise." Kid's observant.

Now that Gold is in front of me, in person, I sort of recognize him. Calculus? No. History? No. Religion. Yes, we have religion together. Maybe—maybe not.

This is not a good sign for my future prospects as private investigator. It indicates a lack of observation skills, a crucial talent required for the trade. This bears reflecting upon. Later.

"Josh's chewing on his toenails," I say. "He likes to do that on Sundays, I don't know why. *I* came here to see *you*."

"Yeah, what for?"

Need a way to disarm him. I smile charmingly. Has no effect on Gold.

"Don't smile too hard," he says. "It looks like it hurts." Then: "So, what do you want?"

"I'd like to talk to you," I say. "Want to come for a spin?" Clever, Jim. Get him in Josh's Jeep and—no escape.

He hesitates. Aha! He has betrayed his weakness. Nobody has ever invited Gold to do anything before. And he wants to go. Alexander Gold wants to, needs to, be liked.

But then he says, "No. You can talk to me right here."

Damn. Tough little monkey.

"No, I can't," I say. "Your mother is—hovering."

Bingo. Kid turns around, says, "Mom. Stop hovering." She melts away, to the distant depths of the bungalow.

"Come sit outside," I invite him. "Let's talk a minute."

He hasn't thawed, but he moves outside and sits down on the low wall that encloses the porch. I remain standing. I'm not sure whether he'll have the advantage if I sit, too—or if he has the advantage because I'm still standing. I need to grasp the psychology of these situations better. Infiltrators can't infiltrate if they don't understand what's going on in the other guy's head.

"So, Alex," I say. "I understand the cops think you killed Mac." *Smooth, Jim. That's* the way to introduce the topic. No pussyfooting.

"So now *you're* here to gawk at me," he says, then holds up his arms and twists around slowly, letting me inspect him. "Yuperoohoohoo!" he yells. "I did it, world. I killed MacKenzie Malone. I'm the one! I'm the murderer! And if you don't watch out, I'm gonna come and kill you, too!" He drops his arms and turns his head and stares straight at me with his blue eyes. What does he see when he looks at me like that? "So," he says, "you've gawked, I've given you a little peep show, now why don't you leave?" He waits a second, then: "Now. Or rather, why don't you leave two minutes ago and pretend this conversation never happened?" He opens his front door and starts to go inside.

This is not going as planned. A confession gained via sarcasm is no friend to my mission.

Besides, I haven't found out what *I* need. What does he know? What did he see? What did Mac say before he died? Vital clues.

Jesuit's Invisible Kid must have a lot of dirt to dish on everybody. Including me.

"Fuck," I say and grab on to his shirt to keep him from going inside. "Don't go."

He looks at me like a scientist scrutinizing a research specimen. "Let go of my shirt," he says. His tone is quiet, menacing.

Now is the time I need my sidekicks. I look back at the Jeep. Machete has the music on so loud, the car is pulsating. He is smoking and staring at the mountains, which are practically at this front door.

I am forced to concede that Machete is a total washout as a violent sidekick.

"Let go of my shirt," Gold repeats, "or you'll be sorry."

"No," I say, then add, for effect, "sir."

Without warning, he karate chops my arm. Shit! Then, a swift kick to my side.

"Fuck!" I scream. "Fuck! That fucking hurt. Where'd you learn to do that? Is that how you killed Mac, you psycho?!"

"If it is," he says, "then shouldn't *you* be worried right about now?" And he grins evilly at me. "Now run away, little boy, and quit playing P.I."

But I recover quickly and try another tactic. "Aw, come on, Alex, just talk to me. You found him, right?"

"Jim Hill," he says, "you are an idiot. And you're lucky I'm not feeling like practicing any moves on you right now."

He starts going toward his door again but González pops out of the bushes and grabs him by the arms while Crazy Diamond grabs his legs. I start whaling on him with my fists. He's squirming in their arms and looks like he's too much for them, so I grab a rock from the yard and smash it on his forehead.

"Fuckadoodle!" he screams at me, then goes limp in our arms. *Fuckadoodle?* This guy really is a geek.

Machete has run out of the car and around the side. "Jesus," he says. "Why'd you hit him on the head like that, Jim?"

"It was the only way."

We drag him to the car, watching the street for signs of cops and the porch for signs of Gold's mother. Inside the Jeep, we tie his hands and legs together.

"He hit me," Crazy Diamond says, like he can't believe

it. "I'm gonna have a black eye. This asshole gave me a black eye."

"Should've kicked you in the groin and made your dick black," Gold says, waking up.

"Girls like black dick," Machete offers. "What'd you expect, Omar? That he'd be a pussy and come with us quietly?"

"What's this about, anyway?" Gold asks. "Why am I sitting in the back of Alvarado's Jeep?"

"We need to gag the prisoner," I say.

We all kind of look around the floor for something we can use.

"Oooooh, you guys had this really well planned, didn't you?" Gold says, kicking the back of the seat with his bound feet. "You're a regular black ops commando unit."

"Ow!" Josh yells as one of the blows hits him. "He hit my kidney. Somebody switch places with him. I can't drive like this."

Gold's hardly a willing participant in his own demise, so it's a real struggle to get him switched with Greg. I have to hit him twice to get him to cooperate. It splits the knuckle on my right hand.

"How's the ol' hand, Jim?" he asks.

He's starting to piss me off. I know that isn't professional. If I get mad, he won't tell me what he knows. I already know he didn't do it, that he's not Mac's murderer. But I still need to know what he knows. "We don't have anything for a gag?" I ask again. "We have to get him to shut up."

"He can't confess if he's gagged," Machete points out.

Gold giggles and I threaten him with the back of my hand. He can see the knuckles bleeding from when I'd hit him before.

Everybody can see them. Crazy Diamond whistles. Machete asks, "What?" and then he sees them, too.

"You'll break your hand if you try that again," Gold scoffs. "You should take a few karate lessons, Magnum P.I."

"So, where're we going to take him?" Crazy Diamond asks.

Now I admit, I should have thought of that. I can *hear* Gold sneering, I swear. I kick him with my foot. "González's. The garage is separated from his house and there's a room over it. Nobody will hear or see us there." I'm beginning to really hate the motherfucker. Kind of like I hated Mac. Well . . . Mac was just annoying, you know? All that religious shit. Such a hypocrite. But wait a minute, is this about Gold or Malone? Maybe both? Why not?

"No way, man," Greg says. "If my parents find out, they'll kill me."

I put all my energy into throwing my look at Greg. My mother says that if I wanted to, I could change a man into dust with that look. But my mother also says it's normal to eat dirt. She's from the South. After about thirty seconds, Greg starts to squirm.

"Wait," Omar pipes up. "My dad owns a warehouse off Piedras. Nobody will ever look there."

A superior venue secured, my mission is back on track. "All right, all right, let's go, let's go, let's go," I say, hand out the window and banging against the side of the door. Josh revs the engine and we're off to Phase Two.

The Fronchies, a Fag, and the Fucking Truth

It takes Crazy Diamond a while to get us into the warehouse. "There's bolts on the doors," he explains, like we're all blind. "Anybody got a bolt cutter?"

"Sure, Omar," Josh says. "I always carry one in my back pocket."

We find a side door without a bolt—but it's locked.

"Why don't you try busting down the door?" Gold asks.

All four of us run straight at it and throw ourselves against it. *Ouch!* Doesn't budge.

Gold laughs. He's having way too much fun. "Always looks easy when the cops do it on TV, doesn't it?" he taunts.

We find a dumpster and Omar climbs on top of it. With a rock, he smashes the glass in one of the windows, then crawls through. A few moments later, he opens the door.

"Do you think anyone will notice the broken window?" Greg asks.

"Nope," Omar says. "Besides, so what if they do? There'll be nothing in here."

"Except Gold," I remind him.

"Oh. Yeah."

What a numbfuck. "Hey, Machete, go get Gold and bring him in here," I command. "It's time to question the prisoner."

We arrange it all as artfully as on TV. Empty warehouse, wooden chair, suspect with hands tied to the back of the wooden chair, a single lightbulb hanging just over the prisoner. The four of us stand around him.

"You know, kidnapping is a felony," Gold says.

"So is murder," I point out.

"I didn't kill your friend," he says. "But, since I'm apparently everybody's favorite suspect, maybe I should just go ahead and kill one of you."

I hear it in his words, in the slight crack in his voice. And that's when I know, if I ride him hard enough, long enough, he'll break and tell me everything.

"Is that self-pity I hear?" I wag a finger at him like he's a bad little boy. "*Tsk-tsk.* You know what they say about self-pity, don't you? How it's mental masturbation?"

Crazy Diamond breaks in with "How did you just happen to be in that neighborhood when Mac was stabbed?"

Gold looks at me when he answers Omar. Knows *I'm* the one challenging him. "There's a girl I like, okay? She lives next door to González."

"Vero?" González asks. "Man. I should have known." He breathes heavily, all agitated in that fat-boy way. Greg's normally your average pudgy Mexican American, not real aggressive, not real manly. The whole macho Mexican thing? A stereotype, in my observation. But I can tell what he's thinking: here's the guy who'd killed his best friend, right in front of him.

"I know Vero," Josh says. "I've fucked her."

"You've fucked this entire town, Machete," I point out. "I'm sure you're a walking disease. When I get home, I'm gonna tell Stacy to go get an HIV test."

"Vero's got a boyfriend," Greg says. "Some guy who hangs out with Rafa. José or some shit like that."

Josh says to me, "Didn't we meet José Friday night, when Rafa dropped by?"

I almost open my mouth to distract him—those are things people here don't need to know—but Gold does it for me. "You guys really need to get your act together," he says. "Is this about you guys or about me or about Mac or about Vero?"

Greg's face puffs up. Think he's gonna blow! But the timing's off. Better that he waits. So I save him the hassle. "Shut up!" I yell, and slap Gold on the face. Not real hard—not yet, that will come later—but it stings my hand so it must have hurt him.

"You better decide which you want him to do, Jimbo," Josh says. "Shut up or talk?" The way he asks it, it's like he isn't really in on this. But he is, believe me. If he hadn't been screwing my sister last night . . . God, I could kill him for that. Right now. I just want to smash his stupid stoned face.

I take a deep breath to calm myself. Josh can be dealt with later. "Okay, fine," I say, turning to Gold. "Tell us what you know."

"Everything?" he asks.

"Everything."

And once he starts to speak, he can't shut up. First, he starts ragging on the Fronchies. That's fine. None of us are total Mexicans. If Rafa or Bernie was here, that'd be a different story.

Then he points out that none of this would have started if Bernie wasn't such an asshole. "You think Mac got killed on accident?" he asks. "No fucking way. Somebody *planned* this! Mexicans are assholes," he says. "If Mac and Bernie hadn't thrown down, Mac'd still be alive. Bernie's behind it, you better believe it."

Motherfucker is *playing* Crazy Diamond. I can see it. Omar's getting red and nodding his head. González is buying it, too. But that's *my* job. So what should I do? Sit back and let him do the hard work—or step in and reassert myself?

He's smart, this guy, smarter than all of us.

I start pacing, circling the chair. I am a lion, stalking my prey. Alex meets my eyes and holds them. A cool customer.

"Come on," Machete says, all reasonable. "Why'd Bernie come to Mac's rosary if he did it? That makes no sense."

"To pretend he's innocent," González says, nodding his head slowly.

"So far, Bernie's maintained his innocence under enormous pressure," Josh says slowly. "Even when Jim and Omar beat him up after the rosary last night, he didn't budge. He's not acting very guilty in my opinion."

"Hey, Machete, we didn't beat him up, just interrogated the suspect," I say. "You don't seem to get it. We need to be using a code when we talk about these things. A code. We use a code to protect ourselves. *¿Comprende?*"

God, I have to be careful not to lose it. Gold will use it against me if I do.

"You're a real ass sometimes, Jim, you know that?" Machete nudges Gold with his foot. "Okay. Go on. What else you got?"

"If the Fronchies didn't do it," Gold says, "then that fag did."

There's this long silence. Then: "What fag?" I ask.

He sneers slightly and nods at Josh. "Your boy, Daniel Tucker."

Mothafucka. Never woulda guessed. "How do you know Daniel Tucker's a homo?" I ask. Everybody else is speechless.

"How do you think I know everything I know?" He grins. "But this time, my knowledge is a little more, shall we say, biblical. He sucked my dick in the restrooms just last week. For free." He closes his eyes and moans, "Ohhhhh, oooohhhhhh, uhhhhhh, uhhhhhh," like he's having an orgasm.

I know he's lying. No guy would admit this.

Machete's nostrils are flaring. "You son of a bitch!" he screams suddenly, rushing over and whaling on Gold with his fists. "Dan's not a fag! Fuck you, Alex, you lying son of a bitch!"

"Hey, calm down," I yell, grabbing Josh, trying to pull him off of Gold.

Not quite sure why I restrained him. But again, the timing's not right. If Josh expends all his anger on Alex now, there will be none left for later, for whatever I can stir up that's bigger than this, better, more newsworthy.

"Well, he's just not," Josh says, his hands folded across his chest, glaring at Alex like an ornery two-year-old.

I can't stand little kids. One time, there was this little three-year-old who lived next door to us, and he was always screaming at night. I guess he didn't want to go to bed, the little fucker. I tried hitting the little guy once to see if that would shut him up. I told him, "You better quit crying at night or I'm going to come and get you." Didn't help. Nothing worked until I started giving him juice laced with Mom's vodka every evening around dinnertime. He was always playing just outside his door. His mom thought it was cute, me giving him juice every day. Sure made him start sleeping the night through, I'll tell you what. They moved away a few months ago and now I actually miss the little son of a bitch.

"Like you all didn't know already," Alex says. "Dan's got a crush on practically everybody except Josh."

Think. Has Tucker ever touched me or looked at me kind of funny or anything? Gives me the creeps just thinking about it.

"That's sick, man," Omar says. "I'm gonna beat his ass the minute I see him."

"No, wait," Josh says. "No, you're not." But he looks sick, too. "You know this sack of shit is lying through his teeth. He's just trying to get to us."

"So Dan did it?" Greg persists.

"Yeah," Alex says. "He was in love with Mac. Mac probably threatened to out him. You know how Malone could be a real self-righteous prick."

Time to get this back on track. "I know you don't think it was Tucker," I say. "So here's your choice: you're gonna tell me who you *really* think it was or I'm gonna beat your ass."

Alex tries hard to keep his look even. He almost does it, but not quite. Still, his look challenges me. He's scared but defiant. I've seen that same look in my sister's eyes when she was a little kid, and I'd barely touched her. Okay, I did a little more than touch her. And I'll never forget that look. That look still gets to me. Makes me feel all guilty and shit. Fuck that.

"Fine." He's deliberate and slow. Trying to get his voice under control. "I think it was Rafa. Rafa and two of his buddies."

Fuck. Josh looks up. *Double fuck.*

He'd been standing over by the window, ignoring us and chewing on his fingernails. Brooding about his fag best bud. "Rafa?" he asks.

"Why would Rafa do it?" Greg demands.

"All I know is, I saw Rafa and his homeboys driving down Baltimore just before I drove up it to see if Vero was up to something. They were leaving, I was arriving, and there was Mac, almost dead." Alex looks at me when he says all of this. Actually, he hasn't stopped looking at me.

"Yeah, but what was his motive?" Crazy Diamond asks.

"Maybe that José guy was with him," Alex says. "Maybe he was protecting his girl. Mac was always talking shit about Vero."

"Did you recognize who was with him?" Greg asks.

Alex shrugs.

"What does that mean?" I ask. "Yes or no?"

He just shrugs again.

Does he know or doesn't he? Even I can't tell. The rest of the guys are completely confused. Exactly the way Gold wants it.

Bastard's due some respect. He's coming dangerously close to something . . . dangerous. And he's poked at something in Josh's head, that's obvious.

"I don't want to hear this anymore," I announce. "Let's beat the fucker to a pulp and go."

Omar's nodding his head. "Jerk knows way too much about everybody."

"I'm not down with that," Josh says. "The only reason he knows so much is because everybody ignores him so he has nothing to do but watch us. That's not his fault."

See? Josh is a cool guy, a softy. "All right, Machete," I say. "You go outside and wait in the Jeep. We'll be out in a minute."

I let Crazy Diamond and González beat on Gold as much as they want. Then I take a few turns. The guy needs somebody to beat some sense into him. He's pretty bloody by the time we finish.

"Oh, hey. Guys?" he says all of a sudden from the floor where he's lying, still tied to the chair. "I have HIV."

We all look at each other. Then we look at our hands, sprinkled with Alex's blood.

"And Ebola and West Nile and mad cow disease!" *Shit.* We haven't broken him. I decide then and there to leave him tied up for the night, to come back in the morning. Maybe.

As soon as we get out to the Jeep, Josh asks, "Where's Gold?"

"We left him," I say. "We'll come back in the morning and get him."

"Nothing doing," Josh says.

"Oh, come *on,* Josh, let's just *go,*" Greg says.

"Nope." Josh takes the keys out of the ignition, sits back in his seat. "I'm not driving away from here as long as he's still tied up."

I suppose we could jump him, take the keys by force, but I'm tired.

When I go inside, Alex has managed to work his knots loose to the point where he is almost free. He stops what he's doing when he sees me. He says, "I took your beating just now, but I won't take it again." His voice is shaking. Just a little. I hear it. He almost lost it after we left. I can always tell.

"Go ahead and finish untying yourself. I'll watch," I say.

It takes him approximately two minutes. I'm impressed. "Where'd you learn to do that?"

"You'll never know." He rubs his wrists.

We step outside and he sees the Jeep with all the fucktards sitting inside, waiting. "I'll walk home," he says, waving at the guys and setting off. It's like he isn't even mad, holds no grudge against us, just has no interest in being around us anymore. An odd bird, this Gold.

I climb into the Jeep and we sit there for a moment, watching him walk through El Paso's downtown streets. We took something from him. I can see it in his back as he walks away.

"Now that is one weird dude," Crazy Diamond says.

"I like him," Josh says. "A lot."

I hate him. He might be invisible to everybody at school, but we are not invisible to him. He knows stuff. A lot.

The Race Riot

Daniel Tucker

Us vs. Them

There has to be a dozen of 'em here. We haven't even met for choir practice before first period and Jesuit's swarming with cops, cops talking to different kids in the halls, cops consulting with teachers. I keep my head down and hope nobody notices me as I squeeze my way through the crowded hallways.

My locker's next to Josh's. He's there with his head stuck inside, like he's hiding. He pulls it out for just a second. His face is all gray and his eyes are totally puffy.

"You look like shit, man," I whisper.

"Thanks," he whispers back, then sticks his head back in the locker.

"Are they just here about Mac or what?" I ask.

"How would I know? Leave me alone."

What's with him?

"Hey, Josh," I say. "Get your head out of your locker when you talk to me, man."

"Sorry." But he doesn't look at me. "I just don't want them to notice me. I'm afraid if I duck out, they'll think I have something to hide."

"Nobody's gonna think that, Josh." I open my locker. Doesn't do me much good. I don't keep schoolbooks in there. Just some music and a poster of Jimi Hendrix. Secretly, though, I'm more into Bono—such a great fucking voice. Nobody else succeeds with the kind of shit he sings—the way he wails, the way his voice cracks and soars. He's an original. And so sexy. Josh asked me one time why I liked "Beautiful Day." I told him it's 'cuz of the lyrics—how even though you're having a shitty time in your life, you can still find something good to think about. Josh smiled at me and said, "Have you ever heard the song 'Tomorrow' in the movie *Annie*?" And then he started singing in a falsetto, *"Tomorrow! Tomorrow! I love you! Tomorrow, you're only a day away!"* Silly bitch.

"Hey, Dan," Josh says suddenly. "Do you ever feel like there's an Us and a Them?"

"Every day," I say. "You have no idea."

"I don't, huh?" He looks hostile for a second. I don't think I've ever seen Josh look hostile before. "Anything you want to tell me, Dan?"

"No," I lie.

"Fucking liar," Josh says. "I'm outta here." And he splits before I have the chance to say, "Huh?"

What the . . . ? What did I say? What does he know?

I've always thought Josh wasn't into divisiveness or labels, more of a "live and let live" kind of guy. But the rest of the guys at Jesuit—they fall into all these little factions, the Republicans vs. the Democrats, or the Catholics vs. the, um, Non-Catholics. The worst faction is probably *Los* Beaners vs. *¡Los Pinches Gringos!* The weird thing is that some Mexican Americans seem angrier than anyone about Mexicans. I don't get it. How can you hate your own people?

I'm freaked about what Josh said, but I go to choir practice, needing that release. Mr. Torres isn't there. Instead, some young, good-looking cop with blond hair and a body most guys would kill for waits until we quiet down. Then he tells us, "Everybody, please proceed directly to the auditorium."

Some dumbass raises his hand. "Why? What's going on?"

The cop seems kind of nervous as he says, "No questions. Just proceed directly to the auditorium."

Dumbass doesn't know how to keep his mouth shut. "But what for?"

"Just do as I say! Now!" the cop suddenly snaps. He stares at Dumbass with that beady laser-like cop gaze. Kid seems oblivious.

Wish I could be Dumbass.

I could definitely get into the whole "cop as sex object" thing. That uniform. Those handcuffs. A little light bondage? But what if my cop fetish is 'cuz of my dad? That's *sick.*

So we all troop over to the auditorium, and we sit there, everybody in those little seats, all of us buzzing, "What's going on?" There's some whispering here and there—

Kids who hadn't heard about Mac are getting the news. You can see it going around the auditorium. The kid next to me starts to say, "Hey, you heard—?" and I cut him off—"Yeah, man, I already know."

Where's Josh? Did he manage to sneak out?

The good-looking cop is over by the door, watching all of us like we're going to explode or something. I settle back in my chair to watch him.

They just leave us to sit. Two cops at every entrance. Nobody's getting out of here.

Dumbass starts leading everybody in a chant. "Hell, no! We won't support Mexico!"

Some of the Mexican kids start shouting, *"¡Viva, Mexico!"* and *"¡Cinco de Mayo!"*

Idiots come in all shades.

I try to compose lyrics in my head. I should continue my song about Mac, but every line seems cheesy, like I'm writing an Elton John love song. When I realize I have mentally written a line that goes *"You were the shining star in a dark night,"* I stop. What's *wrong* with me?

My mind wanders back to Josh. Will he turn out like Pop? You know, really talented but wasting it all on drugs? I'm not attracted to Josh but I think I feel about him a bit the way Ma feels about Pop and me, worried all the time. Sometimes I'd like to tell her about me, but that'll just make her worry even more. She'd go on and on about how I'll probably catch HIV and how I won't be able to have children and how probably I'll be at some bar some late night, a little too drunk, and some men will beat me up and gang-rape me and leave me for dead tied to some fence in the middle of Wyoming like that Matthew Shepherd kid. God, now she's running on in my head. You know what? I don't even need her to protect me in real life because all I have to do is start to think about it and everything she says or would say goes through my mind. Is that because she's right? Or is it just a mother thing?

Suddenly Brother Rodarte enters and addresses "the assembly."

"Young men," he says, "Jesuit High School experienced a tragedy on Friday night. One of our finest young men, MacKenzie Malone, was brutally murdered."

Would he have referred to Mac as "one of our finest young men" on Friday afternoon?

"The culprit has not yet been apprehended," he continues. "And the police informed me this morning that *another* Jesuit student, the young man who found Mr. Malone and called the police, is missing. His name is Alexander Gold. Mr. Gold has been a student at Jesuit for two years."

There is a silent hush. *Who* is Alexander Gold? I see everybody looking around—

Nobody else seems to know either. He's been here for two years?

Brother Rodarte seems to be struggling with himself. At last he says, "Young men, I have failed you. During your four years here, you look to me for guidance. I am your guardian, your protector, your shepherd. And now I fear there is a wolf among my lambs." He bows his head slightly. "This is why I have requested several police officers to remain with us for at least the next week. We will have a special Mass for Mr. Malone this afternoon at one p.m., which will include a prayer for Alexander Gold. That is all. You are dismissed."

We are ushered out of the auditorium to our next class. The hall is buzzing.

"I bet that Alexander Gold did it," I hear Ralph López say as I pass him in the hallway.

"I bet he's dead, just like Mac," Andrew Boyd answers.

"What if somebody's going around knocking off Jesuit students? They should be sending us home with personal police escorts." This from Jim Hill, yakking up a storm in the hallway.

As soon as he sees me, he stops talking. As I pass, his eyes follow me. He has this weird cut above his eye. "Hey, Jim," I say, "what happened to your eye?"

No answer. What the hell? I'm halfway down the hall before he speaks again, loudly. "Did you notice both Mac and Alexander Gold are Americans? And white? Isn't that interesting?"

Idiot! Just because Gold's last name isn't Hispanic doesn't mean he's white.

They should send us home. School today seems pointless. And I'm feeling a little pit of fear at the base of my stomach. Shit. *Is* there a serial killer?

That good-looking cop stops me in the hall on my way to class. He has a little notepad and a pen. "What's your name?" he asks.

"Daniel Tucker."

He starts to write it down. Then he looks interested. "Hey, weren't you one of the last ones to see Malone the night he—?"

"Yeah," I cut him off.

He stares at me a second. Then: "Do you know this Alexander Gold?"

"Nope."

I can hear Mom in the back of my head. *Tell them everything you know, Danny. If you don't tell them everything you know, they'll find out, and then you'll be indicted for obstruction of justice and you'll go to jail and your entire life will be wasted, ruined, completely gone, you'll have no friends, money, or pride; and you will be miserable in jail, too, because you're gay so that probably means you'll be raped every day and—* GOD. *Get out, Mom, you maniac.*

"You ever had any classes with him?" the cop persists.

"Not that I know of," I say.

He looks at his clipboard and starts ruffling through papers. "Shows here that you're in the same math class."

"Oh," I say. "Well, I don't know him."

The cop tilts his head sideways and scratches it. "How can you have a class with somebody five days a week and not know them?"

It's a fair question. "Bet you'll be hearing that a lot today," I offer.

I want to offer my phone number, too, but he seems too butch to be gay. Not that you can't be macho *and* gay but—he's not one of us. I can tell.

He lets me go and I head upstairs for my class. Damn. I have to find my boy. Josh knows something, something more than he's letting on. I can smell it. But sneaking out is out of the question. Cops are at every entrance.

Wait, Josh has a cell phone. If I'm caught by a teacher, it's a twenty-dollar fine and my phone is confiscated. But . . .

I give him a quick buzz.

"Yeah, man," he answers.

"Where are you?"

"At home. Burnin' one down."

"Get the fuck out," I say. "Quit smoking and take a shower. Hide your shit or flush it down a toilet. I heard they've already got lists of who didn't come to school and they're sending cops over to talk to the truants."

"Why?"

"Oh, come *on*, Josh. Like you don't know. Like you haven't heard. The missing kid? Alexander Gold? It's all over school."

"What? He's not missing," he says. *Click.*

"Wait—!" Too late. I call him back, but he doesn't answer.

In that moment, dread settles in my stomach. Son of a bitch. I can't believe it. Josh knows something about Alexander Gold. But what could he know?

I call four more times. Josh never answers.

White Boys RUnning

Just fifty-two hours after Mac dies, Mom makes me go to school. I'll be missing all of Tuesday because of the funeral. Mac has to be buried on Cinco de Mayo. Unbelievable.

I can't go to school. If I go to school today, I'm going to hurt somebody.

"Mom," I beg but she gives me an absolute "NO" before I get any further.

I try to reason with Dad, but he just backs Mom up. "Go to school today," he says. "If you still need to take time off after the funeral, we'll talk about it. But right now, it's better to stick to a routine."

How is Mac's death part of my routine, Dad?

Why didn't I kick Alex Gold in the balls when he was tied up? I didn't, so now anyone's will do. How many of those fake fuckers really liked Mac? How many pretended to be all sorry and everything at his rosary? Who'll come to his funeral just to skip school? If I could be in charge of the funeral, I'd only allow those of us who actually gave a shit about Mac to come. And I wouldn't let in any beaners. Everybody'd have to show their U.S. passports.

The first thing I see as I enter school is Josh, exiting. "González, leave while you have a chance," he whispers.

But I keep walking through the weirdly empty halls. Then I see this massive, burly cop striding toward me. "Hey, kid!" he yells.

Oh, crap.

"How come you're not in the auditorium?" he asks.

"I just got here," I say.

"Well, get in there before you get in trouble." He jerks his thumb behind him.

I breathe a prayer of thanks to the Virgin of Guadalupe, Saint Frances Jerome, Saint Ignatius, Saint Anthony, and all the other saints I can think of. Not that they'll help a person like me. Not after yesterday. Especially since I don't feel sorry about what I did.

I sit in the auditorium forever before Brother Rodarte gives his little speech about what fine young men we all are and how we should all cooperate with the police (Yippie! Maybe they'll find out who killed Mac!), who will be wandering through the halls asking questions because Alexander Gold is missing.

Whaaaaat? Where the fuck is he? How deep am I in this? Shit, shit, shit.

I scan the auditorium. Jim's not here. Of course. Crazy bastard. Just when we need him. Maybe he'll show up later. There's Bernie, smirking at me. What's that about? Is it because Mac's dead or because another American is MIA? Could he possibly know what we did to Alex?

I am gonna hurt one of them. Fucking Fronchies.

We're dismissed to classes and I spot Jim in the hallway but he's talking to someone else. Hopefully I'll snag a chance to talk to him during lunch.

Fourth-period class. History. Mr. Ortiz asks us all to sit down. He has a great big roll of butcher paper that he's unrolling all around the classroom. Then he stands up and says, "Gentlemen, I have some markers here. First we're going to spend a few minutes on the floor, writing about how we feel about what's gone on. You can write whatever you want. Then we're going to talk about it."

Is this some test or some trick, like the police are using Mr. Ortiz to figure out who might be involved? So far, I shouldn't be a suspect, but you never know. What if I write something that gives me away? Having the police involved in this Alex thing is bad.

I hunch over the floor, purple marker in hand. I'm thinking about what Alex said about the Fronchies, and what he said about Dan Tucker, who's writing in a corner over there. I just want to get up and kick his faggot ass. I never knew he was a fag before but now I can see it written all over him. I think about what Alex said about Rafa. Man, he shouldn't have said that about Rafa. Rafa's my homey. He was Mac's homey. He wouldn't have hurt Mac. No way.

I position the marker over the butcher paper. Then, instead of writing, I lift my shirt and draw a little circle around my belly button. Then I draw two dots above the belly button. My mom used to draw these faces on my stomach when I was a little kid. It looks like a face, somebody surprised, like Mac must have looked when he was stabbed.

"What *are* you doing, Mr. González?" Mr. Ortiz asks. He's gaping down at me.

"Uh, nothing," I say.

He shakes his head. "Then start writing. Pronto."

Why is nobody in the entire world, not even my oh-so-concerned mother, taking into consideration the fact that Mac was *my best friend,* mine alone? I am *not* just like every other Jesuit boy.

I look around. Omar's drawn a picture of the Mexican flag, then circled it in red ink and drawn a slanted line through it. Good for Omar. Bernie looks like he's drawing a cartoon of some sort. I squinch in a little closer to get a better look. It's Mac! My God, he's drawn a caricature of Mac, Mac as some kind of buffoon, with priest robes on, his tongue out to the side, little dizzy circles over his head like he's drunk or drugged or stupid or something. Below it, he's written, "We'll miss you, Mac!"

Mr. Ortiz claps his hands. "All right, gentlemen, return to your seats and let's talk about this."

First thing that happens is Omar raises his hand. "Sir?" he asks. "Do you think Mac got killed 'cuz of a race thing?"

"What do you think?" Mr. Ortiz says, pulling the old teacher trick.

"I think he got killed 'cuz he's white and he didn't think we should celebrate Cinco de Mayo," Omar states positively.

Chris Cruz snorts.

"You disagree, Carbon Copy?" Omar asks.

I look at Bernie out of the corner of my eye. He's enjoying this, nodding his head and grinning. *"We'll miss you, Mac,"* right, *Bernie? Maybe I can do something so we can miss Dirty Bernie Martínez instead?*

"I got a better idea," says Bernie into the air. "How about Mac could be an asshole? How about somebody got really pissed off at him and let him have it?"

You're a dead man, Bernie. Just you wait.

"So Mac deserved to get murdered?" Omar asks in this deadly voice.

"Well . . ." Bernie trails off in a "that's what I'm saying but I don't want to say it" sort of way.

Chris siiiiiighs, to let us know he's being veeeery patient. "There has to be an explanation other than the one you're positing," he tells Omar, "because I don't think that's a very realistic one. I mean, Mac was white, sure, but this school is full of white guys and none of *them* got murdered. I just don't buy your 'it's gotta be the Mexicans' response."

"Alexander Gold is missing," says Ricardo. "He's white and American."

"How do you know he's white?" Chris asks.

"I remember him," Ricardo says, but we all know he's lying. "I do! I remember him!"

Omar says in a loud voice, sort of hysterical, "If Mac deserved to die because he was an asshole, then most of you deserve to die, too."

Mr. Ortiz cuts in, ignoring Omar. "What do you remember about Alexander Gold?"

"I noticed him," Ricardo says. "He was always watching us. Nobody ever paid no attention to him. *El chingado* probably knew everything there is to know about us."

"You think?" Chris asks.

"Actually," Bernie drawls, "I know."

Omar's boiling mad. Of course, the guy knows exactly where Alex was last night. And that Alex does know a lot of shit about us. "He was probably some drug dealer. Some lowlife, scum-sucking drug dealer."

Where's Omar going with this?

"You think he had connections to the Juárez cartel?" Chris asks, leaning forward in his seat like this conspiracy theory is one he'd like to explore just for the fun of it.

"Todos los gringos son pendejos," Bernie says. *"No saben nada sobre el cartel."* He shakes his head. "Shit, if it wasn't for Americans, the cartel wouldn't even exist. You think a nobody like Alexander Gold, just some kid at Jesuit, had connections to the Juárez drug cartel? Omar, you are so stupid, you should be in public school."

"Oh, yeah?" says Omar, shoving his chair forward and getting in Bernie's face.

"Cállate," Rafa calls from across the room. "Bernie, everybody in Juárez is all over that shit. Bet you are, too."

"Hey, Rafa, shut up," Omar says. "You live in Segundo Barrio. How the fuck you afford that slick lowrider? You think we don't know you're all over that shit, too?"

"Cabrón," Rafa says. He raises his fist as if he's going to smack Omar. "I was sticking up for you, *ése.* Guess I won't no more."

"Just try to hit me, Rafa," Omar threatens, quietly. "Just try."

"Will you two—or you three—cut it out?" Chris says. "Mr. Ortiz, tell them to cut it out."

"What are you, another pacifist?" Omar asks. "Like Ish?"

"No," Chris says. "I just don't think any of this is very productive. Mr. Ortiz?"

"Hold on, let's hear this," Mr. Ortiz says.

"It's an *insult* to Mac and all Americans for us to celebrate Cinco de Mayo," Omar says.

"Come on," Chris says, like he's in some school-sponsored debate and he's trying to be logical. "We live right on the U.S.-Mexico *border.* Of course we're going to celebrate Cinco de Mayo."

"It's not just about holidays, Carbon Copy," Omar says. He speaks reeeeeeeeally slowly, to show Chris's stupidity. "It's about protecting ourselves. Keeping our country *safe.*"

"You're scaring me, dude," Chris says. "You're really scaring me."

"Are Mexicans going to help us beat the Iraqis? Are Mexicans going to protect our country from terrorism?"

Go, Omar! Go, Military Man!

"Give it a break, Omar," Chris says. "We're the ones responsible for protecting our own country. You can't blame Mexicans for not defending us—they're not us. And besides, that doesn't automatically make them our enemy."

Bernie's nodding his head up and down, over and over. I glare hard at Bernie. He finally notices and glares back. He blinks first.

"No, they're not Us, Carbon Copy," Omar says. "They just come here illegally and don't pay taxes and take advantage of our welfare system and have lots of babies so They can *use* Us."

"Yeah, and they bomb U.S. citizens." That's me.

"For the love of God, would you shut up about one loony guy who just happened to be Mexican?" Carbon Copy turns around in his seat to face me. "Like one Mexican represents all Mexicans?"

"Yo, Carb," Omar says. "You want the Mexicans to come take over our country? 'Cuz that's what they're already doing."

"You can't blame Mexicans for everything," Chris says, all reasonable. "A lot of us have relatives over in Juárez. It's like any place. Like here. Some good, some bad." *Jerk.*

"What does that prove?" Omar asks. I have to admit, sometimes he can be a little dense.

"It proves my point." Chris rolls his eyes. Like he's soooo superior.

Bernie jumps to his feet like he's about to go over and start beating on Omar. "I've had enough of your Middle Eastern Lebanese bullshit, *pinche pendejo,*" he says. "You're worried about protecting the country from Mexicans? Like we're a bunch of terrorists? Maybe one of us did come over and bomb the fucking international bridge. But people from *your* part of the world drove planes into the Twin Towers. People from *your* part of the world are at war with people in *our* part of the world. So just shut your fucking Arab ass up."

Now I stand up. "You shut up, Bernie," I say. "You fucking murdering Fronchi."

And the words just start shooting, like I have Tourette's syndrome or something. Mr. Ortiz isn't stopping me, and Bernie looks a little stunned. But I'm loving every second. I owe this to Mac.

I just keep on chanting, like I'm heaping a curse on them. "Fuc-king mur-der-ing Fron-chies. Fuc-king mur-der-ing Fron-chies." I'm just going to keep chanting. I'll never stop.

Daniel Tucker

Let's Blame the Mexicans

I think I've become like one of the others.
I think I've become like one of the others.
—The Mars Volta, "Cassandra Gemini"

Nobody can study, none of the teachers want to do their normal routine, all anybody wants to talk about is the Murder and the Missing Kid.

I overhear one kid pretending he knew Alexander Gold really well. "Yeah, like, he was all into these punk bands and I think he was, like, totally Aryan Nation, so yeah, I bet that's why both him and Mac were killed. It's gotta be some crazy race thing."

Down the hall a ways, some other kid is saying the exact opposite. "I heard Gold was a real religious dude. Another Father Mackey."

And there's Jim Hill, right there in the middle of it all, his freckled face glowing. He's so excited, you'd think he just blew up the school. "Gold was a mama's boy," he says. "All you had to do was look at him wrong and he'd go home crying to mommy. Totally paranoid. He acted like he always thought somebody had secretly pissed in his milk when he wasn't looking."

"Why are you guys talking like this Gold guy is already dead?" I ask as I pass.

"How do you know he's alive?" Jim counters.

"Well, at least I'm not pretending I knew the guy," I say.

"Well, at least I'm not pretending I'm not a fag," Jim says.

What? Shit. I'm outta here.

Has the beast been set free? Is my life as I know it over?

I have to crush this fear into tiny little bits and throw it out of my mind. For now.

I glance at my cell phone to see if Josh has tried ringing back. Nothing. I feel like some girl waiting for a guy to call and he just doesn't and doesn't and doesn't. *What is going on?*

I nod at one of the cops standing near a door and head into the bathroom to take a piss I don't really need.

Man, graffiti is everywhere. All new. Shouting out in large red, white, and black letters.

AMERICA FOR AMERICANS

WETBACKS GO HOME

FRONCHIES SUCK DICK

Who did this? One guy? Lots of guys?

Then I see it. In very tiny black letters, somebody has written over the urinal:

IS THIS WHERE DAN SUCKED MAC'S DICK?

Should I, should I— Are they talking about me? I'm not the only Dan in this school. But I'm probably the only *gay* Dan.

What should I— God, what should I do?

Will it blow over if I just don't come to school for a few days? I have to find Bernie. Did he tell somebody about me? Fuck, I'd hoped he'd forgotten he ever knew.

Can I wipe it off? I wonder if anybody else has seen it?

I start rubbing it, rubbing it. Rubbing over and over. I grab a paper towel and wet it and try to clean it off. So far it's sticking. Gotta keep rubbing. I'm rubbing away when Brother Rodarte walks into the bathroom.

He whistles. "What happened in here, young man?"

"It was like this when I came in a few minutes ago," I say.

"Is this your work, Mr. Tucker?"

"Sir?" It's not that I didn't hear him but maybe if he realizes what I'm looking at . . .

He reads the graffiti, including *that* one. I'm, like, right in front of the urinal. He's silent for a looong-ass minute. Then he says, "No, I guess you probably didn't do this."

He seems disturbed. By me? Queers must give priests and brothers the heebie-jeebies.

I'd still rather be gay than celibate. At least I have sex to look forward to. He has nothing.

"I won't ask if it's true," he says finally. "But have you talked to anyone, son? Anyone at all?"

Maybe it's the fact that my secret life has been written over the urinal at school. Maybe it's the fact that he called me "son" and nobody has ever called me "son" except for my junkie dad. But, yeah, okay, I'm looking at the floor so he can't see me wipe my eyes.

"You mean, like a priest?" I ask. If I went to confession, what would I confess? My sexual fantasies? I mean, I'm still a virgin and I don't think it's a bad thing to be gay. I don't want some priest to tell me I'm an evil, sick person because of *that*. "I wouldn't even know what to say."

He's still staring at that question. "I found out a few years ago that one of my best friends from seminary—he's gay," he says. "You might find one or two priests who would listen to what you have to say, son." He pauses for a second. "I'll get someone in here to paint over this. But now it's time for you to go back to class."

There's got to be an unguarded door somewhere.

"I'll walk you back," he says. "Fourth period, right? American history?"

Suuuck. There goes my escape.

I scramble to my feet and follow him out the door to Mr. Ortiz's classroom. He opens the door for me. Such a gentleman.

"Will you please get someone to clean that up right away, Brother?" I whisper.

He nods and pushes me gently inside.

The class is drawing pictures and writing messages on butcher paper.

Omar sneers at me when I sit down.

"What?" I say.

He turns around in his seat so his back is to me.

Is everybody staring at me? Can't panic. Can't panic until somebody says something, until I hear something, until I know for sure if everybody knows. Until then, have to act like everything's normal. Have to.

Mr. Ortiz is standing in his usual lounging position in front of his desk, legs splayed out in front of him, arms crossed. He's real young, fresh out of college. I like his muscular, compact body. "Well, guys," he says. "Let's talk about it, since I don't think anybody will be able to stomach a lecture today."

Omar's yapping, yapping, yapping. Big ol' blabbermouth. Thank *God* somebody's talking, taking attention away from me. Suddenly he turns around in his seat and looks at Bernie and Sergio Camarena and Theodore "Teddy" Sanchez, all Mexicans. "If you like your country so much, how come you're going to school in the United States?"

"Jesuit's a better school than anything in Juárez, you know that, Omar," says Sergio Camarena. "My parents want me to go to Harvard, so they sent me here."

"So you admit your country is inferior?" Omar asks, just aching for a throw-down.

"You can be patriotic and admit there are problems with your country," Chris says. "Isn't that what the Cinco de Mayo Bomber was saying? How he needs America to eat but he still loves his country?"

"Do you think that's what he meant, Carb?" Sergio says. "Because when I read the Bomber's letter, I thought he was just tired of being treated like he was scum and, even more, he was tired of being treated like a criminal all the time."

I don't hear Chris's response, but the next thing I hear is Omar saying, "See? That's the attitude They have. That's why I think They did it."

I can practically see the capital letters in his head whenever he uses the words "Them" or "They" or "Us."

Is he just talking about Mexicans? Aren't I a Them? Just a white Them. Do I share something in common with the Fronchies? The problem is . . . Mexicans are probably bigger fag haters than Anglos. A Latino-macho Catholic thing.

"How? How exactly can you know that, Chavarria?" Chris asks. "Huh? How?"

"Mac beat up one of theirs," Omar says. "So they killed Mac. Just makes sense, man, that's all."

Mr. Ortiz watches this like it's a tennis match, the ball being volleyed back and forth. He's always been Mr. Cool Guy, King of the Kids. He wouldn't know how to put out a fire if it burned him in the ass.

"True that," Bernie says. "I'm Mexican. We protect our own. So . . . you're Lebanese. If I'm a Mexican murderer, does that make you a Muslim terrorist? Huh? Are you a Muslim terrorist?"

"Just 'cuz my family is Middle Eastern doesn't make me Muslim," Omar mutters.

"No?" Bernie says. "Then quit pulling racist bullshit out yo' ass."

"No, *you* quit, Dirty Bernie," Greg says suddenly. "Fucking murdering Fronchi!" He stands up in his seat and starts this chanting, like he's gone idiot all of a sudden, like that acid he did the other night fried his brain. "Fuc-king mur-der-ing Fron-chies. Fuc-king mur-der-ing Fron-chies." Like he's reciting a mantra.

We're all staring at him until Mr. Ortiz clicks into action, as if he's been released from a trance. "That'll be enough, Mr. González," he says.

Greg abruptly shuts up. But there's fear and hostility and worry and anger pulsing in this room and I can tell we all feel it. I'm the enemy, too. Does being white trump being gay? Should I be glad I'm white? How weird.

Nothing's been the same since the Fight on Friday, and everything's changed even more drastically in these last few minutes. Nobody knows who anybody else is. But we all know there are enemies among us. Maybe even a killer.

Isaiah Contreras
Cafeteria Incident

Assembly was weird. Fourth-period class was weirder. Our math-teacher-turned-philosopher-for-the-day was all into discussing the danger of creating outsiders who take out their rage on the rest of society—just like the Cinco de Mayo Bomber had done—and questioning who's to blame. Us, for making them the outsiders?

Teachers. Cops. Everybody's running scared.

So after all that, I'm on my way to lunch and I run into Omar shoving Chris around in the hallway. Chris is crouching against the wall, saying, "I don't want to fight you, man."

"Omar, if you don't cut this stuff out, you're going to get into really deep shit," I say.

Omar backs off when a cop rounds the corner and sees us.

"If you guys love Mexicans so much, why don't you just move to Mexico with Bernie?" Omar asks.

Chris comes out of his crouched position. "I'm not going to discuss this with you," he says, like a big priss.

Am I a pussy, like Chris? I don't think so, 'cuz I've stood up to my dad a few times. But maybe I just did that 'cuz of my mom. It always makes her all happy, like I'm her hero.

"You just watch yourself, Carbon Copy. Just watch yourself." Omar spins on his heel, all dramatic, and stalks off.

I watch him walk away. "What's up with that?" I ask.

He points his chin toward Omar's retreating back. "Guy's losing it."

"Are you all right?" I ask. "It looked like he was whaling on you pretty hard."

"Yeah, I'm fine." He rubs his arm. "I know the administration's taking this Mac and Alexander Gold stuff seriously but— I think they're ignoring some other important stuff. I feel something coming."

I start to laugh at him, but then I realize he's dead serious, so I quit.

We head off to the cafeteria.

♦ ♦ ♦

I mean, it's always like this, things bubbling up to the surface every now and then, but now it seems totally out there, and a little scary. The cafeteria is actually divided, all the Mexicans sitting on one side, the south, and everybody else sitting on the opposite side. It's so—what's that movie, *West Side Story*?

"Whoa, what up?" says Chris.

It's weirdly quiet. I mean, people are talking, but in low voices. Everybody on the Mexican side is talking in Spanish. My mother's Mexican, so's my father, but I was born here in El Paso. Never lived on the other side. So where do I sit? I sneak a look at Chris. His parents were both born here, they're not naturalized Americans, like mine.

"*¡Ése!*" Somebody's calling me from the Mexican side. "Ish! *¿Qué haces con ese pinche güero?*" What're you doing with that fucking white guy?

"Leave me alone," I say, deliberately in English.

I start to sit down on the Mexican side, dragging Chris with me, but there's this low hissing sound from all the Mexicans sitting at the table. Are they hissing at me or at Chris?

Chris looks sick.

On the American side, my real side, Chris's side for sure, the guys start to pound the table. *Bam-bam-bam-bam-bam-bam-bam.* They're pounding for Chris, and they sound like they're going to pound until he sits down with them.

"This isn't good. Where are the teachers?" Chris asks, standing up and walking out. As soon as he leaves, the hissing and the pounding abruptly stop.

I look around. Not a single teacher in sight. The Mexican women who cook and clean are all standing over by the food, looking scared. One of them is crouched down behind a table like she's taking cover. Another is holding a huge salad fork like it's a weapon.

Mac's death and that missing kid—they're both American and white, right? So maybe there *is* something racist going on? *Is* some Mexican to blame?

How can I take sides? Can pacifists do that? And anyway, why aren't the Americans okay if I sit on their side? Am I more Mexican than American? Just because of my parents' citizenship? Haven't we been here *long enough*?

A long time ago, I was taking a social studies class, and we started talking about Mexican migration. Somebody was yakking on about how Mexicans come here and have babies and those babies are American citizens and then those Mexicans can become Americans, or at least get their green card through their children.

That's how my parents did it. But I don't think my parents did that on purpose or nothing. *Did* they?

The first jeer comes from the American side, a random cliché: "Why don't you just go back where you belong?"

A long silence. Then: *"¡Pinches gringos!"* Sergio Camarena yells.

Mutters all around.

"If we're so stupid, how come you want to be just like us?" someone from the American side yells. I can't believe it. It's Greg.

One of the Mexicans yells, "This land used to belong to Mexico and someday we're gonna reclaim it! *¡Viva Zapata!*"

Somebody from the south side lobs a metal napkin dispenser in the air. It hits one of the tables on the north side with a hard clank.

Then somebody from the north side grabs a ketchup dispenser and squirts it directly at the guy who lobbed the napkin dispenser. In a second, three people are coated in ketchup. Looks way too much like blood.

Next Ricardo grabs up spoons and knives and forks.

What, isn't nobody going to be normal, sane? Greg looks like an overripe tomato about to pop. Omar looks like he's gonna rip right into him. And Rafa? He's stalking toward the Americans with clenched fists and a look on his face like he's about to pound somebody, anybody.

Wait—now he's got Jim Hill around the throat.

"EVERYBODY FUCKING STOP IT!" I shriek. And suddenly . . . everybody does.

Silence. Rafa stops mid-stride. Ricardo quits gathering silverware.

Take that, bitches.

"Why should we listen to you?" says Manuel Hernández, our resident priest-to-be, clutching a fistful of forks.

"Why do you have those forks?" I respond.

Right then, some teachers bust in. "What's going on in here?" asks Ms. Smith, my English teacher.

Now it's Students vs. Teachers, and I notice that all the forks and knives have disappeared and the three guys who were covered in ketchup are slouched behind their friends so teachers won't see them.

"Uh, nothing, ma'am," Omar says, stepping forward. "We were just talking about the situation, that's all."

"We heard yelling," she persists. "It sounded—" She pauses. "It sounded like you, Isaiah Contreras." And she turns to me, surprised. 'Cuz I'm never in trouble. "Was that you, Mr. Contreras? Did I hear you use the f-word?"

"Ohhhhh, *that*." Omar grins. "Ish just got a little out of control, that's all. You know how he holds such strong opinions. We calmed him down." He nods around the room like, "Thanks, everybody."

I will strangle him.

Ms. Smith turns to me and says, "Mr. Contreras? What do you have to say for yourself?"

"Uh, I'm real sorry, ma'am," I say, all humility and sincere fake regret. I can't rat anybody out. That's the rule.

"All right, then," she says. "But I think you should come down to the principal's office for a little chat, don't you?" She holds out her hand to me like I'm two years old.

And the guys? They love my humiliation.

Pacifism, whatever it is, is a tough road to take. I've seen the destruction violence causes. See if I come to these guys' rescue next time. Yeah. Next time, I'm going to be a different kind of pacifist. The kind that just stands back and watches. As they all kill themselves.

Gregory González

Mac Is Kinda Like Jesus

Lunch is fifth period. We hustle into the cafeteria, Dirty Bernie and me jostling in the doorway. "Soon, Bernie," I mutter as I try to squeeze my way past, but I'm a little too chunky, can't quite get by him.

"You gonna lose it like you did in class, Greggy?" he asks.

Omar shoves me from behind, knocking me into Bernie, who loses his balance. "Real soon," I repeat as he sprawls on the floor.

Jim Hill enters the cafeteria behind us. He claps his hands loudly, shouting, "Okay, beaners to the left, Americans to the right."

People look up from their plates.

"Come on, come on, come on!" he says, clapping his hands impatiently. "Let's go! Beaners to the left, Americans to the right. ¡Ándale!"

One guy loudly shuffles around in his seat, then stays put. A beaner stands up from where he's sitting and stomps over to the south side of the cafeteria. He's the only one who moves.

"You all think you're such hot stuff just because you're American," says Robbie Muñoz, who's Mexican but has lived in El Paso most of his life.

"Buncha racist pigs," says Bernie. "That's what you guys are."

"Man, I am sick to death of hearing that," says Jason Ronchetti. "Just because I'm white, I'm automatically racist. Just because I'm American, you think it's okay to bash on me. You think just because your skin is brown you aren't racist?"

"I wasn't even talking to you, *bolillo*," Bernie says. "I know what you are."

Suddenly one of the Mexicans throws a tray at us! I duck to avoid it but it hits my ass. Damn, right on the tailbone. And it's on. Right now.

I run over to the Mexican side and before I even know it, I've launched myself at that stupid beaner. I'm whaling him across the face like he's Alex Gold or Bernie Martínez or anybody else who had anything to do with Mac's death. 'Cuz— my best friend, you know? The only innocent one out of all of us is Mac.

"I'm gonna grind your stupid face into the dirt," I yell. One guy grabs me by the collar and another shoves me roughly into a seat.

"See what you started, motherfucker?" Omar screams at Bernie. "See?"

Bernie's waving his arm in its sling around at Omar. "I didn't start nothin'," he yells. "Mac did this."

Omar starts to lunge at Bernie, but then wheels around and sits down. There's an instant hush. The scene freezes.

"Yo, Omar, why'd you chicken out?" Jim asks. He's sprawled on a table, leaning back, just watching.

That's when Isaiah Contreras and Carbon Copy walk in. Ish instantly takes stock of the situation. I can see him sizing us all up.

"What's going on?" Ish addresses this to Bernie and Omar.

"It's Us versus Them," Omar says shortly, nodding at both sides.

"How come?" Ish asks.

"*¡Ése!*" One of the Mexicans is gesturing at Ish to get him to join their side. "*¡Ey, ése!*"

"Leave me alone," Ish yells, in English. "This is a Catholic school. Isn't there some Bible verse that says in Christ there is no Jew or Gentile or male or female or anything like that? We're all basically the same, right? You think God really gives a damn about national borders and who's on which side? You really think God cares about that?" He sits down on the Mexican side, dragging Chris with him.

"Yeah," Omar says. "I do think God cares about that."

"So God hates Mexicans, too?" Ish asks.

I think about how we all have these "God Bless America" bumper stickers on our cars since 9-11. About how we have to protect ourselves and God *has* to bless that, so God *must* be for some of us more than for others. How could God have no opinion about who's right or who's wrong? God's all about right and wrong, right?

"God doesn't love any murderers, rapists, terrorists, or drug dealers," I yell at Ish.

But some drug dealers are rich. So are they blessed by God? I can't get this straight in my head. If Mac were here, we could talk this out.

But Mac is gone . . . forever. Dead. I knew it before but not like this. Gone. Forever. Dead. Somebody's going to pay. Somebody has to.

Ish waves his hand at all the Mexicans sitting at the tables behind him. "You think any of these guys are rapists, murderers, terrorists, and drug dealers?"

Sanctimonious bastard.

I start pounding on the table, hoping to shut him up. It works. Pretty soon, every guy on my side, the *American* side, is pounding, too. I figure we outnumber the Mexicans three to one. I see the Mexicans start to look a little scared. *Yeah. Good. Be scared.*

One of them throws something metal at us. It clatters on the table. I get hit in the side by a fork.

I grab it and launch it back at the Mexicans. Then Rafa springs up and puts his hands around Jim's throat. I start to head over there to help Jim but I stop when I hear this piercing scream.

It's Ish. He's standing up on a table. He puts his hands out in the air on both sides of him, like a cop stopping traffic. And he screams: "THIS IS FUCKING INSANE. IF YOU DON'T STOP IT RIGHT NOW, THOSE COPS IN THE OTHER ROOM ARE GONNA COME BACK IN HERE AND START TAKING PEOPLE DOWN TO THE STATION. STOP IT RIGHT FUCKING NOW!"

And we do. We all stop. Because he's right. We're not finished with this, no way, but this is not the time. I lean in close to Bernie. I say, "To be continued, Bernie-boy."

Ish hears me and says, "This isn't a Schwarzenegger movie, Greg."

It isn't?

At that moment, three teachers race in like the building is burning down and we all sort of melt away, sit in our seats like good little Catholic schoolboys.

♦ ♦ ♦

Next period, we have the special Mass for Mac. It suddenly occurs to me that Mac is kinda like Jesus. Jesus was murdered, right? And maybe Mac was murdered for what he believed in. It puts Mac in a whole different light, like maybe he's holy or something. Except Jesus was murdered by his own people and I bet the dude that stabbed Mac was a damn Mexican. Maybe one that had one of those inferiority complex things?

I feel like I'm back in that long hallway where I can't reach the door with the big M blazing across it.

I trudge up to receive Communion. I haven't confessed my recent drug use or kidnapping Alex or the fight in the cafeteria. I feel guilty about that but right now I need . . . something. Besides, if I *don't* receive, everybody'll wonder why.

Soon-to-Be-Dead-Meat Bernie is just ahead of me. I watch as the priest gives him the wafer and murmurs, "Body of Christ," looking Bernie in the eye. Bernie chews it, makes the sign of the cross, moves away.

And now I'm looking my priest in the face, opening my mouth to receive. Our eyes meet, and I can't look away. "Body of Christ," he murmurs, and I make the sign of the cross. I still can't look away. I'm frozen.

He's waiting for me to leave and I know that, but all of a sudden, I can't. I need something more from him. Like a guarantee that it'll all be okay. I stand there looking at him until he blinks and whispers, "Are you all right, son?"

I nod and move on so the priest can finish up. Back in my seat, I stare up at the figure of Jesus above the altar, and I think about Jesus and Mac and wonder whether there are parts of the

Bible that didn't get written down, like maybe Jesus's disciples went around cutting off the fingers and ears and feet of the Jews who had shouted, "Crucify him," before they knew that Jesus rose from the dead, before they figured out this whole thing wasn't about revenge. But then, maybe—wasn't it all about revenge? Didn't Jesus say something about whoever is not against us is for us? Doesn't the reverse hold true as well? So isn't it all about being on the right side?

I wish Mac was here to figure out this shit with me. I miss him.

Daniel Tucker

Who is Mine Enemy?

Most of my heroes don't appear on no stamps . . .
Nothing but rednecks for 400 years if you check.
—Public Enemy, "Fight the Power"

I feel guilty for not going to the 1 o'clock Mass, but, shiiiiit, there've been way too many Masses for Jesuit boys lately. Too much drama altogether. Anyway, the Catholic Church hates my fag guts. I can't confess, I can't take Communion, not unless I lie my fag ass off. If they take down the names of people who don't go, guess I'm one fag in hot water. Son of a bitch, this is ruining my life.

Ma gets all hysterical when I come home. "Are you skipping school, Danny? Are you doing drugs? Are you going to become a criminal like your father? You know, all it takes is skipping school once, then it becomes a habit, and the next thing you know, you're in jail."

"Ma, no. If I was, I wouldn't come home so you could be all over my ass."

She laughs at that one. "Okay, okay. What're you doing home then?"

"There's some Jesuit kid missing," I say. I'm hoping for . . .

something from her. Instead, it sends her off into ballistic mode.

"What's going on over there?" She launches right into it. "Does somebody have a vendetta against Jesuit? It's probably some Mafia thing, the Mexican Mafia, somebody has some problem with Jesuit and this is the method of revenge. Maybe it's the Juárez drug cartel. Those people, they always take care of their own. Mac was probably killed in some drug transaction. Do you think he was involved in drugs?"

"Ma, it wasn't the Juárez drug cartel. Mac wasn't dealing drugs."

"How do you know?" she asks. "Anyway, I guess he would be small potatoes. Unless his parents are involved somehow. Do you think any of the priests at your school are in the know? You know, dirty money paying tuition or hush-hush fees or something?"

God.

"I'm gonna pull you out of that school," she finally says.

"Do it, Ma," I say. I don't even think about it. "I'll clean out my locker tomorrow." *For once, follow through, Ma. Please.*

"I'll homeschool you," she says.

"Ah, Ma, no," I say. "I can't be homeschooled. I'm in a band. Have you seen homeschoolers? They're all geeks."

"So?"

"So are you really going to teach me calculus?" I ask.

"Oh," she says.

"Exactly," I say. "How about public school instead?"

"I'll think about it," she says.

Yes! I can work her on this! She's never ever considered public school before.

"Listen, I'm going to go call my buddies and practice in the garage," I say.

"And I'm going to call around and find out more about what's going on over there."

"I've told you everything I know," I say. "I doubt anyone else knows anything more. At least, not anyone who'd tell *you* anything."

"I have my ways," she says, smiling mysteriously.

Yeah, I'll just bet, Ma. You haven't even figured out who I am.

◆ ◆ ◆

The guys come over to practice. So yeah, we're practicing in the garage, working our new song about the creep in the walls—it's an extended metaphor about drugs—and our drummer, Manny, finally puts down his drumsticks and says, "Hey, Dan, there's something I think you should know."

"What's that?"

"You know my kid brother goes to Jesuit?" he says.

"Yeah. So?"

"So he came home today with some story about how you're gay."

So they know. It's a cliché and everything, but I actually feel some icy coldness grip my stomach. Everything is now clear to me. It was all there on the bathroom wall. *They fucking know.* It's why Josh acted funny. It's why Omar looked at me that way. It's why I heard giggles in the hallway. And now I know—being white doesn't trump being gay.

I'm dead.

While I'm processing, the guys stand around scratching

their butts. Finally I say, "So, you guys want me out of the band or what?"

"No, man," says Matt, the other guitarist. "We don't care. We're college dudes, you know? We already knew you were gay. I mean, you never told us so we figured you weren't ready to come out yet. But we thought you should know that your high school buddies are talking about it."

"So anyway, the only reason we're telling you is 'cuz we think you should watch your back," Alfredo, our bass player, says. "Some spooky stuff's going on at Jesuit. You don't want to be next."

"Yeah, man," says Matt. "Be careful, dude."

Manny continues, "And I hate even more to say this, but some of the kids are saying that you're the one that killed that kid, because you were in love with him or something."

"What?" It always comes down to this, right? The deviant gay kid gets blamed.

"Yeah," Manny says. "I mean, we know you couldn't stab someone to save your life. But that's what some kids are saying."

I want to throw up. Now. I say, "Be right back," and I go inside and I bend over the toilet and just wait. The saliva builds up in the back of my mouth, the way it always does right before you hurl, but nothing's coming. How did they find out? Bernie? He's the only guy at school who knew, who could have told. He probably told to get the heat off himself. Guess he's more of an asshole than I thought.

I straighten up and look at my watch. It's past 2. That means he should be out of Mass by now, maybe even heading back to Juárez. I dial his number and wait. It rings and rings and rings. I sit down on the toilet seat for a second. Then I dial again.

He answers, but he's out of breath, like he's been running. *"Bueno."*

"Bernie. It's Dan Tucker."

"Fuck," he says. "I don't got no time right now. What's up, *joto*?"

I jump right in. "Did you tell people that I'm, you know . . . ?"

"What?"

"Did you tell people that I'm, you know"—I pause for a second, then choke on the word as I say it—"gay?"

Bernie swears. *"¡Chingao!"*

"What?" I ask. "What?!"

"I don't go around telling people things like that," he says. "I'm not into homos, you know that," he adds, "but I got a favorite uncle who's gay. *Pues,* he has AIDS. He's dying, you know? I've never told nobody nothing about you, I swear on *La Virgen de Guadalupe.*"

I didn't know about this uncle. I just know Bernie showed up one time for one of the monthly meetings at the Gay & Lesbian Alliance. The topic that week was HIV. I remember our conversation in the hallway after the meeting. "You won't—?" I started to say, and he answered, "Not unless you do."

So if Bernie didn't tell, who else found out? And how?

The thing is—does Josh know?

"You sure?" I ask.

"Dan, I'm in the middle of a fucking fight here," he yells into the phone. "No! I didn't say nothing. Leave me alone, you *pinche* fag."

"You're in the middle of a fight?"

"Yeah, *joto,* right in front the cathedral. Those guys are trying to beat my ass and I'm gonna give 'em some."

"Is Josh there?"

"How the hell should I know?" *Click.*

I'm already running down the street toward Jesuit. Have to find Josh. I don't care if they've got machine guns and they're spraying the crowd. This is my boy we're talking about.

God, it's like I'm in fourth grade. All I can think about is finding him, asking him, "Are you still my friend?" What will I do if he says no? Probably start to cry. I don't give a fuck about anybody else.

Since last Friday, this is what I've been reduced to. Yeah, that's me. A crying, friendless faggot.

Alexander Gold

Pulling Something Out of Our Collective Asses

Listen, you fuckers, you screwheads: Here is a man who would not take it anymore. A man who stood up against the scum . . . the dogs, the filth. . . . Here is someone who stood up.

—Travis Bickle, *Taxi Driver*

As I walk away from the warehouse, I wonder, should I disappear? Where? Those guys have it in for me, and that Jim Hill is a real head case. Is this fun for him? What if he's the one who killed Mac and this whole thing is one big power trip for him? Nobody suspects *him,* everybody suspects *me.* But still, *why* would he kill Mac? Just because he's psycho, or does he have the hots for Vero, too? Seems like she was everybody's ho. Mac, Josh, José, me. Not that she ever put out for me. But still, if she'd put out for Mac, I might've wanted to kill him, too.

My nose is bleeding. I taste blood in my mouth, that metallic taste. Damn. There's no way I can go home like this. I flash to that scene in the movie *Friday,* where Smoky runs over to his friend who's just been slammed to the ground and yells, *"You got knocked the fuck out!"* It's nice to be distracted for a second.

It's dark out here. Not many people around downtown El Paso at night.

Jim managed a pretty mean punch. I have to hold my nose closed to keep from bleeding all over everything and then I decide what the fuck, who cares, let me just bleed all over everything, use my shirt as a Kleenex.

I have to *think,* think about how I can approach this. Go to the cops, tell them what happened, and see what they do? Go home and forget about the whole thing? Disappear, leave El Paso, just get on with my life somewhere else? I could cross the border, melt into Mexico, become someone else. I don't speak Spanish, but I could pick it up, right? Or . . . I could just hole up for a few days, wait until things get really hot and heavy for Jim and Josh, and then return, as it were, from the dead. Bet everybody'd notice me then.

What am I saying?

I check my wallet. Exactly ten dollars. If I'm careful, I can probably eat for a couple of days with that money. But jeez, it isn't going to get me far. I have to figure out something else. Have to come up with a plan. A Travis Bickle plan. Bickle might have been a nutcase but he wanted to save somebody. He wanted to help, to cleanse the world of evil bastards. His motives were pure.

Who do I want to save? Myself?

What if I just go to Jim Hill's apartment right now and kick the living shit out of him? Or what if I pay Josh a little visit and find out what he knows? 'Cuz he knows something—I could see it in his eyes when I said that thing about Rafa.

I don't know Josh's address but I can find out. So off I go.

◆ ◆ ◆

Josh's house is only about six-plus miles from the warehouse. Between walking and jogging, it takes me just under two hours to get there. I feel like I'm in a movie—the wounded hero, walking bravely on for miles and miles, alone and bleeding, to reach his loved ones. Except there's no love for me where I end up.

Josh's mom is concerned when she sees how bloody I am. "Don't worry about it, Mrs. Alvarado," I say. "Can I just use your bathroom to clean up and call my mom to come get me?"

"Did somebody beat you up?" she asks.

"Nah," I lie. "I was skateboarding and I wiped out. Hit my nose. I figured I'd come here since it was the closest place."

"Where's your skateboard?" she asks.

Whoopsie. "Um, it got broken so I just left it at the park," I say. "It's pretty trashed."

She shakes her head at me as she shows me the bathroom and gives me a towel. Thank God she doesn't ask what park I was at.

"It's really late," she says at last. "What were you doing out there skateboarding at this time of night?"

I shrug like it's no big deal, like I do that all the time. "That's probably why I kept wiping out. *Way* too dark out there."

She troops out to the front hallway and calls up the stairs, "Joshua, you have a friend here who wants to see you."

I wonder what she'd do if she knew everything Josh was mixed up in. *My* mom would cry, then faint.

I head up the stairs. Josh looks like *he's* going to faint when he sees me on the landing. "We made it so you could walk home," he says, sounding like a little boy. I have a sudden picture of Josh in prison. It isn't pretty. He might deal drugs but he's not hard-core. He'd never make it.

"I came here to talk."

Josh takes that in for a minute. "Let's go in my room," he says.

I'm blinded, it's so white in here. White walls, white carpet. Even the bedspread is white. "I'm gonna get blood all over everything," I say. "I've cleaned up but I'm still splattered."

"Ah, so what?" he says. "We've got Clorox."

I don't bother sitting down. "You know something," I say. "You know something that you should tell the cops."

"I don't." His denial is immediate, too immediate.

"It's a good thing I'm not the police," I tell him. "They'd know in a second that you're lying. Don't you ever watch *Law and Order*?"

He shakes his head. "Too busy doing other things."

"Smoking dope?"

"What's it to you?" He looks directly at me until I look away.

"I don't care about that, Josh." I look around the room. There's a Bob Marley poster up on the wall, Marley smoking a big joint. He's the only thing in the room that isn't white.

Josh is still watching me.

"Look. I didn't kill Mac Malone. I had nothing to do with any of it," I say.

"I know," he says.

"So then," I say, "between the two of us, we can probably figure out who did it."

"You mean, we can pull something out of our collective asses?" Josh asks.

"Why not?"

I can tell Josh is not yet ready to spill the beans. So we'll play Twenty Questions. I'll start.

I ask Josh where he was during the Fight.

"Raf and I were discussing a deal," he says.

"Did you see anything, notice anything?"

"No. By the time we finished talking, Bernie looked like he was dead and everybody had stopped yelling. I heard plenty in the next couple of hours. 'Didja see Mac's eyes?' No. 'They looked demonic.' Come on. 'Shit, he looked freaking possessed.' Give me a break. 'Was Mac on drugs?' Fuck you. 'I bet he smoked crack.' Double fuck you. 'How do you know?' He's too smart. So put that in your crack pipe and smoke it—"

"Do you know for sure he wasn't doing drugs that day?" I interrupt. It's a test question. I'll pretend I don't know anything, like I didn't catch Mac snorting that one time. Like I don't know he'd stopped taking his Ritalin.

"He liked *la coca*," Josh admits. He's fiddling with something, a pen or a marble or something.

"How do you know?"

"How do you think I know?" He doesn't need to add "dumbass" because I suddenly know I am a dumbass.

Oh. Right. "So was it a bad habit?"

"Yeah, I guess."

"How bad?"

"He owed me. A ton." Then: "He'd started giving me his Ritalin medication to pay off part of his debt."

We're silent for a minute, until I say, "Somebody could construe that as a motive for murder, Josh."

He straightens up. "Yeah, they could. Obviously. But I didn't do it, okay?"

And yeah, I really do believe him. "Back to school. What else happened that day?"

223

"I don't know. There was lots of shit talked about in the halls. 'Nobody likes Mac anyway.' *I* like Mac. 'No, you don't.' Don't tell me who I like and don't like. And 'Hey, didja hear, Bernie's in the hospital? He's in a coma.' Where'd you hear that? 'Everybody knows.' Buncha gossipy girls, that's what we are."

"Yeah, I heard people saying that kind of stuff, too."

"Everybody had a motive," Josh says. "I had a motive. As you pointed out. Look, I'm just the dealer. You're the shadowy background guy. So why don't you pull something outta *your* ass right now?"

"Dan Tucker had opportunity. And motive."

Josh glares at me.

Okay, okay. If I'm gonna get Josh to tell me what he knows, I have to start thinking outside the box. Outside the box. Outside the box. Outside— "Vero!" I realize. "Vero lives over there! Do you think she might have seen something?"

Josh practically jumps up and down. "It coulda been her that did it! Why didn't we think of this before?"

"Because nothing points at her," I say.

"But she lives right there."

"So? A lot of people live there and they didn't kill him."

"You like her, huh?" he asks me.

"So?"

"She's a slut, you know."

"That doesn't make her a killer." I can feel myself losing *my* motive here. I just can't, don't *want* to believe Vero would be involved in something like this. "What's her motive?"

"She's the Jesuit ho," he says. "Everybody knows it, she's tired of it, so she knocks Mac off 'cuz she's mad."

"No way."

Josh sighs. "You don't know women, do you?"

He's right. Or at least, I don't know women the way Josh knows them.

"One thing I do know," I say. "Women don't kill by stabbing."

I'm saying what I'm saying and he's responding but I still feel like I'm playing a part, like I'm watching myself in a movie.

"What are you doing here, Alex?" Josh asks finally. "If you wanted revenge, why not go to Jim's house, beat him up? He cooked up that little scene. You and I don't have anything to do with each other."

"This isn't about me. How could you think this is about me?"

"Well, it *is* about me," he says.

"Get over yourself, Josh. This is so not about you."

"Yeah, it is," he says. He's drumming his fingers against his sides, a nervous tic. He leaps up from the bed and leans against the wall, like he doesn't want to sit as long as I'm standing. "I can't talk about what I know."

"Tell me what the fuck you know," I say. My voice is even and strong. I've analyzed Josh. He'll respond to calm force.

"Maybe what I know isn't . . . isn't worth repeating?" he says, his voice faltering.

"How can you know?" I ask. "Maybe what you know is exactly what the police need to figure this out."

"I hate cops," he moans.

"Spit it out, motherfucker," I say. Again, calm but forceful.

"I was hanging out with Jim," he admits. "And Rafa did come by with José, to drop off some X that I'm going to sell. I

225

took some and so did Jim's sister, who sort of has the hots for me, and we went to her bedroom for a while. You know," he says. He doesn't even blush. "Anyhoo, I came out at some point and both Jim and Rafa were gone. Jim came back a little bit later and we smoked a joint and I went home. By the time I left, the cops were arriving at Mac's house, I just didn't know it. I passed some cop cars and an ambulance while driving, but I didn't know where they were heading. I make myself scarce when cops are around, so I just went home."

Here it is. Most of it.

"Do you think Jim did it?"

"I don't know. But he could have. It was the right time frame and they did go to Mac's."

We look anywhere but at each other. "Was it just Rafa and José that came by or did Rafa have anyone else with him?"

"Just Rafa and José."

" 'Cuz I saw three guys in that car."

"Fuck," Josh says.

"You have to go to the cops."

"They'll put me in jail."

"You don't have to tell them about the X."

"You think they won't find out?"

"Okay, they'll find out," I point out. "But it's probably better for you if you come clean with them, tell them what you know and why. Maybe they won't even care."

"Oh, they'll care."

"What's worse, drugs or murder?" I move my hands up and down in the air, like I'm weighing justice and mercy. "I think you'll be okay."

"I can't do it, Alex," he says. "I just can't." He fingers his bedspread. He won't look at me. He seems . . . ashamed? Terrified?

"You may not have a choice." I'm already at the door, ready to go. I've said what I need to say and now I know what Josh knows. It isn't anything absolute but Jim's a crazy fuckadoodle, we both know it, and this is exactly the kind of thing he'd do. For kicks. Just stab Mac to death, to see what it was like. Up close and personal.

"What're you going to do now?" Josh asks.

"Disappear, at least for a few days."

"Don't you think the cops will assume you're guilty?"

"Maybe. But I'm hoping to light a fire under Jim's ass. Give him his turn in the hot seat. They'll trace my last movements. My mom saw Jim."

"That'll put me in the hot seat, too." He looks glum.

"Sorry," I say.

Josh returns to the original topic. "I just want to know why, you know? It just doesn't make sense. It doesn't make sense that Mac is dead. Fuck. He's dead! I don't get it. I don't get that *anybody* killed him, but that *Jim* killed him? I just want to know why. Maybe there is no why. But I want to know if there's a legitimate explanation. Before I go to the police. Is that too much to ask?"

I don't know how to answer that one. "Hey, Josh, I have a question *I* want to ask," I say. "Why are you stoned all the time?" I can't help it. I have to ask.

"You see where we live?" He gestures wildly around the room but I know he's referring to everything outside. "At the end of the earth! Who wouldn't do drugs?"

I gesture just as wildly. "Josh, do you see where we live?

Who *would*? Can't you see you'll get caught? It's just a matter of time." I think about the military zone I've lived in my entire life. Sure, it's been worse in El Paso since the Cinco de Mayo bombing. But life hasn't really changed by more than a few degrees. This is the way it's always been. I think about the desert outside, the mountains, the city of El Paso that always and never sleeps. I think about the police, the Border Patrol, the DEA. We're under so much surveillance here, we can't take a dump without the possibility that someone will get in our business.

"I know," he says. "My older brother and all of his friends have been arrested at least once. But you have to do something to survive." He's numb. Carefully and comfortably numb. Pink Floyd said it best.

"Yeah, I guess you're right," I agree. "You have to do something to survive." I'm supposed to go now, but I have one more question. "Josh. One more question."

He is carefully refraining from gritting his teeth. "What?"

"What are you going to do about Dan?"

He chokes, then laughs a little. "What the fuck are you talking about?"

"You know." I'm not going to say it exactly.

He's quiet for a long time. He's definitely struggling. I'm not sure if he's mad at me, or exorcising some personal homophobic demons or what, but I can tell he's struggling.

One or two minutes is a long time to be standing in a room in silence, looking at some guy squirm. It begins to feel like nobody can break this silence.

Then he looks directly at me and says, "Dan Tucker is my best bud."

"And?" I ask. I'm still waiting, I don't know for what.

"You've never had a real friend, have you?" he asks. But it's really a statement, not a question.

Damn. I've held it in for years. I held it in throughout the kidnapping and beating. I've never ever let anyone know that it matters. But now in this moment my eyes are hot and wet and gushing. Stupid tears roll down my cheeks. I'm wiping them but they keep coming. *Shit, get ahold of yourself, Alex.*

Josh ignores it. Nice of him. Really nice of him. He is a good guy.

"So?" I know the answer, but I want to hear it. Because I like Dan Tucker. Not that he's ever noticed me, but, given that he's gay, he's been in practically the same position I've been in all these years. An outcast. A Them.

"He's my best friend," Josh repeats. That's all there is.

By now, I've sunk to the floor and I'm sitting on the carpet. The beating I took earlier is beginning to catch up to me. I could go to sleep right here.

We sit. I'm not sure which one of us is going to stir or say something first. I feel like I could sit here for the rest of my life.

Isaiah Contreras
You're Either For Us or Against Us

Brother Rodarte calls my mother, tells her what happened, promises that, "given the volatile situation right now," I will be "severely reprimanded."

No one even asks me for my side of the story. As I'm sitting there listening to them talk to my mother about my "sudden outburst," Brother Rodarte suggests that "perhaps" I "should stay home for a few days."

"Please understand, Mrs. Contreras, that we're not suspending him," he says in his smooth voice. (How I hate that voice. How I hate him.) "We just think he needs some time to cool off. A lot has happened and many of the boys are just a little bit on edge. He may return on Thursday or Friday with no repercussions."

"I have a exam in religion on Wednesday," I point out when he hangs up the phone. "What do you mean, no repercussions? Am I going to get an F for missing the exam?"

Yeah, I know how I sound.

"I'm going to ignore that tone of voice, Isaiah," Brother Rodarte says, the Big Man. "I know you're overwrought. We will arrange for you to take that exam on Thursday or Friday. You just go home and get cooled down and straightened out."

So now I'm gonna go home and watch TV and play video games for a few days. Yeah. Who gives a shit if Jesuit goes up in flames? I'll just watch 'em burn baby burn. Not a very peaceful attitude, but fuck. They just dumped on me, why should I give a shit about any of them?

♦ ♦ ♦

I go to Mass, but I refuse Communion.

A lot of the guys involved in the cafeteria incident—I feel like I should think about that in capital letters, the Cafeteria Incident—take the Eucharist. I mean, I don't know their hearts so I'm not supposed to judge, right? But they shoulda at least gone to confession first. Hypocrites. Godless fucks.

I hunch up in my pew and cross my arms and just sit there. I don't even listen to the sermon. I'm not even here.

I start thinking instead. About where people go when they die.

I know what my religion teaches me. Catholicism is so literal, like heaven's a real, physical place and so is hell, and when we die, we are mysteriously transported there (wherever we deserve to go) and that's where we spend eternity, which never ends. Up or down. I don't really *get* that. Once you leave your body behind, how can there be some physical place where we actually go? Maybe it's like a soul dimension? All airy and shit?

And why does there need to be a heaven or hell to understand or explain the things on earth? 'Cuz everybody seems to need it. For Buddhists, it's Nirvana or whatever. For Hindus, reincarnation. For Christians and Muslims, heaven and hell. I wonder if there's some religion somewhere that just teaches people to lead a good life and not worry about what comes after death. Is that what atheists believe? Is the only reason religion exists because we need to explain death somehow? Like, if we didn't die, would we even need religion?

I don't usually think such deep thoughts. Maybe Mac *was* reincarnated, but he's staying inside part of my brain, making me question everything I've been taught. He loved this kind of shit.

◆ ◆ ◆

So I'm waiting outside the church after Mass, just hanging out until my mom comes to pick me up, and all these guys file out and start messing with me.

"So, did you decide which side you're on, Ishy-poo?" says Omar. "Are you American or are you *Me-hi-cano*?"

"You're either for Us or against Us," intones Greg. He's flanked by Ricardo and Omar.

This is *loco*. "What are you trying to do?" I ask. "Pretend this whole thing is some big terrorist thing? Are Mexicans the new nine-eleveners?" I'm no good at debate, not like Chris, but I can hear a bit of Carbon Copy in my reply.

"Look, all I'm saying is, we have to protect our own," says Omar.

"Fine," I say. "But you've lost sight of what this is really about, *amigo*. Mac's *dead*. Somebody *murdered* him. Even if it was a Mexican that did it, it wasn't goddamn *Mexico* that murdered him." Then I realize I'm still on the front steps of the cathedral and I just said "goddamn." Shit. I should make the sign of the cross, but, dude, I can't with the guys right here.

"You *know* it was Mexicans did this," Omar says. "Do you know who Bernie's uncle is? He took over the Juárez drug cartel after Amado Carillo died. And Bernie threatened to kill Mac at the hospital. That's a fact."

Bernie's uncle, the latest drug lord? Got to be just a rumor. But even if it's true . . . "Maybe Bernie's involved," I say. "But that's not all Mexicans."

"With Us or against Us," Greg repeats. "They stick together. So should we."

"You're insane," I say.

"You think they'll defend you?" Omar jerks his thumb at Bernie, Sergio, Teddy, and Rene, a group of Mexican nationals standing behind us. I can always tell who's Mexican and who's Mexican American. It's a gift.

I look down at my shoes. Yeah, I can tell. Because I am an Us. I mean, I even call my mother "Mom." No *"Mami"* for me.

"Why would you even *want* to be Mexican?" Greg asks. Like I'd be stupid to even consider it.

"I wouldn't," I say. Wait. Have I just taken sides?

Omar slaps me on the back. "So we can count on you?" he says, and doesn't wait for a answer. "Hey, Dirty Bernie," he yells. "We shall meet again, *chin-ga-do.*"

"What are you, Luke fuckin' Skywalker?" Bernie yells back. "I guess that makes me Darth Vader. Hey, *Ish,*" he says suddenly. "I thought you were on *our* side."

Omar claps his arm around me. "Ish knows what side he's on," he says.

Bernie juts his chin out at me. It's the El Paso way of saying, "What's up" or "What's the deal, yo?"

"Tienes familia en el otro lado," he says to me. *"Familia."*

Sometimes, when I've gone with my mom to visit my aunts and my *abuelita* in Juárez, Bernie's come over to see me. Or my mom'll drop me off at his house. He's got a nice house with a swimming pool. And, of course, big Rottweiler dogs and other security à la Juárez—thick slabs of sharp glass cemented to the top of the wall all the way around the perimeter. Does that mean his family is involved in drugs somehow? I mean, his mom don't work and his dad's been at the house most of the times I'm there, hanging out with his brothers. Seems suspicious to me.

"Yo sé," I reply. *"Pero tengo familia aquí, también."*

He persists. *"Pero,* most of your family is in Juárez."

Fuckers won't leave me alone. "Look," I say, "I'm just waiting here for my mom."

After they leave, I realize nobody's mentioned that missing kid, Alexander Gold. Where is he and what does he have to do with all of this, anyway? Why doesn't anybody care about him? Who *is* he? I guess everybody's just concerned about their own stuff. We've forgotten he's even missing.

I'm no prophet. But I have this feeling. Like something's gonna blow.

♣ ♣ ♣

Mom picks me up with the kind of look she has when she and Dad fight, which is . . . practically all the time. "What did you do, *mijo*?" she asks right away. "What did you do? *¿Mijo?*"

"Nada, Mom," I reply. *"Nada."*

She looks at me and says, *"No seas mentiroso,* Isaiah."

234

I scoot as far away from her as possible. "I told you, I didn't do *nothing*. I got set up by some of the other kids. Why do you *always* blame me?"

She gets that same scared look and I realize I sound like Dad.

"Look, I'm sorry," I say, sinking down into my seat. Ashamed. The last thing I ever want to do is make my mom scared.

"*Es* okay, *mijo*," she says, reaching over and patting my knee. "*Es* okay."

◆ ◆ ◆

As soon as we get home, Mom says, "*¿Mijo?* There's a gordita in the refrigerator," but I just go straight to my room.

Leti follows me and hovers in my doorway. "What's wrong, Ish?" she asks. I can tell she wants to come in, but I'm in no mood for her right now.

"Nothing, Leti," I say. "I'm fine."

She looks at me with her big round brown eyes until I relent. I say, "Come on in. Let's read a book together."

She bounces happily onto the bed and snuggles up against me. "Where the Wild Things Are!" she demands.

God. Little sisters are just like puppies.

I reach over and grab the book from my shelf. As soon as I start reading, my little sister leaning up against me—as soon as I hear my own voice saying the first words of the book, about Max being in a bad mood—I feel better. Little kids. They're so basic.

The Race Riot

Greg

Outside St. Frances Jerome Cathedral, I meet up with Omar and Ricardo. They're talking to Isaiah Contreras, that big fat pussy, who tries to convince them that this isn't about race. I try to tell him, "Hey, Ish, you're either with Us or against Us," but he laughs at me.

"Come on, Greg," he says. "You can't separate people into two sides like that. I mean, you're Mexican American. How can you be against Mexicans?"

"I am American," I point out. "I was born here."

"Yeah," he says. "Shouldn't you also be *loyal* to your ethnicity?"

"I am a loyal Mexican American," I say.

"Shee," he sighs.

"Look," I say, trying to reason with him. "Mexicans come here to make money off us and stuff, but then they hate us. I am Us. Think Cinco de Mayo, last year."

"This is not about Cinco de Mayo," he says. "It's not about 9-11. We're not at war with Mexico. Some weirdo just strapped a bomb on his back and went ballistic. So we're going to blame every single Mexican just because of some crazy fuck?"

"They were celebrating in the streets, man," Omar says. "*Our* streets, not just theirs. You saw them."

"It was *Cinco de Mayo*," Isaiah says. "They weren't celebrating the bomb, you dumbass."

"No, they were celebrating 'cuz one of their own got back at the big bad U.S. They're jealous of us 'cuz their country is inferior," I say.

Isaiah shakes his head at me. "*They* are your people, Greg," he says. "Your people. My people. How can they be inferior?"

"Do you *really* think you're Mexican?" I ask. "Would you even *want* to be Mexican?" I can't imagine being Mexican. I mean, you're either wealthy—and that's practically nobody— or you're living in some disgusting shack in the Juárez hillsides.

Just then, Dirty Bernie runs over. "Isaiah," he yells, "what are you doing with these *pinches* Americans?"

I want to throw down right then but I hold back. He'll get his. Just wait a *lee-tle* while longer.

"I'm not taking sides," Ish contends. Stubborn prick.

Everybody kind of snorts at that one. "You can't *not* take sides," Omar says, and Bernie chimes in, "You've got family *en el otro lado. Family.*"

"So?" Ish replies. "I've got family on this side, too." Lucky for him, his mother pulls up to the curb. "See ya later," he crows. "Try not to do anything stupid, you guys."

He gets in his van to go home. With his *mama.* He seems soooo relieved to go. I'd like to stomp his balls until they fall off. Mac died and he's all reasonable about everything. Traitor.

"Hey, Greggy," Bernie says, and makes a stabbing motion with his hands. "When did you become such an Americunt?"

"You're just the same as that fucking terrorist!" I scream.

He giggles. I mean, he *giggles*. "Americunt," he whispers again.

When my hand cracks his jaw, it's the best feeling in the world. I could just keep on hitting this fucking beaner asshole forever.

"It's on!" I hear Omar yell as he goes jumping over the cathedral steps. I glance up for just a minute and see him tackle Sergio Camarena to the ground.

Bernie

I threw a punch at Greg and now I'm gettin' outta here. I'm running down the steps when my cell phone rings. *Who the fuck?* *"¿Quién es?"* I want to know immediately, now, a minute ago, before I even answer the phone.

"Daniel Tucker," he says.

Why's that *joto* calling me now? "Look, I don't got no time for you," I say, but the whiny bitch won't shut up.

"Did you tell anyone I'm, you know . . . ?" he chokes.

I got more problems than everybody thinks. It's not all about Mac and Bernie, Bernie and Cinco de Mayo, Bernie and Jesuit, Bernie and *los gringos*. I'm Dirty Bernie here but I got another life with my family in Juárez, *¿sabes?* A family with problems.

"No way, José," I say. "Didn't tell nobody."

Should I tell him about my uncle? *Pues* . . . okay. But the motherfucker better keep it to himself or he's gonna get some. That's our biggest family secret. Ever.

Omar

Shit-for-Brains thinks I'm Muslim. Just because my mom's Lebanese. The level of ignorance scares me. We're Orthodox. That's almost Catholic.

I'm solid American, through and through. My dad fought in the first Gulf War. He's leaving next week for Iraq.

How dare he question my loyalty?

"Americunt," Bernie whispers, and Greg slugs him so hard, he splits his cheek open.

Sergio's already running away, cowardly pussy.

"We're on," I yell, running after Sergio.

Rafa

Híjole. Gringos everywhere.

Which side am I on? *No sé.* Since two years ago, we've lived in the U.S. *Aiyi. Pero . . . toda mi familia es mexicana.* And it wasn't no Mexican killed Mac. Why they got to blame the most obvious choice?

I got some excess energy to burn in the worst way. So . . . I'm gonna fuck up the first Anglo walks my way.

¡Ándale!

Dan

Jesuit's not far from my neighborhood, just a few blocks to the north. I don't like to run—somebody told me once I run like a girl—but I still run all the way there.

I round the corner and hear it—screaming. St. Frances

Jerome Cathedral. Jesuit students are everywhere, punching each other out. One guy punches another guy and he flies straight backward, tumbling down the steps that lead to the entrance of the cathedral. Those steps are made of cement. Hard.

Josh? Maybe Josh is around the corner?

Check around the corner. Nope, not here.

What about the other side, away from all the guys fighting?

I round the third corner and—hit the pavement. One guy on my back, pounding me in the head, another kicking my legs, and a third one standing over the other two, yelling, "Fight, you fucking fag!"

One of them hits me in the eye and my flesh tears apart. I'm staring at drops of blood on the sidewalk. They shove me over and I'm staring at the sky. What the—

"Crap, my—"

B e r n i e

El chingado's all over my back, like those nightmares you can't wake up from. *No puedo hacer nada.* Think, Bernie. Pull back your arm. Concentrate on Greg's head. Aim. Fucker, it's your bad arm. Hit him anyway. Fuck, my—

D a n

"—nuts," I scream but he's not listening. The pain travels all the way up my spine and into the brain. Why does it hurt your head when your dick's kicked?

"Please, dear God, just stop. God, just stop."

"Queers go straight to hell when they die, you know," this kid with a big nose says.

Do I even know this guy?

Bernie

Does he have to kick me *en los huevos*?

Hurts like I'm not gonna have children no more.

Greg

Now I have Bernie on the ground and I'm kicking him, kicking him, kicking him.

I hear him once or twice, pleading, "Greg, stop. Please stop. *Por favor.*"

He staggers up, pulls his arm back, and swings it forward. It knocks me right in the chest with a crack. He screams, as if it hurt him worse than it hurt me. Just as I hit the pavement, I see his sling go flying down the cathedral steps and Bernie goes running after it, his arm dangling by his side.

I start to go after him but now there are guys everywhere, hitting and kicking and punching and beating on each other. I'm smacking somebody I don't even know. His spit hits my face.

Bernie

Why do they think all Mexicans are into illegal shit? Drugs? My dad's a damn dentist. Most of his clients are Americans. They cross the border for good cheap dental work.

Why do they think all Mexicans wanna be American? I sure as hell don't. Especially after today.

Rafa

Yo, *güero,* this one's for *mota.* *¡Órale!* This one's for my woman! This one's for *la familia!* *¡Órale!* This one's for La Raza! This one's for Mexico! *¡Viva México!* *¡Órale!*

El chingado has flecks of blood between his freckles.

Don't usually see that. When me and *los vatos* go cruising on Friday nights, looking to race somebody down Montana Street, even when there's trouble, it's with other Mexicans, some *cholos.* Never seen no Mexican with freckles.

Greg

That's when I look up and notice the TV cameras. Shit. I gotta get out of here before my parents see me on the news.

Maybe I can sneak around the side of the cathedral.

Guys are running everywhere. One leaps off the cathedral stairway onto some kid walking past. They tumble to the ground and roll out into the street in front of oncoming traffic.

Jim

The Infiltrator observes a moment of silence, like a prayer.

The scene before me is exquisite. The cathedral spire sticks straight up into a clear blue sky. Young Jesuit men tumble across the cathedral steps, like little kids playing tag. Let your eyes wander down the hill, past downtown El Paso—the view of Mexico is superb. Smog floats lightly above the city of Juárez.

The more I watch, the more I like. It's like drinking your sixth beer of the evening. If they made my story into a movie, this would be the big scene . . . the best. Guys taking swings every which way, until they don't know who is hitting who. And me, I'm just watching.

Complete satisfaction. That's what I feel.

Suddenly I see a cop car rounding the corner.

Time to leave. Have fun at the station, all you bad little boys. The Infiltrator is outta here.

R a f a

El chingado's sneaking away. I shoulda choked him when I had the chance in the cafeteria.

Instead, I'm beating up this white kid from my religion class. Eric . . . Moody? And I'm thinking about the conversation me and Jim and José had on Friday night in my car. Every time I think of another thing we said, I slam my fist into Eric's head. *Bam.*

"Hey, Rafa, you think Mac hates Mexicans?"

Bam.

"Jim, do *you* think Mac hates Mexicans?" It seems to me someone's always out to trick you. Better not to answer. If you answer, you're responsible. People will hold you to it. Better to turn the question around, back to them.

Bam.

"I'm not gonna answer that one," he said. Then: "Hey, Rafa, Josh is fucking my sister right now. Think I should beat up the son of a bitch when I get home?"

Bam.

"I don't know, do you think you should beat up the son of a bitch when you get home?"

"You shouldn't talk about your sister like that," José told him. "But if you don't like what your *vato*'s doing, you should lay it out on the table, man."

Bam.

José, he's one good *vato.* Told Jim exactly like it is.

Bam.

"Rafa, Rafa!" Eric's repeating, over and over. "I surrender! I surrender! Please! Please stop!"

I've been banging his head into the cement for the last minute and a half.

"Okay," I say. "I'll stop. But not before I wrap your *chones* around your head."

"What?" he says.

"Yeah, give 'em to me or I'll find a way to get 'em myself."

I stand over him while he takes his pants off, then his underwear. He starts to hand them over.

Fuck! The cops! I'm outta here.

Greg

Some kid is grabbing my arms from behind. I twist my head around. Oh my God, it's a cop and he's slapping handcuffs on me. My mom is going to kill me!

That's when I hear a bunch of kids standing over by the steps, watching and chanting, "Fight! Fight! Fight!"

The cop shoves me toward his car. I don't see anybody else in handcuffs yet. Just me. What, do they think *I* started this?

"Please, Officer," I tell the cop, all good-boy polite. "What's going to happen? I have to go to my best friend's funeral tomorrow. The one who was stabbed. MacKenzie Malone. He lived right next door to me. We were friends forever, best friends. Please, Officer? Give me a break."

He just shakes his head. "You've got more to worry about than that right now, young man."

Omar

Gonna pretend this stupid kid is Bernie, accusing me of being a Muslim terrorist. Smash his face to the ground. Grind it in the cement. *Yeah, you all bloody? Take that, bitch! And that!*

Greg

I sit back in the car and look out the window. It only takes a few minutes for the cops to stop most of the fighting. They lead a few guys away toward cop cars. Soon there are four or five shoved in each car, three in the back, two in the front. Sergio Camarena is shoved in my car. He sits next to me, glaring.

I kick him with my foot.

He kicks back.

The cop reaches in and yanks him out. "You're just going to get yourself in worse trouble, son," he says to me before handing Sergio off to another cop.

They replace Sergio with Omar. We glare at each other.

What have we done?

Omar

I mean, the heat was bad after 9-11. I was totally pissed off about the Cinco de Mayo Bomber, too, but . . . secretly . . . I was relieved. Took the heat off me—I mean, my kind.

Heat's gonna be bad after this, too.

Greg

And there's Dirty Bernie. He sits on the cathedral steps, holding his broken arm and howling, tears and snot and blood streaming down his face.

Did I do that to him? *Could* I hurt him that bad? Two paramedics hustle over to him and try to calm him down. They help him onto a stretcher.

A couple of guys are getting medical attention. One guy with a bandage wrapped around his head is talking to television cameras. One guy's butt-naked!

A reporter steps up to the car we're inside with a tiny notebook. The photographer with her starts flashing pictures. I'd cover my face, but I can't, I'm handcuffed.

"Go away," Omar says. "We're not talking to you."

Dan

After a while, I get up and hobble around the side of the cathedral. By the time I get there, I can see the cops have things mostly under control.

I don't see Josh anywhere. He probably split as soon as the police showed up. That boy has a radar for cops like I've never seen. Was he even here?

Greg

That's when I notice the cop sitting in the front seat.

"You fucked up good this time, didn't you?" he asks, looking straight at me. At *me*! Why not Omar? Why not that other dude in the front seat? What about *them*?

No kidding, asshole. I look out the window and I realize I don't know if any of these guys had *anything* to do with Mac's murder. They're just mad.

I'm just mad. Mad and sad and left behind. How could someone hate my best friend so much that they'd stab him like fourteen times or however many times the doctors said it was? It's insane.

Still, I just beat Bernie up pretty good. What would I have done if I'd had a knife? Wouldn't it have felt great to plunge it in him over and over again? Am I the same as any other killer?

The cop starts the car and we drive away. I can't believe I'm on my way to jail. My parents will bail me out, I know that, and get the best lawyers, and the punishment won't be huge.

But I still have to live with this—that I'm alive and Mac's not.

God, please, take it away. Make me numb. No, don't make me numb, God. Just help me to deal with this better tomorrow, okay? I haven't been handling my shit too good lately. Help me to deal with it better tomorrow.

Dan

I walk home, real slow. My dick hurts and blood is dripping off my eye. Thank God Ma's not around. She'd legitimately freak. *Danny, you're hanging out with all the wrong kids. It starts off with a black eye but it doesn't stop there. There'll be all sorts of beatings and finally, they'll find some guy with HIV to rape you and you'll get infected and you'll die a horrible death. Before you know it, you'll be dead like that poor Malone guy. The last thing I want is to go to your funeral. You can't die before I do. You hear me?*

I can't take her right now. I just have to clean up and somehow figure out where to find Josh. Once I know what's up with Josh, I'll deal with Ma. And everybody else.

I look at my cell phone. He hasn't even called back and I've called him like ten times. I try again. His voice mail. I say, "Josh, man, I have to talk to you. Please call me back. Please." God, I sound like I'm going to cry. God, I sound like such a fag, I can't even stand myself. "Please," I beg one more time, and then I hang up.

See, this is why I kept it a secret. A guilty, shameful, sucky secret. I mean, I know all the bullshit about a true friend will be a true friend no matter what, but it's bullshit, right? A lot of guys will stick with you no matter what until they find *that* out. Then you're automatically an enemy. Then they think you've got the hots for them, even if you've never done anything that could remotely be considered a come-on.

All of a sudden, I lean over the curb and gag until drops of puke drizzle out onto the street.

Wiping my mouth, I look around. Did anybody see?

I've gotta protect my own ass. Everybody's my enemy.

Isaiah Contreras
The Jesuit Riot

Dad comes home at about the same time I turn on the 5 o'clock news. He steps inside the kitchen, says hello to Mom, and the next thing I hear is him cussing in Spanish and she starts in with the pleading. It's always the same old same old—he don't like how she never wants to go out, she don't like how he spends money, neither one of them is happy.

I've seen this replayed too many times, her waving a spoon at him, him sitting at the kitchen table, chair pushed back, staring at her like she's a crazy woman. He don't listen so he never understands why she's upset. She can never get him to understand.

If one of them don't stop, it always escalates. That's the worst. I can't sit there and do nothing if my dad hits my mom.

The phone rings and I grab it.

It's Chris. "Turn on Channel 9," he says. "Then call me back."

I leave the kitchen and the fight and turn on the TV in the living room. There's the front steps of the cathedral, with what looks like a hundred Jesuit students pushing and shoving. There's a big ol' cop leading some kid off the steps with a broken nose and a big black eye. Dirty Bernie! *Third time in a week, Bernie. What'd you say this time?*

The reporter, this young, pretty woman, is speaking in the typical "something important is going on" voice that reporters have. She's standing in front of the cathedral. In the background, I see a couple of cops milling around and that big yellow crime-scene tape across the front doors of the church.

I turn the volume up.

"This riot occurred on the steps of the cathedral minutes after a special Mass was held for MacKenzie Malone, the Jesuit student murdered on Friday night in Kern Place," she says. "Malone was stabbed fourteen times outside his house on Friday night and was discovered by Jesuit student Alexander Gold shortly after he was stabbed. Gold was reported missing this morning. So far, police aren't disclosing any suspects. At this time, it is unclear how the riot is related to the two incidents, but there appears to be a racial element involved. If you listen carefully to the tape, you can hear some students shouting racial slurs."

The TV cuts back to the scene of the riot for a second so we can all hear the clearly shouted chant. The camera pans in, and I can see Gregory González kicking some kid on the ground, all the while chanting something the news station bleeps out. *Shit.*

The TV cuts back to the reporter. "Some people are concerned there will be another riot tomorrow at Malone's funeral, which is scheduled to be held on Cinco de Mayo. Cinco de Mayo, a traditional holiday celebrating Mexico's independence from France, is also the day when a year ago a Mexican national suicide-bombed the Santa Fe Street Bridge here in El Paso."

The report cuts to footage of the international bridge after the bombing, the jagged cracks in the car lanes, the shell that was left of the inspection station. Then the screen goes back to the reporter. "Police say they will vigorously enforce security at Malone's funeral."

I call Chris back. "Jesus."

"I know," he says. "I guess the Cafeteria Incident was just a precursor."

Precursor? No wonder he did so well on his SATs.

"What happened to Greg?" I ask. "Did you see him?"

Just as I ask that question, the camera angle narrows in on the riot again. A cop sprints toward Greg and grabs his arms from behind. Greg tries to keep kicking the kid on the ground. The kid turns his face. It's Bernie! Again! Shoulda known.

As the cop twists Greg's arm, his face is screwed up in pain but he keeps straining and kicking until the cop pulls him back far enough so Bernie gets up and runs away. Looks like he was in automatic mode.

"Guess Mac's death hit him pretty hard," Chris said.

"No shit," I say. "Look at that." I see Omar, too, and Ricardo, and a bunch of other guys we know on the television screen.

Chris stays silent as we keep watching. Sometimes I wonder how he gets his anger and frustration out without swearing.

"Don't you ever get mad?" I ask.

"What?"

"Don't you ever get pissed off?"

"My mom says that if you get mad and act on it, you could do something you'll regret, something you can't ever fix. She says you're letting someone else turn you into a person you don't want to be, allowing someone else to control your behavior. So I don't let anything bother me too much."

I think about that and decide it's sort of stupid. If you had a mom as nice as mine and a dad who beat her up all the time . . . Sometimes getting mad is completely normal, you know? But there has to be a better way of dealing with anger than what I've seen at home.

"Think we'll have school tomorrow?"

"There's no way," Chris says. "School's canceled for sure."

"I wonder who'll get expelled," I say.

"They can't expel the whole school," Chris points out.

Leti and my other little sister, Angie, plop down on the sofa beside me. I change the channel to some cartoons. "Hey, lemme call you back later," I say.

"Later, bro." *Click.*

My parents have their own riot still raging in the kitchen. Angie's sucking her thumb. She does that when they fight. Sometimes I'll take her thumb and stick it in her mouth for her so she won't start crying. That just makes Dad even madder.

"Hey, Mom, Dad," I yell from the living room. "Turn on the news. Channel 9. There's something about Jesuit."

Silence from the kitchen. Then I hear the TV blaring and my mother's *"¡Dios mío!"*

"How's that for parochial school *discipline,* Dad?" I yell. I know I'm being a ass. He don't say nothing in response anyway.

I go into the kitchen. Mom's standing with her back to the sink, her hand over her mouth. Dad's still at the kitchen table, watching. I can't tell what he's thinking.

"Pues, Isaiah, *¿qué está pasando?"* he asks me, without looking up.

"Don't know," I reply in English, like usual—that always annoys him.

"*¿Conoces los vatos?*" Dad says.

I know one of them's Greg, but I look closely at the TV like I'm trying to figure out whether I know him or not. I also see Rafa, holding an ice pack to his eye. Omar's standing over by a reporter, and he's answering some questions. Wait, there's Bernie. He's shaking a fist at the camera. Dumbass Dirty Bernie.

"Nah," I say. "*No los conozco.* They must be in a different grade. I'm not even sure if they all go to Jesuit."

Mom knows most of these guys. She knows I'm lying.

"*Bueno,*" Dad says, with finality. "You don't need no *vatos* like that for friends. You study hard, go to JUTEP like Gabriel."

Gabriel's my older brother, and the thing is, he hates UTEP. He tells me to go anywhere but there, that if I do well at Jesuit, I could go someplace like Yale or Harvard. Get out of this shitty town. But ever since Mac caught me cheating, my grades have dropped and I have no shot. Fuckin' Mac.

"You don't know nothing about this, eh?" Dad asks then.

"Nope," I lie.

Mom starts picking at her sweater. She says, "I'm gonna go to the grocery store. Isaiah, you help me. *Vámonos.*"

She's not asking. "Okay, Mom, lemme get my shoes on," I say.

Angie and Leti whine about coming: *oh please, oh please Mommy, can't they come, too?* I join in with, "It don't bother me if they come."

"No," she tells them. "Today *es* just me and Isaiah."

Angie starts pouting but soon it's just me and Mom, in the van, heading to Albertson's.

"What?" I ask as soon as I get in the car.

"You know all those boys," she says. "I saw Bernie and Greg."

"I know."

"*Dígame.* Tell me."

I don't have nothing to lose at this point, so I just dig in and tell her. "Mom, it's no big deal. It's just some kids think this is a Mexicans versus Whites thing, that Mac Malone died 'cuz he's American. We almost had a riot in the cafeteria this afternoon—that's why I got sent home. I was trying to stop it from getting like what we saw on TV and that's why I got in trouble."

"*Mijo,* why didn't you tell them?"

She means the principal.

"They didn't ask." Adults never understand these things. You can't rat out other guys, even if they rat you out. It's just not done.

"So, you just become in trouble for nothing?" she asks, and pokes at my chest. She manages to jab me right where it hurts. "*¿Por nada? ¿Por qué,* Isaiah?"

"Ow, Mom." I rub my chest and glare at her. "What was I supposed to do? They weren't gonna believe me or nothing anyway."

She starts yelling at me in Spanish. About how you have to stand up for yourself and shit like that. She yells until we get to the store and then we get out and walk toward the entrance and she's still yelling.

"Okay, Mom," I say. "I get the point, okay?"

"No, *es* not okay," she says. "*ES*—NOT—OKAY. You have to stand up for things."

"Look, I wasn't in no riot."

"*Yo sé,* Isaiah," she says, patting me on the cheek. *"Pero necesitas hacer algo, ¿sí? Para la paz."*

"Mom, I'm *always* the peacemaker. You should know this better than anyone." I'm always afraid Dad'll get out of control, like the last time, when he threw Mom against the wall and broke her arm. The doctor said she was lucky she didn't break her neck. That was just last year. Right before Christmas. *Feliz Navidad,* my ass.

She's quiet now. But you can never underestimate Mexican moms. When we get to the vegetables, she starts in again. Who am I choosing for my friends and am I hanging around with the wrong bunch of people and we didn't see Josh Alvarado in the riot, why don't I hang around Josh no more?

"Because Josh is a drug dealer," I blurt.

She gives me this hurt wide-eyed look. Reminds me of Leti.

"I'm kidding, I'm kidding," I say. "Of course he's not. Josh is a good guy. And Carbon Copy wasn't there," I say. "He's my buddy, too."

She searches my face, then nods slowly.

"What're we here for anyway?" I ask. Her basket is empty.

"Nada." She looks around at the fruits and vegetables. "*Pues, nada.* I just want to talk to you, my son. I can't talk to my son? Just don't forget, Isaiah. *Es* up to you. *Es your* job to be a good example *en* Jesuit. *¿Entiendes?"* Then she grabs my face and kisses both my cheeks and I laugh, a kind of nice mother-son way to end this.

It's like all my life of fixing fights between Mom and Dad has come down to this one moment. Now I have to decide, which way am I gonna go? Am I gonna help my buddies work through this? Or am I gonna let them set fire to themselves and watch them burn?

"Yo entiendo," I say. I understand. *"Claro."* It's clear. I know what I've got to do. Of course. There's really no other choice. For me.

"Vámonos," she says, and we head toward the exit.

Isaiah Contreras
The Savior of Jesuit High

I'm weirdly fired up from Mom's confidence.

The first person I visit is Dan, figuring he'll be easy. He's never been a fighter.

He opens his front door. Yeesh—his eye is purple and swollen and there's a big bloody slit across the eyelid. Yuck.

"What?" he asks.

I look at the ground, then at the painting in the hallway that's behind him. "I just came to see you."

"What, so you could gawk at the faggot?" He starts to slam the door.

"No, wait, Dan!" I manage to get my foot in the door. "What are you talking about?"

"Oh, you haven't heard?" he said. "Well, you might as well know, 'cuz it's all over school that I'm gay."

A pause.

"You are?"

Another.

"No!" he yells, and then: "So fine, I am, what's it to you?"

"Well," I say, "just that if everybody at school knows it, you probably shouldn't come back."

"No kidding," he says, and he points at his eye. "How do you think I got this?"

"Dude, I'm sorry."

"I just need to talk to Josh. I haven't talked to Josh yet." He looks suddenly panicked. "You think Josh will care?"

"I don't know," I say. "Have you called him?"

"Thousand times."

"Left a message?"

"Check."

"Gone by his house?"

"I don't have a car. Ma's out."

"Look, I have to talk to Josh, too," I say. "So why don't I give you a ride?"

"Let's go!"

We hop in my mom's Toyota Tercel. Dan keeps drumming his fingers on his jeans.

He directs me to all those new houses over by Franklin High. I can't *believe* Josh's house. "Ooh la la."

"I know."

We sit there staring at it.

"So, Josh doesn't deal for the money?" I say.

"Nope."

"You ready?" I ask. He doesn't move. "Why're you so nervous?" I ask. "He's your boy."

"Why the fuck you think I'm so nervous?" he asks.

"Jeez, man, you don't have to yell at me. I was just saying, that's all." Maybe gay guys are more sensitive than regular guys. Am I some kind of prick because I don't think he's a *regular* guy? But . . . you know . . . he's *not*. So what is he? *"Vámonos,"* I say.

I knock on the door and Mrs. Alvarado answers. She throws up her arms in a big hug and kisses Dan hello. "What happened to your eye, Daniel????"

Dan shrugs. "Had a little accident, no big deal."

"What's with Jesuit boys lately?" she says to me. "Another Jesuit student came here yesterday, bleeding all over the place. Said he fell off his skateboard."

Yesterday. *Before* the riot.

"Who was that?" Dan asks.

"Just some friend of Josh's. There's something going on, but Josh won't talk to me about it." She leans toward Dan. "What's going on, Daniel?"

"Uh, I don't know. Can we just go speak with Josh, Mrs. Alvarado?" he asks.

She closes her eyes and nods. "Maybe you can get Josh to leave his room," she says.

Dan leads the way as we head up the stairs. When I look back, Mrs. Alvarado is still watching us.

Dan don't knock, he just goes in. For a split second, I wonder—is Josh gay? Are they lovers? Am I about to get myself into the middle of something? Ah, fuck, what does it really matter? As long as neither of them hits on me.

Josh looks pissed at the two of us for bursting in on him. "Welcome to hell," he says. "Can I take your order?"

"Hey, I've been calling you!" Dan says, like he's about to cry.

Josh looks at Dan and Dan looks at Josh and you can tell they both know what they're not talking about—but neither one of them wants to be the first to ask the Big Question.

"I left you like a thousand messages," Dan says. No actual tears, but his eyes are kind of pink and wet and glassy. "Why haven't you called me?"

"I'm not your boyfriend," Josh says. "I don't owe you anything."

"Dude, that's cold," I say.

"But are you still my best friend?" Dan busts out. *Holy shit, he is such a girl!* How come I never noticed before?

Josh takes that in. Even I have butterflies in my stomach.

"Yeah," he says at last. "I guess so. But how come you never told me?"

Dan looks like he's going to really cry. As in, sob. God. *Please don't cry, Dan.*

"I was freaked out," he says simply.

"Well, hey, don't be." Josh reaches out and punches him on the shoulder. "We're still good. You stupid bitch." He clears his throat and they both laugh. They both sound so relieved when they laugh.

True *compadres,* you know? Must be nice.

"Awww," I say. "I'm so happy to be a part of this feel-good moment."

"Why *are* you here?" Josh asks.

"There was a riot at school today," I say. "Americans punching out Mexicans, Mexicans punching out Americans. Mac's funeral is tomorrow. So I'm going around to see a bunch of the guys, make sure nobody does nothing stupid."

"No worries," Josh says. "I'm not interested in beating on any Mexicans. I know they didn't do it."

"They might have," Dan says. "You never know. They were pretty pissed at Mac."

"No," Josh says firmly, "I *know* they didn't do it. 'Cuz I know who did."

Holy crap.

"It's not you, is it?" Dan asks. He's back on the verge of tears.

"Nuh-uh, it's definitely not me."

My mouth is hanging open. I've got to get ahold of myself. "*Órale,* man, you gotta go to the cops," I tell him.

"If I go to the police," he says, and he looks miserable, like his life is about to be over, "I have to turn myself in. You know. For selling. I'll go to jail. And I'm seventeen. That means no juvie hall for me. Real jail."

No one knows what to say to that. We're all quiet for a few seconds. Then Dan speaks up.

"Quit being a pussy, Josh," he says. "I don't want you to go to jail, but you're talking about murder here. And that other kid, what's-his-face, is missing, too—he might be dead for all you know."

"He's not dead," Josh says.

"How do you know?"

He points to the corner of his room. "Gentlemen, meet Alexander Gold."

My God. There's some white kid sitting there.

"Dan, Ish," he says, nodding in greeting. He knows us? I've never seen him before in my life, I'm positive. "Don't waste your breath. I've been trying to get him to go to the cops since yesterday evening."

"You look like something the cat puked up," Dan tells him.

"Yeah, well, you wouldn't win any beauty prizes yourself."

Dan turns away from him. "Enough. *Who did it?*" he asks Josh.

Josh squirms a little and then it comes out. "Jim Hill," he says. "I *think.*"

"Come on," Alex says. "Quit trying to protect your twisted buddy."

"I think Jim did the killing part," he says. "But the thing is, Rafa was there, too."

I'm surprised that I'm not really surprised. There was always something off with Jim, ever since we were little kids. But Rafa? He's kind of a *cholo* wannabe, or at least he hangs out with them. But him being . . . a, how you call it, accessory to murder?

"But how do you know they were even there?" Dan asks.

"Because I was hanging out at Jim's house. Rafa was gonna drop some X off for us. He's got his buddy José with him, you know, Vero's dude, right? Anyway, so they come by and they say, 'We're gonna go fuck Mac up.' Rafa said something about how Mac beat up a member of La Raza and now he was gonna get his. José, I think he just felt like he needed to avenge his girl or something—you know how Mac's always talking shit about Vero. I don't know why Jim decided to go, but he said he was going along with them, he'd be back in a few."

"Where were you?" Dan asks.

Josh looks down at his own feet. Then he says, "I was fooling around with Jim's sister."

"Josh!" Dan says, all parenty. "She's a little kid."

"She's fourteen!" Josh says. "In my book, fourteen is fair game."

There's still something not quite right about all of this. "But how do you know what they did?"

Josh explains: "When I came out of Stacy's room, Jim was changing his T-shirt. I think he probably had blood on it. By the time I left his place about fifteen minutes later, the cops were already on their way up Baltimore. Also, Alex here says he saw Rafa and two dudes tearing their way out of Kern Place. A coupla minutes later, he found Mac."

"But why?" I ask. "Why would Jim do this?" Something in me doesn't *understand* the whole violence thing. This *and* the bigger stuff—this war we're in, or suicide bombers, or someone I know killing someone else I know. I just don't get it. Is the whole world crazy? "So why'd they do it?"

"Maybe Rafa was still mad about that whole flag incident, you know?" Josh offers. "Remember when he climbed up the flagpole on the Fourth of July and took down the U.S. flag? And Mac got all righteous and tore up a Mexican flag, just to make a point? Maybe that's why Rafa was mad enough to do something, to even the score. Or maybe Jim finally just went extra psycho. Or maybe José got sick and tired of Mac talking shit about his girl all the time."

"Josh," Dan interrupts, "none of those reasons justify *any* of this. And you *are* going to the cops. You have to. And I'm going with you."

"I can't," Josh pleads.

"Now," Dan says. "I'm gonna call my dad's lawyer. He's a bit slimy but he'll know what to do. It's your first offense. You may not even go to jail. If you have a lawyer, you can negotiate a deal. Ish, you're going to go see Rafa, right?"

I hadn't thought that far ahead, but it's a relief to see Dan take charge of this situation. "Right."

"I'll come with you guys to the station," Alex says. "I have to make a statement myself." He slaps Dan on the back. "You're all right," he says, like he's surprised a homo could be all right. But maybe that's not what he means? I could be wrong. I've been wrong before.

"Ish, see if you can't get Rafa to come down to the station," Dan says. "It'll be better for him to turn himself in. It's gonna happen anyway."

"His ass is going to jail for sure," I say. "Even if he didn't do it, he still withheld information about a murder."

Everybody looks sorry for a second. Rafa's not a bad guy, for all he pretends to be a hood. He's mostly a good guy who hung out with one wrong dude. Like all of us.

What *was* Jim's motive? Did he even have one? Or was it just the same Jim I remember when I was a kid, the one who'd burn ants alive just to see them pop?

Isaiah Contreras
Git On wit' Yo' Badass Self

Should I be scared to go see Rafa? Rafa was there, after all. He saw a real live murder.

I've never been to Rafa's house in Segundo Barrio but I know the neighborhood pretty good. We lived there with my crazy aunt when I was a little kid. She moved back to Juárez a few years ago so I don't hang out there no more, but even last year, we'd go swimming in the Armijo Center once in a while.

Talk about profiling. It's like a war zone down here. Border Patrol everywhere. I get stopped. Twice. All they want is to see my driver's license. After that, they let me go. Guess I'm American enough for them.

Rafa lives in a little brick house, low to the ground. It's old, been here a hundred years, I bet. There are yellow rosebushes in the front yard and one of those statues of *La Virgen de Guadalupe* set inside a little altar and surrounded by faded pink and yellow plastic flowers. I've heard that Rafa even has a tattoo of *La Virgen* on his back.

A ginormous Rottweiler guards the house, the roses, and *La Virgen.* He's sitting patiently in the front yard, ready to rip into me if I dare put one foot inside. They don't have no doorbell on the gate or nothing, so I yell, *"¡Hola! ¡Hola! ¿Está Rafa? ¡Buenos diiiiiiias! ¡Hola!"* and start rattling the gate. The Rottweiler barks, and finally this little Mexican lady comes out.

"Hola, Señora, busco a Rafa," I tell her.

"Un momentito," she says, going back inside.

A second later, Rafa tumbles out of the house. He thrusts his head up and chin out—it's the Raza way of greeting each other in El Paso. I greet him back the same way.

"Ish, what up?" he asks. *"¿Qué pasa?"*

I'm checking him out to make sure I'm not gonna die if he goes off, but I don't see no knives hidden inside his wife-beater or scroungy jeans.

We sit down on the curb next to my car. It turns out that big ol' Rottweiler is a puppy, and a cuddly one at that. Rafa lets her out and she snuggles right up to him, happy as all get-out to have her ears scratched.

"Órale, Rafa, you know what's going down?" I ask.

"Órale, Isaiah, do *you* know what's going down?"

Typical. I give him a look. "Yeah, Raf, I do know. *You're* going down. That's why I'm here."

"Entonces, cut the bullshit. *Dígame."*

So I just burst out with it. "Josh Alvarado's on his way to the cops with that kid, Alex Gold, the one who was missing. Josh is gonna tell the cops that you and Jim Hill and that guy that was with you, José, said you were going to beat Mac up and when he left Jim's house half an hour later, the cops were already at Mac's. Alex is gonna tell the cops that he saw you leaving the area just before he found Mac. So bottom line, Raf, the cops are probably gonna come arrest you."

"*¡Chingao!*" Rafa swears. "*¿Quién es,* Alex Gold? *¿Quién es? ¿Ey? ¿Lo conoces?* Do you know who he is?"

"Look, man, that's not the point," I begin to say, but he cuts me off.

"*¡Cállate!* Lemme think a minute."

We sit there in silence for a few minutes. Then he says, "Lemme explain. Lemme tell you how it happened."

"I'll hear you out," I tell him, "but I'm not the one you need to tell. You're gonna have to go to the cops."

"Fuck that!" he says in a voice loud enough that I'm pretty sure his mother could hear him inside the house. "How can they rat out a friend that way? Huh?"

"Hey, keep it down." I wonder if his mother heard?

"*Mami,* she don't know English," he says. "*No te preocupes. Ella no entiende nada.*"

"So tell me what happened already," I say.

"It was like this," he says. "I didn't know we were going there to kill him. You hear me? I swear on *La Virgen* that I didn't know. *No sé nada.*"

"Okay. *¿Pues . . . ?*"

"We were just going to fuck him up, teach him a lesson, teach him not to mess with La Raza. That's what me and José wanted to do. Plus, José's girl, Vero, had a thing for Mac, you know? She told José that one time Mac showed her his dick and it was all hard 'cuz Mac wanted to do her. José got flaming mad about it, wanted Mac to know he needed to leave his woman alone. I was just mad about Bernie. So we go, right? But we have to stop off with a delivery for Josh." He stops.

"I know about the delivery, Raf," I say, so he can proceed.

"José and me, we tell Josh and Jim what's up, what we're

going to do, and Jim decides he's gonna join us. The mother-fucker. The motherfucker."

I want Jim Hill to be guilty just like everybody else, but is he too convenient a scapegoat? All of a sudden, I know what's coming.

"We pull up and the house is dark. We're thinking should we look around, see if we can figure out which window is for Mac's room. We can't ring the doorbell, you know? 'Cuz then after we beat him up, his mom will know it was us. And I can't have no police nosing around my family. That's what *I'm* think-ing. I don't know what Jim is thinking 'cuz I'm not psychic. Not psycho or psychic. Get it? Ha-ha."

"Not the time, Rafa," I say, trying to be helpful. "You'll make it worse for yourself if you make those jokes in front of the cops."

"Hey," he says. "This is *my* story. Let me tell it *my* way." He pauses, then continues. "So we're waiting there, wondering what to do, when this car pulls up to the curb. And whoever's in this car just dumps Mac out and goes screeching off, right? So there's Mac, looking kind of, I don't know, maybe drunk, right? So it's the perfect moment. *'Vámonos,'* I say, and the three of us get out and walk up to Mac."

Rafa stops but I roll my hand at him. "Keep it coming, Raf, keep it coming. *Ándale.*"

"Then . . . then . . . then everything got fucked up," he con-tinues. "I threw a punch, and the next thing I know, Mac's gasp-ing and blood is bubbling up out of his mouth. That's when I see, Jim's in back, *stabbing* him. *In the back. El cabrón* is stabbing him *in the back.* I'm realizing Mac's gonna die while I'm in the middle of beating him up. So I decide just to get the fuck outta there. I run to my car and José runs, too, and I'm thinking I can get outta there before Jim catches up to us but the guy has survival skills. He must be friends with the devil, *¿comprendes?* 'Cuz when I get to the car, he's already in it! I look back and Mac's on the ground, jumping around like he's getting electrified. Or is it 'electrocuted'? What the fuck do I know? I look back and Mac's blood is gushing and the dude who killed him is *in my car.* So, like, I leave, but I'm scared 'cuz José is yelling at Jim and Jim takes out his knife and says, 'If you don't shut up, I'm gonna wipe Mac's blood all over your T-shirt, motherfucker, and then I'll tell the cops you did it.' So José shuts up. But I'm sure he was thinking what I was thinking. How do we get this sick bastard out the car? So I go straight to Jim's apartment and I yell, 'Get out, get out, *vámonos,'* and he just turns around, like nothing, like nothing—*¿sabes? Como todo es un chiste grande.* And he says, 'See ya Monday, Rafa,' and to José, he was like, 'Nice to meet ya, bro!' The dude is crazy, I tell you. Jim Hill *está loco en la cabeza.* I mean, he *needs* to be locked up. *¿Sabes?"*

We're sitting there on the curb and the dog is thumping his tail on the ground and there's a enormous almost-full moon shining down on us, but nothing feels real. I mean, how can this be real?

"So have you talked to Jim since then?"

"No, man. He came by yesterday with Josh. They was gonna get that Alex guy, beat him up, find out what he knew."

"What did you do?"

Rafa sticks his chin out so far, it looks like it hurts his neck. "I went to my *tío.* I had him clean out the interior of my car, just in case Jim got blood in it."

"But you didn't kill him."

"I was an accessory, you know? You know what that is, Isaiah?"

"I've watched enough cop shows, okay?" I sigh.

"If I turn myself in, what happens to my family? They'll look into us, you know?"

Suddenly I do know what he means. The family business. Drugs. He can't have the spotlight shine on his life. But it's way too late for that.

"Josh and Alex are probably already at the station," I say. "You'll be better off if you go to the cops now. They'll go easier on you if you confess."

"I gotta go call my *tío*," he says. "He'll know what to do. Maybe I'll go back to Mexico."

"You can't hide in Mexico forever," I say.

He slaps his hand on my back. "This is my problem, Ish. My problem."

"*Voy contigo.* I'll go with you," I say. "To the cops. *Si necesitas.* If you want me to."

He snorts. "Git on wit' yo' badass self," he says. "*Tú eres el vato,* Isaiah. A good guy. One of La Raza, you know? *Pero . . . voy a ir,* okay? I'll go, but I'll go with my mom."

"Okay." I don't know what else to say. "Take a lawyer with you."

He nods. *"Claro."*

Rafa's already rushing inside when I leave, yelling, *"Mami? Mami?"* I guess he's gonna tell her before he loses his nerve.

The front door slams behind him. I can already see him in prison, locked up. I've never known nobody who went to prison before and now I know at least two. Maybe three, if Josh goes. Too bizarre.

I get in the car. I'm gonna go home and give my mom a hug. Not that that can fix this. But fuck it—I want a hug from my mom anyway, 'cuz even if it don't fix nothing, I need to know she loves me.

Daniel Tucker

The Confessional

"Reeking of marijuana is probably not in your best interests," I tell Josh after Alex leaves. "Better take a shower." Other than his quick trip to school, I guess he and Alex have just been sitting here for the last two days. Gross.

I shower, too. There are numerous confessions ahead of us today, and at least one of them will be mine. I want to feel clean when I do it.

"Will you tell my parents?" Josh asks as he heads into the shower.

"No way, bro. That's your job," I say.

After we've both showered, we head downstairs. I'm hoping Josh's parents will be cool, since they have experience with this kind of shit. His older brother was arrested for possession twice. His sister got pregnant last year. She's trying to juggle UTEP and a baby.

"I mean, how bad can this be in comparison?" Josh asks.

"Dealing's a whole other category," I say.

We gather Mr. and Mrs. Alvarado in their white living room. They're sitting on a gigantic white overstuffed sofa and we're standing in front of them. Two little schoolboys, confessing their sins.

"I'm going down to the police station," Josh says. "I have some information about Mac's murder and I guess I should tell them what I know."

Mr. Alvarado is leaning forward on the couch. His feet dangle off like he's a little kid. I never noticed how short he is.

"Why have you been sitting on this information all weekend?" he asks.

"Well, it might, uh, implicate me in certain activities," Josh says.

"Joshua, do you need a lawyer?" Mr. Alvarado stands up.

"What kind of activities?" Mrs. Alvarado asks. She stands up, too. I know the sinking feeling she must have. At least she's not freaking out like my ma would.

"I've called my dad's lawyer," I say. "He's meeting us at the police station."

"Joshua," Mr. Alvarado asks, "were you involved in this boy's death?"

"No!" he says.

"Oh, thank God." And Mrs. Alvarado sits down again.

Of course, they both drive us to the station. Mr. Alvarado calls one of his own lawyer buddies first. "He says he's already down at the station," he reports, hanging up. "That's puzzling."

"Not really," I say. "Did you watch the evening news? There's got to be a dozen Jesuit students being booked for that riot at school today."

"Riot?" Mrs. Alvarado is beginning to look freaked and frazzled. "Were you involved in a riot, Joshua?"

"Again, no," he says. "I didn't kill anybody and I didn't beat anybody up. But it's possible that in the course of the investigation, the police might find out that, ahem . . ." And then he says it: "I've been dealing drugs." He says it so soft and slow, trailing off, that his parents don't catch it.

"What?" Mr. Alvarado says. "You've been feeling rugs?"

"It sounded like he said he needs healing hugs," Mrs. Alvarado says.

I giggle. I can't help it.

"Um, no," Josh says. "I've been dealing drugs."

They both look stunned. There's a minute of silence. Then: "Since when?" Mr. Alvarado asks, while Mrs. Alvarado says, the color rising in her cheeks, "When we get home tonight, I'm going to slap your ass into next week."

"He might not be coming home with us, honey," Mr. Alvarado says, gently.

"Then I'm going to slap your ass at the station," she says, "right before they lock it up."

Jeez, tough mama.

Josh looks miserable. What will be worse, telling his parents or the police?

◆ ◆ ◆

It's like a Jesuit reunion down at the station. Omar's sitting in the hallway with his dad, who looks none too pleased to be there. Greg's up ahead with both of his parents. Scenes from the riot are playing on the station's TV. The scene now flashing is Greg stomping Bernie in the nuts. Mr. González is watching with his arm around Greg. He flinches, but at least he doesn't move his arm.

"What're you doing here, fag?" Omar whispers to me as I pass.

Josh swivels around and leans in close to Omar's face. "I'm warning you," he says, slow and even. "Leave. Dan. Alone. Or else."

"Dude." Omar scoots backward in his seat to get away from Josh. "Did you hear that, Dad? He was threatening me."

"You're going to receive more than threats today, young man," Mr. Chavarria says.

Alex is up at the front desk with a woman who must be his mom. He nods at us as they lead him away into a back room.

The cop sitting at the front desk looks a bit like the one I was fantasizing about earlier today. "And what can I do for you folks?" he says, looking cheerful.

"My son has some information about MacKenzie Malone's murderer," Mr. Alvarado says. "We'd like to speak with some officers."

"You'll have to wait your turn," he says. "There are at least ten Jesuit boys here, all claiming to have some information."

As we head out toward the dim hallway to wait, my dad's smarmy lawyer arrives. I introduce him to the Alvarados. He suggests he speak with Josh alone and the two of them head off down the hallway together, Josh trudging off with him like he's carrying something heavy and my dad's lawyer bouncing gleefully because it's just another day, another opportunity to work the system.

* * *

The next morning, I walk over to the cathedral and enter the side door where a secretary guards the main office. I don't really want to do this and I'm scared of what will happen, what the priest will say to me. But it can't be any harder than what Josh had to do.

Last night, we all crowded into a room with two detectives, who sat at a table, facing Josh. Josh's confession was way less private, with way less mercy. Plus, nobody was sworn to secrecy except Josh's lawyer. But when Josh started to speak, the detectives leapt to attention. They knew it—here was real information, stuff that corroborated what they'd already heard from Alex. If Ish was successful, they'd hear Rafa's side of the story, too.

Josh called me at around midnight. They had arrested Jim and he was being held at the downtown station. Although he hadn't spoken to Jim, he'd been required to identify him for the detectives through one of those one-way mirrors. He said Jim was alone in the room and that he kept whispering at the table in a voice too low for him to hear.

Will we ever learn the truth—whether it was Jim or Rafa, whether they acted alone or in cahoots?

I realize I've been standing in front of the secretary for several minutes without speaking. She smiles encouragingly at me, and when she finally notices that I am focused on her, she asks, "What can I do for you?" She's an older lady, with short gray hair, wearing a purple suit and a name tag that says "Jean."

"I was wondering if I could see one of the fathers, for confession."

"We don't normally have confession on Tuesday mornings," Jean says. "Can you come back on Wednesday between five p.m. and seven p.m.?"

"I'd rather not wait, if possible. Can you ask if someone's willing to see me? And can we use one of those booth thingies?"

She seems to register my bruised face, says, "One moment," and disappears through a door. After about a minute, she returns, followed by a young Hispanic man in his early thirties. He smiles at me, then disappears again through the door.

I *would* have to get the good-looking priest, wouldn't I? *God, please don't let me get a hard-on.*

"Father Manny will be pleased to see you," Jean says. "Please follow me. I'll show you the way."

She leads me down several hallways and through a chapel into the cathedral. She points to a confessional on the right-hand side. "I believe Father Manny said he'd be in that one," she says, and nods at me to go forward.

What am I doing here? Am I about to be told that the fires of hell will rain down upon me because I'm an abomination unto the Lord?

I seat myself on this dinky little stool behind a curtain and I peer through the little mesh screen that separates me from Father Manny. He smiles at me.

"I'm guessing you've never confessed before," he says.

"No," I admit. "I don't know the, uh, proper way to do it."

"That's okay. I'm not sure there *is* a proper way to confess."

Whoa. Should a priest say that? "So there's no set formula?"

"I think we can dispense with it for today. Tell me what's on your mind."

I just dig in. I don't know the man, I'll never know the man, and I need to get this off my chest. "First of all, you should know that I'm gay."

"All right. Is that what you're confessing?"

No recoiling in shame or horror. A good sign. "No, not really."

"You're not ashamed of being gay?"

"No. I like who I am."

"If only we could all say that," Father Manny says, "the world would be a better place. All right, young man, proceed."

"Well, you know that guy who got murdered on Friday night?"

"MacKenzie? Yes."

"Yeah. Well, we went out earlier that night, the night he died, and I, I, um . . . made a pass at him."

He whistled. "And you're feeling guilty about it?"

I don't answer that. "He didn't invite it or anything. And I didn't plan it. He was feeling bad about getting suspended and I was just comforting him and suddenly I—I went too far."

"Well, do you think that's the only thing bothering you? Or is there something else, too?"

"It's just that . . . Well, some of my friends just found out I'm gay. And I go to Jesuit."

"I see," he says.

"Yeah, well, some of the guys are going to be awful. I mean, they already beat me up. But my best friend, he was great about it. He told me that we're friends no matter what." I choke back the tears when I say this. I don't want Father Manny to know I'm on the verge of crying. I sneak a peek at him. All I can see is his profile.

"That must've been a relief," he says.

"Totally," I say. "I wish I had told him before this. We've been friends since second grade."

"That's a long time to keep a secret from a friend," he says.

"Yeah. I should have told him before. I should have trusted him."

"So . . . is that what you're really ashamed about? Why you've come here?"

I realize suddenly that *is* it. Why hadn't I let Josh see who I really was all these years? Why didn't I trust him like a friend is supposed to? This was something to feel guilty about, much more than coming on to Mac, which happens to people all the time—hitting on somebody who, it turns out, isn't interested in you.

"Yeah," I say. "I think that *is* what I feel bad about."

"Friends can be the most important people in our lives," he says. "They see us through the good, the bad, and the ugly. Have you apologized to your friend?"

"Not yet," I say. "But now I will."

Whatever I felt bad about before this talk—it's gone now. I wish I had come in here months ago. Years ago.

"I think that's about it," I say. "So maybe we could wrap this up?"

"Sure thing, kiddo," he says. Then he recites his little spiel about how my sins are forgiven and suggests that I go through the Stations of the Cross as penance.

I'm not sure what I'm supposed to do at each Station of the Cross. I never paid much attention during my catechism classes. But that's okay. I stand or sit or kneel beside each one and I say thank you to the great God of the universe out there, whoever he is, not only for giving me a great best friend but for making it so Father Manny didn't rip me a new one for being gay.

It takes me about an hour to go through each Station and think about things. When I emerge from the cathedral into the sunlight, I feel like I'm being born again—but not *that* kind of born again. Here are the steps where all the guys were fighting just yesterday. Here's the corner where I puked after they beat me up.

Things won't heal overnight. Most of those guys will hate me now. I wasn't wrong about that. But Josh will be cool. Maybe I'll even find the courage to tell Ma . . . ?

What *is* different is how I feel . . . more alive. Free. Like if they put me onstage right now, to sing to the Pope, the goddamn president of the United States, and Bono himself, I would rock their world. Yeah.

Isaiah Contreras
A Cinco de Mayo Funeral

Mom decided we wouldn't celebrate Cinco de Mayo this year, we'd just go to Mac's funeral. Her sisters in Juárez made a big fuss about that but she said, "I don't wanna hear another word about it. *Pueden celebrar sin nosotros.*"

They could celebrate without us, it's true, but they all told her it wouldn't be as much fun without me and my sisters. My aunts in Juárez all have kids. So I think they were just trying to make her feel guilty. My mom's good at that, too. Must be in the genes.

If you didn't know no better, you'd think the entire town was celebrating Mac's funeral. There's a wild Cinco de Mayo parade going on right in front of the funeral home. How would Mac feel about that? But, I mean, if death doesn't give you some kind of perspective on things like that, what will?

I walk into the funeral home and hear some sad-ass organ music. The funeral director is this old guy with greased-back hair and an old-school navy blue suit. "This way, please," he says as he ushers us toward a large room at the front of the building.

It's packed. Which is good. I wonder if Mac is glad, too.

I scan the room. Jim's missing. Rafa's missing. *Thank God.*

Josh is here, though—*interesting*. He's sitting next to Dan. Greg's here, of course, along with Omar and Chris and a lot of other guys from school.

Last night, I called almost every Jesuit guy in this room. I told them everything I knew and asked them to be cool at the funeral. A lot of them had spent the afternoon at the police station. That mostly calmed them down so I probably didn't make no difference. They all look subdued, anyway, in their suits, with their moms and dads. I've never seen Jesuit guys acting so polite.

Several of them told me they'd been booked and let go, that if the school presses charges, there might be a trial, but otherwise the cops would pretty much let it slide. Jesuit probably won't press charges 'cuz they'd lose too many students if they did. Some parents are already yanking their kids out of Jesuit, sending them to Radford or public school. I heard one kid's getting homeschooled because of this.

Omar said he saw Alex come into the station and pretty soon after that, Alex's mom came in. She was weeping. He said he went over and apologized to her and she just looked at him like he wasn't even there, just kept crying, which made him feel even worse. His dad was pissed and told him he'd shamed the family.

Brother Rodarte's here, and that priest from St. Frances Jerome, Father What's-His-Name. I can never remember.

There's that girl Mac liked. José's girlfriend. Vanessa or Veronica or something like that. She's pretty, but I wouldn't say she's *that* hot. I know she's not to blame or nothing but I can't help but wonder if we'd even be here if she had never been born. Girls, man.

Okay, I gotta stop thinking about it. It's not my problem

anymore. The cops will do their job and I can just go on with my life. Right?

The casket is up front. Mac's in there and I think, *I'm not going up there, no way.* My dad makes a motion for us to head up the aisle and pay our respects. He reaches around behind me and pushes me forward with a hand on my back. So I'm marching up the aisle. Fuckin' A. Mac's all white and shit. He's got makeup on to make him look more natural, I guess, but it makes him look weird. Nice suit, though. He was one tall dude. Funny, I never noticed how good-looking he was.

I just—I just can't believe this. He's in this casket and this casket is going to be lowered into the ground and dirt's gonna cover it.

We sit down wherever we can find seats. My dad stays near me, his hand on my back, a constant pressure that says, *Remember where you are,* mijo. *Keep it together.* The only other funeral I went to was my grandfather's, in Juárez, and that was your traditional long-ass Catholic funeral.

Within minutes, the service begins.

The funeral director gives some "all religions welcome" kind of greeting, commenting how, in death, we can find the peace that may have eluded us on this hard earth.

My head jerks up when he says that. I guess I'd never thought about Mac struggling through life, looking for peace. Well. I mean, I hope he has that now. Some peace.

They ask for guys to come up and say something about Mac. Everybody's looking around, quietly panicked. Greg'll never do it, even though he should, as Mac's best friend.

Now I feel my mom's hand pressing hard into my back and my dad nudging me on the side.

So I stand up and I go forward and I look out at this crowd of strangers and this is what I say:

"I grew up with MacKenzie. We played soccer together and went to school together all the way from kindergarten until he died last Friday."

I take a deep breath and look over the crowd. I think they're listening. So I keep going.

"I wish I could say I knew everything there was to know about Mac and it was all great, all good. Well, I can't say that. I realize I didn't know him as well as I thought. And now it's too late. If I could, I'd like to become friends with Mac again. I'd like to hear what he's thinking, what he thinks is funny, what makes his brain start to go off the way it did. I can't do that. None of us can. But I like what the man here said." I look around and point at the funeral director. "The last few days, lots of us, we got pissed—uh, I mean, angry—and we wanted to do something about Mac being dead. I can understand that. But I don't think Mac would've wanted us to do what we did, no matter what happened last Friday. Mac thought about a lot of stuff. Like God. And heaven and hell. And I think he'd want this place to be more like heaven than hell. So that's what I'm gonna do—I'm gonna start working to make this a better place. It'll never be heaven, exactly, but we can do better. Thanks, Mac. Peace, man."

They start clapping—I mean, clapping at a funeral? Is that okay? It's not like anything I said was so profound.

But I see some Jesuit guys clapping and that gives me a tiny bit of hope. That things could change a little. Fuck. That's all we can ask for, I guess.

What is hope like for Jim, lying or sitting or whatever the

fuck he's doing in his jail cell? I still think of him as a friend, somehow, even though he's always scared me. Weird.

Rafa must be in some jail cell, too. The thought of him locked up makes me feel sick to my stomach.

If they let us visit them in prison, I'll visit Rafa for sure. Not Jim. But . . . maybe Jim. Yeah, maybe.

Yeah, Jim, it's Ish here. Peace to you. Peace to you, wherever you are. Amen.

Coda

Jim Hill
Waiting

I've been handcuffed to this table for hours. When I asked for a lawyer, they laughed, said, "It'll be a while, but sure thing, kid." That was forever ago and I've just been sitting here ever since, thinking.

Mom's sure gonna be pissed.

Worse, she's gonna cry.

The first time I was arrested, I was eleven. They caught me spray-painting the side of Old Lady López's garage. She was too old to go outside. She'd sit in her wheelchair at her living room window, yelling at us kids when we walked past. We weren't doing any harm, just throwing stones and shit. Why'd she have to yell at us all the time?

I never understood the big deal they made—it's not like people haven't heard the word "cunt" before. They whitewashed it and her garage looked even better than it had before. If you think about it, I did her a favor.

I still think it wasn't a big deal. She couldn't even go outside, so she never would have seen it if the authorities hadn't decided to get involved. The fucktards compelled Old Mrs. López's children to prosecute. No big deal, just a fine, which my mother paid. Not without complaint, mind you, but she paid.

As we left the courthouse, she asked me, "Where did you *learn* that word, Jimmy?"

Told her I heard one of her boyfriends call her that.

The second arrest—I was twelve. Six months after my mom paid the fine, López's garage burned down. They suspected arson and me. Not a shred of evidence. It didn't matter, her kids were going ballistic, thinking their mom was in mortal danger. They were even going to sell the house, move their crazy old mom somewhere else. They were *that* scared of me. *Good.*

But the fire trucks arrived in plenty of time to evacuate Loca López from her house and put out the fire. I saw the whole thing.

And the insurance companies kicked in and built her a new garage, which was even better than the original. Not only that, they replaced her porch so she had some fancy equipment that allowed her to wheel right through the front door and out of the house. And her kids pitched in and got her floodlights and alarms and an emergency police responder button on her wheelchair that she could push at a moment's notice.

Again, another favor, courtesy of me. Look at the crapload of technological improvements I brought to the withered old bitch's life.

That time, I went to juvie. Jail sentence of two years, which was reduced to nine months for good behavior.

I don't remember much about that. What I do remember is not worth relating. I did my time and was glad to get back home.

✦ ✦ ✦

When the cops came for me this time, I was sitting on the couch with my sister and mother watching *The Simpsons*. A cozy family moment. Decent human beings would be loath to break it up, but not the El Paso Police. Oh, no.

They knocked once and didn't even wait for a reply before busting down our door, fourteen of them running in and shoving me against the wall before I could even say "motherfucker." In a few seconds, I went from watching Homer Simpson trying to strangle Bart to being slammed against a wall with a picture of me, my mom, and my sister back when I was just a little kid.

"James Wyman Hill?" this Mexican cop asks my back.

"Yo," I replied. I had one hand free, one hand pinned behind my back, so I held up two fingers in the air, my nose shoved against the wall. "Peace, man! *¡La paz, hombre!*"

He grabbed my fingers, bending my free arm back around, and handcuffed me. "James Wyman Hill, you are under arrest for the murder of MacKenzie Meredith Malone. You have the right to remain silent. Anything you say can and will be used against you in a court of law. You have the right to an attorney. . . ."

All the while, this detective is searching me like he's looking for weapons of mass destruction. *Wait. Meredith? Mac's middle name was Meredith? Ha!*

"Guess they think I'm an Al-Qaeda operative," I told Mom as the cop posse surrounded me, crowding into our dinky living room and spilling out into the courtyard. Fourteen cops. Just to handcuff a skinny-ass punk like me?

Then Mom started wailing. "What did you do, Jimmy? What did you do? Jimmy? Jimmy!" She had a cigarette in her mouth and it fell out onto the carpet and started smoldering.

That's the last thing I saw before they shoved me in their little pigmobile. Motherfuckers bumped my head on the car door, didn't even say sorry. "Fuck you, too," I said.

No reply.

I pondered the arrangement while we drove. Two cops sat in the front and two sat in the back with me. What'd they think I was gonna do all handcuffed in the back of a cop car?

The cops in the front turned on the music just loud enough to drown out their voices. Then they started to talk in low tones.

Drove me nuts. What were they saying?

Two cop cars led, two followed. We were a procession, five cars long, all the way downtown. Four miles. I figured juvie hall, but, no, it was the county jail this time.

Bummer that I turned seventeen last month. Still, maybe I can work my age to my advantage. We'll see.

County houses most of the hard-core, maximum-security prison population for El Paso. Located in a tall, gray, hulking beast of a building right next to the County Courthouse. The prison looks like it has no real windows, just these little slits running up and down the sides, like angry eyes squinting at downtown El Paso. I've heard rumors that, a long time ago, mothers would bring their children to the streets below and have them wave up at their fathers, guys who were locked away. But from the street, looking up, I couldn't see inside at all. Maybe they changed the façade so people couldn't do that anymore.

If I knew what was coming, I could prepare, could figure out some way of working the system. But I don't know what they know and they're not telling me.

Haven't seen population yet—all the dudes I'll be hanging

out with until the trial. They haven't gotten to that part of the game yet. I hope I get to see my lawyer before they book me and send me in.

Maybe they're watching me behind these mirrored windows, the kind they have in interrogation rooms.

I am resolved. I will not say a word. Not one fucking word. Okay. Maybe one.

"Lawyer!" I scream, pounding on the table. "Lawyer! Lawyer! Lawyer! Lawyer! Lawyer! Lawyer!!!!!!!!!!!!!!!!!!!"

The glass is impassive. Bounces back my decibels.

They've left me in here to rot.

Maybe they've got Josh in another room, or Alex—Greg? Those pussies would definitely talk, except they don't know anything.

But I am in trouble if they have Rafa.

They must have Rafa. That's why they're not in here busting my balls. They don't need to. They already have everything they need.

It hits me: I am so fucked.

I know what I've done and I know what I'd do again if I had a chance. I know who I am and how the system works. I'll get a lawyer. He'll come bustling in, with papers and briefcase and cell phone, and he'll tell me not to talk, not to say a word, and he'll ask for the details of the case, and I'll be processed.

Maybe they're hoping I'll cave before my lawyer arrives.

See, I also know what I will and won't do to get out of here. Yeah, I'll talk, if my cooperation buys me a shaved sentence. Or I'll say nothing. I won't give them anybody related to the case, because that is *not who I am*. But I can make stuff up, if I need to. I just have to plan ahead, create a believable enough lie about somebody where I know there's enough evidence to indict them. Rafa, for sure. I can make stuff up about him. Whatever I say might even turn out to be true. And I can give them Josh. Josh, the big drug dealer.

The first thing I'm going to tell my lawyer when he gets here is that I don't want to see her, not at all, not even at the trial— she can't come. Because if I see her, I will lose it.

I know how this works and I am *not* going to cry. I'm not going to show one iota of weakness that they can use against me. I'm going to sit here silently except, every once in a while, I'll demand my lawyer.

See, I know all this. But I also know one other thing, and it's the thing I can never say, but it's inside of me, aching to come out, just this one thing. But I can't say it. Or maybe I can say it so they can't hear it. Because I have to say it, to myself, very, very softly.

If I say anything else . . .

I put my head down on the table and I look at the patterns in the grain and I think really hard, because this need has become a mantra in my head.

To the table, I speak very, very softly.

"I want my mother."

There. I'll only say it once.

I chance it one more time. Press my head against the table. Whisper. "I want . . ." I want, I want, I want . . .

C'mon, Mom. Come save me.

Acknowledgments

I grew up on the U.S.-Mexico border, knowing that it was a place you either loved or hated. Luckily, I learned to love it, not just because it is the place I call home but also because it is the place where the truth—both ugly and beautiful—is revealed every day by people who live there. And for loving it and for speaking the truth, I want to thank the many people who have influenced the way I see the border—people like my parents and my students in both El Paso and nearby Sunland Park and Las Cruces, New Mexico; Lee and Bobby Byrd and the whole gang at Cinco Puntos Press; my first official editor, Randy Limbird, who gave me several article assignments about El Paso; the artist Lupe Casillas-Lowenberg; and the writers Benjamin Alire Sáenz, Luis Alberto Urrea, Joe Hayes, and Charles Bowden.

Sparta and The Mars Volta—both bands that started in El Paso—provided the background music I listened to while writing *The Confessional*. I wish to extend a special thanks to Jim Ward, lead singer of Sparta, who generously said, "El Paso people are all good in my book" when I asked if we could reprint lyrics from Sparta's song "Tensioning."

Acknowledgments

Of course, thanks should go to my family—parents, brothers, in-laws, nieces, The Dussen, and "Christafari." I also want to thank countless numbers of friends, especially those who read early drafts—Lora, Nash, Isaac, and Denise—or who checked my Spanish—Lori and David.

And last but not least, I want to thank my agent, Jennifer Carlson, and my editor, Cecile Goyette. This manuscript is ten times better than the day Cecile first encountered it. Thanks for the intense scrutiny and the chance to grow as a writer.

Abrazos!

About the Author

J. L. Powers created six first-person voices—plus a supporting cast of cholos, clerics, and variously wayward and steadfast characters—to tell *The Confessional*'s dark and thoughtful tale. Powers admits that "these guys kept me up at night" but also credits this story as a "personally transforming experience." The yen to create the plot began while the author was working on an El Paso literary press and teaching writing at a local college. A large number of students were simultaneously attending a nearby Catholic high school. As Powers got to know them, they offered intriguing perspectives on life on the U.S.-Mexico border, particularly with regard to race, religion, and immigration. Powers, who was recently awarded a Fulbright-Hays Scholarship, is newly married, and is pursuing a PhD in African history at Stanford University. Visit the author on the Web at www.jlpowers.net.